Date: 5/27/11

Hanging in Wild Wind

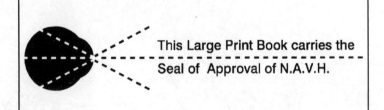

This Large Print Book carries the
Seal of Approval of N.A.V.H.

HANGING IN WILD WIND

RALPH COTTON

THORNDIKE PRESS

A part of Gale, Cengage Learning

GALE
CENGAGE Learning™

Detroit • New York • San Francisco • New Haven, Conn • Waterville, Maine • London

GALE
CENGAGE Learning

LIBRARY OF CONGRESS CATALOGING-IN-PUBLICATION DATA

Cotton, Ralph W.
    Hanging in wild wind / by Ralph Cotton.
        p. cm. — (Thorndike Press large print western)
    ISBN-13: 978-1-4104-3544-6 (hardcover)
    ISBN-10: 1-4104-3544-X (hardcover)
    1. Large type books. I. Title.
PS3553.O766H36 2011
813'.54—dc22   2010048750

Published in 2011 by arrangement with NAL Signet, a member of Penguin Group (USA) Inc.

Printed in the United States of America
1 2 3 4 5 6 7 15 14 13 12 11

For Mary Lynn . . . of course.

PART 1

CHAPTER 1

Vientos Salvajes, New Mexico Badlands

The first slug from the ranger's big Colt sent outlaw Morris Wheeler flying backward through the open door of the Belleza Grande Cantina. The sound of the gunshot sent people scrambling in every direction, emptying the busy dirt street. Even as Wheeler crashed down inside the saloon, upending a table crowded with empty bottles, shot glasses and wooden cups, the ranger had already turned with his smoking Colt, poised and ready. He searched the street warily for his next target.

He saw no one, but he knew there were three others. He'd seen them before he'd even ridden into Vientos Salvajes. He had lain atop a rocky trail and watched the outlaws through his battered army telescope. He'd counted four of Silva "the Snake" Ceran's gang riding toward the bustling badlands town, each of them wearing a long tan riding duster and a broad-brimmed black hat. One of the four he'd recognized as the woman, Kitty Dellaros. The other three were Andy Weeks, Delbert Trueblood and Morris Wheeler. Each was a noted thief and murderer.

He'd seen no sign of Silva Ceran himself, but he had an idea that the gang leader was somewhere nearby, lying low, letting his crew take all the heat that had been on their trail ever since the payroll robbery near the mining town of Poindexter more than two weeks ago.

The ranger stepped toward an alleyway, breaking into a run alongside the large cantina. A flock of frightened chickens burst forth in a flurry of batting wings, squawking above the pounding of hooves. Silva "the Snake" Ceran wasn't there, but in this deadly business the young ranger had learned quickly to take what he could get.

These were Silva Ceran's people; there was no questioning that — *a few of his people anyway,* the ranger thought. Riding with Ceran had become a popular pursuit among the swell of saddle trash who preyed on the citizens along both sides of the border.

The ranger knew very little about Kitty Dellaros, aside from her name and the growing reports that she'd been riding with Silva Ceran of late. As for the three gunmen, he knew them well enough. For weeks now he'd been carrying around in his saddlebags posters of their grim faces. They were desert outlaws from the old Sugar Blanton Gang, and in addition to the posters, each man's name was carefully recorded on a list that the ranger carried in his vest pocket, along with the battered stub of a pencil. He'd hoped to put that pencil to good use today.

As he turned and gathered Black Pot, his Appaloosa stallion, he heard a frightened voice call out from the front door of the cantina.

"Ranger, you must come quickly, *por favor.* This one is still alive."

Sam hurried out of the alley, leading the stallion behind him. Out in front of the open doorway, an elderly man jumped up and down in place, waving his long, bony arms to get the ranger's attention.

Still alive . . . ? The ranger looked surprised. But no sooner had the old man spoken than a gunshot accompanied by a string of cursing and the crash of breaking glass erupted from inside the cantina. "Stay out here," the ranger said, giving the old man a quick once-over, wondering whether

11

this was a trick of some sort.

"*Sí,* of course. I will wait out here," the old man said.

Inside the darkened cantina, Morris Wheeler had dragged himself to his feet and managed to snag a young woman by her long black hair as she stood stunned, staring wide-eyed at him. He was standing slumped against the bar, his bloody left hand entangled in the woman's dark locks, holding her against him. "You moved too slow, little *chick-chick.* Look what it got you. . . ."

"Please don't hurt me," said the young woman, her voice trembling.

"We'll see," Wheeler said, strained and weakened. "You're taking me out of here, little missy. I die, you die. . . ."

"Turn the woman loose, Wheeler," the ranger called from inside the door.

Wheeler turned to face him, his Remington in his bloody right hand. "Or what, Ranger?" he growled. "You going to shoot me again?"

"Most likely," the ranger replied, his Colt leveled as he took a step forward.

"Getting shot don't matter much to me now." Wheeler gestured with his gun down the front of his bloody shirt. "I'm shot to hell already."

"I can get you some help," the ranger said.

"Shit, you can," said Wheeler. "Look at me. I'm dead. You did this, you son of a bitch."

"It needed doing, Wheeler," said the ranger. "If it wasn't me, it would've been somebody else soon enough. We both know that."

The dying man considered it. "Yeah, I guess so." He gave a dark chuckle and shook his head. "Get out of here, darling," he said to the young woman, letting go of her hair and giving her a shove. "Next time . . . don't stand around so long."

The young woman bolted away like a frightened deer.

"Now, as for you, Ranger . . . ," Wheeler said. He cocked the Remington with his bloody thumb.

The ranger's Colt bucked once in his hand, and the shot hit Wheeler an inch to the left of the bloody wound in his abdomen. He staggered back in a full circle along the bar but caught himself. "Gawl-damn it!" he said, pained and outraged. "You did it again." He bowed deeply at the waist.

"Drop the gun or I'll keep it up," the ranger said with no remorse.

"Jesus, Ranger . . . You can't just shoot a man who's already —"

The ranger cocked his Colt, and at the

sound the outlaw stopped. "Wait. Damn it." His Remington slipped from his hand and landed with a hard thud on the floor. "There. Satisfied?"

"What about that help?" the ranger asked. He stepped forward, keeping an eye on the bowed outlaw's hand, which was dangling near the top of his boot well.

"Don't do me no favors. . . ." Wheeler moaned.

"Suit yourself," said the ranger. He took a bottle of whiskey from atop the bar, uncorked it and handed it out to the outlaw.

Wheeler gave him a curious look, but took the bottle from his hand. "Figure a little kindness will get me . . . to tell you where the Snake is?"

"I know where he is," said the ranger, still keeping an eye on Wheeler's bloody hand. "He's at the end of whatever trail those three are on." He gave a nod in the direction the other three outlaws had taken out of town.

"Smart son of a bitch," the dying outlaw growled under his breath. He managed to take a swig of whiskey without straightening. "You're that ranger they're all talking about — the one who killed Junior Lake and his gang." He looked up at the man's dusty silver-gray sombrero and added, "Sam

14

something-or-other."

"Arizona Ranger Sam Burrack," the ranger said. "Yes, that's me."

"That figures. . . ." Wheeler gave a sneer of contempt. "I just wish I could see you once Trueblood and Weeks get done with you. . . ." His voice grew weaker and his words became slurred because of the steady loss of blood.

"Are you going to die or what?" the ranger said coolly.

"Why? Are you going to shoot me again?" Wheeler asked angrily.

"Might," said the ranger. "I want to get on your pals' trail." He watched as the outlaw's bloody fingers flexed near his boot well.

"You want to get a hold of Kitty . . . like every other man does," said Wheeler. "I know what you want. . . ."

Since Wheeler brought up the woman, the ranger pursued the matter. "Is she the Snake's woman?"

"Ha. He thinks she is . . . ," Wheeler said. It sounded more difficult for him to form his words. "She'll throw open her knees for . . . anything that's got a pecker. . . ."

The ranger nodded. "I've heard that."

"I just bet you have," Wheeler managed in a suggestive tone.

"Are you going to die or what?" the ranger repeated.

"I'm going to . . . Just shut up," said Wheeler. He lowered his bloody fingertips inside the edge of the boot well.

Any second now, the ranger told himself.

Wheeler's hand came up quickly enough for a dying man. But the ranger was ready. *A knife . . . ?* He saw the bloody hand try to rise and stab the blade toward him. But in Wheeler's condition, the big knife slipped from his grasp and fell to the floor.

Sam's boot stamped down onto the blade as Wheeler fumbled to grab it by the handle. "The shape you're in, you draw a knife?" Sam said. He pulled Wheeler up by his shirt and leaned him back against the bar.

"It's all . . . I had left . . . ," Wheeler said, sounding weaker, his eyes more and more distant. "You didn't leave me no choice . . . Arizona Ranger Sam *fucking* Burrack. . . ."

"I didn't come here bringing choices," said the Ranger.

The three riders did not slow their horses until they topped a high ridge five miles from town. "Whoever it was, he ain't riding alone," Delbert Trueblood said. He and Weeks looked back across the flat stretch of land below. Tagging behind them, Kitty Del-

16

laros nudged her limping horse to a stop.

"That's what I'm thinking, too," Andy Weeks said to Trueblood, sounding winded, looking worried. "We're lucky we didn't run into them on our way out of town."

"Damn lucky," Trueblood agreed.

"It's one man," Kitty Dellaros said with disgust. She edged her horse a few feet away from them and stepped down from her saddle.

"Yeah?" The two gunmen looked at each other. "How the hell do you know that?" said Trueblood.

"I looked back," said Kitty. "You two sods could have looked back too, if you weren't in such a hurry to run out on Wheeler."

"Watch your mouth," Weeks warned.

"We did look back," said Trueblood. "There're others waiting to trap us back there. Ain't you been listening to us?"

"I'm listening, but I'm not hearing any-thing," the woman said, pushing her hat brim up on her forehead. "I don't know how you sods ever made it this far."

"Call me that one more time," said Weeks, "and see if I don't kick your ass, same as I would a man."

"That goes for me too," said Trueblood.

The woman didn't answer, but she didn't take their threats too seriously. They didn't want her going to Ceran with complaints against them. Instead of replying she shook her head, raised her horse's front hoof and ran a gloved hand along its foreleg with a critical eye. "Easy . . . ," she purred when the horse resisted her touch.

The two outlaws nudged their horses closer to hers. "Is that horse going to make it?" Trueblood asked as he and Weeks stared at her from behind, taking pleasure in the sight of the female form, even in the loose, ill-fitting riding duster.

"No," said Kitty. She lowered the horse's foreleg and patted the animal's hot muzzle. "This is as far as he goes." She raised a short-barreled Colt Thunderer from a holster beneath her duster. She held the shiny nickel-plated gun out at arm's length toward the horse's sweaty head.

"Don't even think about firing that gun," Weeks said quickly. "It's a dead giveaway where we are up here."

"What else can I do?" Kitty said with resolve, staring at the lame horse as if speaking to it instead of the outlaw.

"You can leave him," said Trueblood. "The critters will make fast work of him tonight once they catch his scent."

"Yeah, right," Kitty said without turning her eyes from the horse. What he'd suggested was unthinkable. She took a deep breath.

Weeks shouted, "If you fire that damned gun, I swear to God I'll —"

She squeezed the trigger. The sound of her shot rolled out across land and sky. The big horse's knees buckled beneath it. It collapsed dead onto the rocky ground.

"Damn it to hell!" Weeks shouted, having been cut short in the midst of his threat. "You are the most hardheaded bitch I have ever come across!"

"Shut up, Weeks," Kitty said. She swung the Thunderer toward him, not needing to cock the short double-action Colt. "I just killed a horse I *liked.* Think what I'd do to a sumbitch I can't stand."

Weeks' hand started to go for the gun on his hip. But seeing she had him cold, he stopped himself.

"Both of yas settle down," said Trueblood. He raised his rifle from across his lap and held it loosely, covering the two of them. "We're being dogged by somebody back there, whether it's one man or a dozen. This is no time for us to start falling apart."

"It's one man," Kitty insisted. "It's that ranger, Burrack, who killed Junior Lake and his gang." Her eyes and gun remained locked on Weeks.

19

"Burrack, huh?" said Trueblood. "How the hell do you know that?"

"Because I saw him riding in," Kitty said. "You two wouldn't stop humping your whores long enough to look out the window when I told you to, else you would've seen him yourselves."

"How do you know Burrack?" Trueblood asked, suspicious.

"Jesus . . ." Kitty lowered the nickel-plated Thunderer and shook her head. She looked back along the trail leading across the flat desert land below. "I don't *know* Burrack. I saw him once in Yuma. He always wears that gray sombrero, rides that big Appaloosa. The horse belonged to Outrider Sazes until one of Junior Lake's boys stopped Outrider's clock."

Trueblood and Weeks glanced at each other questioningly. "You sure know a hell of a lot about the man for not knowing him."

"I want to know all I can about any sumbitch who's out to kill me," Kitty said. "Anyway, we've got a problem," she added, gesturing her gun barrel toward the dead horse.

Weeks grinned. "The way I see it, you're the one with the problem. We've got saddles beneath us, ready to ride."

Kitty didn't answer. "Which one of you am I riding with?"

They both grinned. "What's in it for us?" asked Weeks.

"What's in it for you?" She pushed up her hat brim again. "How about this? I won't tell Silva that neither of you offered me a ride out of this hellhole after I lost my horse."

"The thing is" — Weeks grinned — "if we leave you afoot out here, we don't have to worry about what you tell the Snake — not ever again."

Kitty looked at the rifle in Trueblood's grip. Then she looked away for a moment, knowing he was right. When she looked back at the two outlaws her countenance had changed. She gave them both a coy smile. "All right, fellows, I think we all *know* what's in it for you. The question is, when and where?"

"It can't be soon enough for me," said Trueblood. "I got cut short back there with my whore."

"Yeah, me too," Weeks said with a hungry look in his eyes. "There's a water hole up ahead." He nudged his horse over, reached a hand down and helped her swing up behind his saddle. "I've been craving a piece of you for the longest time."

"Silva can't hear about us doing this," said Kitty, settling in behind him.

"Hear that Weeks?" said Trueblood in a mock tone. "Don't you ever tell the Snake what we're about to do." He nudged his horse forward on the narrow high trail.

"What? Tell Silva Ceran we both crawled into his warm spot?" said Weeks. "Do I look that crazy to you?"

CHAPTER 2

Out in front of the cantina, the ranger rummaged through the saddlebags on Wheeler's horse, looking for any sign of the stolen payroll money from Poindexter. He took out a small leather pouch and shook its contents into his gloved palm. Watching him with curiosity, the old cantina owner stepped in closer for a better look at the pouch's contents.

"Welcome to Wild Wind, Ranger," he said, translating the name of the town into English. He gestured toward his cantina. "Anything you want, it is free."

"*Gracias,*" the ranger said absently, without turning his gaze from the palm of his hand. *Gold teeth . . .* He shook the bloodstained teeth back and forth in his hand.

Beside him, the old cantina owner stopped an inch away and craned his neck down. "Aw, *sí,* gold teeth," he said as if answering the ranger's thoughts.

The ranger turned a stern look toward him; the old man stepped back. But he shrugged, then said, "I only try to see if this is enough to pay for his burial. Am I wrong to do so, Ranger?"

The ranger didn't answer. Instead he considered his findings. Since there was no cash in the dead outlaw's saddlebags, it had to mean one of two things. Either Silva "the Snake" still had the gang's robbery money, or else they had stashed it somewhere for safekeeping in the badlands between here and Poindexter.

Handing the few bloodstained gold morsels over to the old man, he said, "Here. This should cover it."

"*Sí, gracias,*" said the old cantina owner, inspecting the teeth, moving them around in the palm of his hand with a long, knotted finger. "If not, perhaps I will sell his horse and —"

"Do what suits you," said the ranger. He gazed out toward the hill line in the direction the three riders had taken out of town. He doubted Ceran would have stashed the money and taken the chance of one of his men coming back and getting it without his knowing. No . . . The Snake still had the money. He'd bet on it.

Before leaving Vientos Salvajes, the ranger

watered Black Pot at the town well and stood the animal in the shade of a tall saguaro cactus, rubbing him down with a handful of dried grass. While he rubbed the big Appaloosa, the young woman from the cantina walked over to him. Her black hair had been brushed and she wore a clean dress, her other dress having been soaked with Wheeler's blood as he'd held her against him.

"I come to thank you for what you did," the woman said to the ranger, her English reasonably good. "If you had not been there . . ." She shook her head slowly, letting her words trail.

The ranger turned from rubbing the stallion. He touched the brim of his sombrero. "Begging your pardon, *señora*," he said, "but had I not shot him, it wouldn't have happened."

The woman looked bewildered for a moment. Then she touched her long, glistening hair and said, "My head is sore, where he pulled me by my hair."

Not knowing what else to say, the ranger nodded and said, "Well, he won't do it again."

"No, he will not do it again," the woman said. She smiled. "I am Ramona."

"Pleased, Ramona," the ranger said. "I'm

Ranger Burrack, Samuel Burrack."

"I am pleased to meet you as well, Samuel," she said with formality. "And I still thank you."

"You're welcome, then," Sam said.

"I work at the Belleza Grande," she said. "The Grand Beauty."

"Yes, I understand," he said. "Next time trouble starts, you need to duck down and get away from it."

"*Sí,* the next time I will," she said with a smile that told Sam he was wasting his breath trying to warn her of the hazards involved in the sort of work she did.

Ramona shrugged. "Anyway, Don Emilio said I can thank you for the rest of the day if I wish to." She smiled again.

"Don Emilio, eh?" The ranger looked over at the Belleza Grande Cantina. The old man stood looking back at him, waving the gold teeth in his closed hand as two men carried Wheeler's blood away on a two-wheel cart.

"He is not a real padrone," the young woman said in a lowered tone, "but he likes us to call him one."

"And he sent you here," Sam said, "to thank me?"

"No. I asked him if I could come, and he gave me permission," she said. She stepped in closer. "I can thank you longer than all

26

day if you like. If you are staying the night . . ."

"*Señora*" — the ranger, letting out a breath, avoided saying her name — "I'm obliged. But I can't stay the night. I can't even stay the day. The fact is, I'm leaving here as soon as this fellow's attended." He gestured toward the stallion.

The woman brushed a strand of hair from her cheek that a warm breeze had swept there. "You go to kill those others who were with him?"

"That's the probable outcome," Sam said.

She had trouble with his words.

He saw it and said, "If they put up a fight, I will kill them."

She paused in contemplation for a moment. "You would prefer to go and kill them instead of staying here with me?"

"No, *señora,* I do not prefer that at all," Sam said, shaking his head. "I would much prefer staying here with you. But this is my job." He dropped the handful of straw and picked up his saddle, which lay on the ground at Black Pot's hooves.

"Your job?" She looked confused. "It cannot wait while you and I —"

"No, *señora,* it can't," he said, cutting her off as courteously as he could. He spread Black Pot's saddle blanket.

27

"That makes no sense, Samuel," she said, half smiling, half pouting.

"No, *señora*," he said, looking her up and down, "none at all." Then he turned and pitched the saddle up onto the big stallion's back.

In moments the ranger had ridden out of Vientos Salvajes, following the three sets of hoofprints left by the fleeing outlaws. He had traveled halfway across the desert floor when he heard the single gunshot resound in the distance. By the time he reached the trail leading up into the hills, he saw four buzzards move in high above the ridgeline and begin circling in a wide, lazy swing. Two more of the big scavengers appeared as he nudged the Appaloosa up the last few yards of steep, rocky trail.

He stopped when he spotted the dead horse lying fifteen feet away. *Three thieves, two horses* . . . This changed things. No outlaw on the run wanted to share his horse, especially out in this rugged, sun-scorched terrain.

He looked all around. Then he swung down from his saddle, rifle in hand, and walked over and stood above the dead animal. His eyes followed the remaining two sets of hoofprints off along a narrow, rocky

28

trail. After a moment he stooped down, flipped open the exposed saddlebag on the dead horse's rump and rummaged through it, seeing what he might learn about the animal's owner.

Overhead, the buzzards swung in lower, but kept a cautious distance as the ranger pulled out items and laid them on the ground. A handful of bullets, a hairbrush, a dirt-streaked riding blouse that smelled of perfume, a weathered, folded paper envelope. Kitty Dellaros was the one left horseless, he now knew, opening the folded envelope and shaking out a cheap tin locket on a thin chain. *For how long?*

Pulling off a glove, the ranger opened the locket and examined the tintype of a smiling young girl inside. *Kitty Dellaros as a child? Could be,* he thought, studying the picture as the chain dangled from his fingertips.

If this was Kitty Dellaros, he imagined all the things life had led her through from that time to this. Staring at the photograph, he shook his head. *You never expected it would be this way, did you?* he said silently to the innocent face smiling back at him. After a moment he closed his hand around the tin locket and snapped it shut. Then he stood up, mounted the big Appaloosa and rode away.

An hour later he stepped back down from his saddle atop a high ridge overlooking a small pool of runoff. With his naked eye he was able to see the three outlaws through a thin stand of pine and mountain cedar. But for a better look, he led the stallion back out of sight and drew the telescope from beneath his bedroll.

When he'd settled in behind the cover of a rock, he stretched out the telescope and began scanning the trees.

At first sight of the woman through the sparse pine branches, the ranger jerked the telescope down from his eye. He blinked as if his eyes had tricked him. Through the lens he had seen her standing naked to the waist. He hadn't expected this. He put the telescope back to his eye in time to see her step out of her trousers and toss them onto a blanket spread alongside her discarded blouse.

Not wanting to take advantage of a woman's private moment, Sam moved the lens away, scanning through the pines to the edge of the watering hole. There he saw Trueblood and Weeks talking back and forth. The ranger could tell they had reached an agreement of some sort when both of them nodded and stepped back from each other. He watched Weeks fish a coin from his vest pocket and shake it back and forth in his closed hand.

Flipping a coin? He continued watching.

On the edge of the water hole, Weeks stopped shaking the coin and said to Trueblood, "Call it."

"Uh-uh," said Trueblood, "you call it. I never win when I call it."

Weeks grinned. "That's good to know. Call it."

"I told you, I ain't calling it," Trueblood insisted. "You call it."

"You want me to flip it and call it?" Weeks asked.

"That's right," said Trueblood.

"Okay then, I'll call it." Weeks shrugged and flipped the coin. "Heads," he said, while the coin still rose and spun in the air.

The two made room for the coin to fall to the ground between them. They loomed over it.

"Heads it is. You lose!" Weeks said.

"Damn it to hell," said Trueblood, sounding bitter in his disappointment. "I never win anything."

"Tough knuckles, you unlucky son of a bitch," said Weeks, laughing, picking up the coin from the dirt.

"Flip it again," said Trueblood.

"I'm not flipping it again. Are you crazy?" said Weeks, his laughter waning as he realized Trueblood was serious.

"If it was the other way around, I'd flip it again for you," Trueblood said.

"That just shows the difference between the two of us," said Weeks.

"Shit." Trueblood brooded. "I just wanted to go first for once."

"What difference does it make? I won't wear nothing out," he said, still grinning.

"None," said Trueblood.

"Then why do you want to be first?"

"I just do," said the sulking gunman. "I've not got any luck — never have had, never will."

"Then I best not say something like *Better luck next time,* had I?" Weeks grinned.

"It'd be wise not to," said Trueblood.

Pulling off his hat, Weeks spit in his palm and ran his hand back across his tangled hair. "How do I look?" he asked.

"Go to hell," said Trueblood, turning and flopping down onto the ground.

At the edge of the stand of pines, Kitty Dellaros called out, "Let's make some sparks fly, boys. The day is getting away from us."

"Oh my God," Trueblood said, his voice

raspy with anticipation as he stared at her naked body. She cupped one hand at a firm, round breast; the other hand she held loosely over her most private area.

"Whew-*iee*," said Trueblood, turning and looking at her from twenty yards away. "If the Snake ever hears about us doing this, he'll sure enough kill us both, and Kitty too."

"Damn it to hell. Why would you mention the Snake at a time like this? You're just trying to spoil this for me," Weeks said angrily. "You *losing* son of a bitch."

"Sorry," said Trueblood. "Get on in there and hurry it up."

"Hurry it up?" Weeks laughed excitedly. "You're talking out of your head."

"Of course, if you boys would just as soon forget about it . . . ," Kitty said, turning and walking back into the pines toward the blanket.

"Whoa, hold on. I'm coming!" shouted Weeks, bounding across the rocky ground behind her, sailing his hat away and yanking out his shirttails as he went. "Don't even think we're not going to do it!"

Atop the ridge, the ranger stood up from behind the rock and collapsed the battered telescope between his palms. He had a good idea of what was about to happen down there. *This is my best chance to take Weeks and Trueblood,* he thought, dusting the seat of his trousers on his way back to the big stallion. *The woman . . .* He had nothing on her — no wanted posters, no outstanding charges against her. She was Silva Ceran's woman.

But being an outlaw's woman was no reason to arrest her, he reminded himself. She had no witnesses placing her at the scene of any of the gang's robberies. If she played her cards right, she could walk away when he finished with the two outlaws. If not, well . . . he'd have to see how it went. He stepped into his saddle and turned the big stallion toward a slimmer rocky trail that looked as if it would cut his time in half.

"Come on, Black Pot. Looks like we're going to interrupt everybody's party," he said, nudging the Appaloosa forward.

CHAPTER 3

Trueblood sat at the water's edge, wishing he'd taken a twist of tobacco from his saddlebags before this thing got started. Now that the show was under way, hot and heavy on the blanket, he couldn't just walk past them to get to his horse and his saddlebags. Even though the reason would be honest enough, he knew both Weeks and Kitty would think he was trying to watch, which, to be honest, he just might be, a little, on the way there and back.

After a few minutes longer, he began to fidget in place, getting anxious, impatient. He wanted a chew; he wanted the woman. *Damn, how I want the woman.* "Hey, hurry it up in there, Andy. I want my tobacco." As soon as he'd spoken, he caught himself and said, "Hell, you both know what I want. Now hurry up."

"Wait your turn, Delbert," Kitty called out, sounding out of breath. "You'll get yours."

"Damn right I will," Trueblood said in firm tone. "But if I don't get it soon, I might not be able to . . . for a while anyway."

"Just . . . take it easy," Kitty called out, in the same breathless voice.

Jesus . . . The sound of her voice and the image of what was going on over there caused Trueblood to get all the more impatient. He waited for a few more minutes, until he couldn't stand it any longer.

"To hell with this," he said, rising to his feet and adjusting the crotch of his trousers. "I'm coming in. It's my turn. You better both think about it. If I get cut out, what's to keep me from telling the Snake about the two of you out here?"

He waited only a few seconds for a reply. When he didn't get one, he turned and started toward the trees. "By God, I'm coming in and getting my part," he called out, jerking his Colt from his holster, just in case Weeks wanted to turn this into a fight.

He walked into the trees along the path the two had taken. He stopped when he saw Weeks' pale, naked feet sticking out from behind the trunk of a slender pine. "You can't blame me, Andy. I see what's going on here. I know when I'm being cut out."

When Weeks didn't answer, he walked on. He stopped at the pine tree and looked

36

down at the rest of Weeks' pale, naked body lying stretched out on the blanket, his dead eyes staring straight up at the sky. A wide, bloody gash made a semicircle on Weeks' throat from ear to ear.

"Good Lord, *Andy!*" Trueblood gasped in shock, but the Colt became poised and tensed in his hand. He backed up a step and looked warily all around, as if expecting to see the woman's dead body as well. He almost called out Kitty's name. But then he caught himself as he heard the sound of both his and Weeks' horses running out of the pines and pounding away along the narrow trail.

"He-iih," Kitty called out to the animals, spurring the one she was riding and leading the other along beside her by its reins.

"Damn you, Kitty," Trueblood shouted. He fired two shots at her, and she ducked low in the saddle, the tails of her riding duster flapping wildly behind her. The clothes she'd been wearing still lay on the ground beside the blanket. Trueblood fired two more shots before he saw the woman and the two horses ride out of sight.

The reality of his situation finally sunk in after a moment of stunned silence. Drawing in a deep breath, Trueblood looked down at Andy Weeks' naked, bloody body. "Looks like I wasn't the unlucky sonsabitch after all. Was I, Andrew?" He looked up in the direction Kitty Dellaros had taken with the horses. Recalling the sight of her standing naked in the sunlight earlier, he said, "Hell, I knew it was too good to be true."

He opened his Colt's cylinder, dropped his spent rounds and replaced them. "I ever lay eyes on that throat-cutting whore again, I swear to God, she's graveyard dead," he vowed to himself. Holstering his Colt, the stunned and disappointed outlaw sighed and slipped away along the stand of pines. He gathered her clothes and walked along a thin game path leading down to a wider trail below. *There's no point in trying to follow her,* he thought. She wasn't going to stop for nothing until she knew she was safely away from him.

Two miles away from the water hole, Kitty Dellaros reined in and stepped down from the horse she was riding, and lowered the duster off one side to inspect a bullet graze across her shoulder. *Of all the rotten luck,* she told herself. She'd had to leave without managing to gather her clothes. She hadn't expected Trueblood to come barging into the pines just as she was getting ready to make a run for it.

Now she was stuck with no clothes. *I'm*

not about to try going back there, she thought, allowing the duster back to droop off her bloody shoulder. Trueblood would kill her for certain. At the rump of Weeks' horse she flipped open the saddlebag and found a wadded-up bandana. Shaking it free of dust, she looked it over, sizing it up as a bandage. It wasn't much, she decided, but it would have to do, for now anyway.

She folded the bandana and pressed it down against the bloody bullet graze. But just as she started to pull the shoulder of the duster back over the bandage to hold it in place, she caught sight of the ranger standing at the edge of a tall saguaro cactus, his rifle in one hand, the reins of his big stallion in the other. Afternoon sunlight glinted on the badge showing from behind his lapel.

Collecting herself quickly, Kitty gave a coy smile and in a cool, even tone said, "My, my, Marshal, you certainly know how to catch a gal unawares."

"Arizona Ranger, ma'am," Sam corrected her, stepping forward. "Arizona Ranger Samuel Burrack." Having noted the bullet graze and knowing her shoulder might be too weak for her to raise her hands, he said, "Keep your hands out where I can see them." He looked her up and down closely,

39

having already seen that she was naked beneath the riding duster.

"All right . . ." She let out a breath. "Just so you understand, Sheriff," she said, "I'm not wanted for anything. My hands are clean." She gave another slight smile and wiggled her bloody fingertips. "See? Bloody, but clean," she added.

"I know you're not wanted for anything right now, Miss Dellaros," Sam said, ignoring her calling him *Sheriff.* This was her way of being playful with him, he saw.

"Oh, you know my name, then, Deputy?" she said, her eyes widened slightly. The ranger doubted her look of surprise.

Yep, she was teasing him with the names — *Deputy, Marshal, Sheriff;* anything but his actual title. But he ignored her. He wasn't going to play any games.

"Yes, I know your name, ma'am. It's Kitty Dellaros. You're Silva 'the Snake's' woman," he said.

"I'm acquainted with Silva Ceran," she said in an evasive manner, "but I wouldn't call myself his *woman.* And I don't know his whereabouts."

"That sounds like the kind of answer a lawyer would advise you to give," Sam said.

"Those lawyers," she said, again with the smile. "What would a poor gal on her own do without them?"

Sam just stared at her, knowing his silence would draw out more than anything he could say at this point. He was right.

After a moment under his gaze, she shrugged. "The truth is, I'm nobody's woman but my own. I like it that way." It was her turn to look him up and down, assessing him. "It leaves me free and open to any opportunity that presents itself."

Sam saw the suggestion in her eyes, but he was having none of it. Looking past her along the trail, he said, "I heard gunshots a while ago. Where's Weeks and Trueblood?"

"They're back there," Kitty said, giving a toss of her head. "The gunfire was them firing at me." She nodded at her wounded shoulder. "We had a disagreement. Luckily all I got was a graze out of the deal."

Sam's eyes went to the bloodstain on the torn shoulder of her duster. "A disagreement about what?" he probed.

She gave him a defiant look. "About me spreading my legs for the two of them, *Sheriff*," she said.

"I see," Sam said coolly, unaffected by her off-color remark. "Where were you going?"

"I was headed back to get something I left with my dead horse," she replied. "I'm still going there, unless I'm under arrest for something." She stared at him expectantly.

"No, you're not under arrest," Sam said. "But you're riding back to the water hole with me." He nodded in the direction of the runoff where she'd left Weeks and Trueblood.

"If I'm not under arrest for anything, Ranger," she said, finally using his correct title, "you've got no right to hold me against my will." She cocked a hand on a slender, well-rounded hip.

"Unless it's for your own good," Sam said. He didn't want to let her out of his sight until he'd seen what all the shooting was about. "For all I know there could be Apache slipping around this way and that out here. I can't leave you alone."

"Uh-uh," she said. "I'm not falling for this. I told you I forgot something in my saddlebags. I've got to go get it."

"If it wasn't for that, would you be riding with me to the water hole?" Sam asked pointedly.

She shrugged her good shoulder stiffly. "Yeah, sure. Why not?" she said. "But I did forget something, and I'm not stopping until I've got it back."

As she spoke, Sam had reached into his trouser pocket and lifted out the locket. He flipped it open and let it dangle from his fingertips. "Is this what you were going back for?"

Her eyes widened in surprise. She took a step toward him before she caught herself. "Where did you get that?"

"From the saddlebags, like you said," Sam replied. He clasped his hand shut around the cheap locket. "It's a beautiful picture," he said. "I can see why you don't want to lose it."

"Give it to me." It was not quite a demand, but not far from it. She took another step forward. The ranger raised his hand, stopping her.

"Not so fast, ma'am," he said. "Here's something else I found when I went through the saddlebags." He pulled a thin leather razor case from his vest pocket and held it up for her to see.

"Yeah, so?" Kitty said. "It's just an empty razor case."

"Finding it empty is what concerns me," Sam said. "If it had a razor still in it, I'd feel much better."

Without hesitation, Kitty spread the front of the riding duster wide-open, revealing her naked body. "Does it look like I'm hiding a razor?"

"No, ma'am," said Sam. He had to keep himself from looking away from her. He wasn't gong to let himself be taken in by his own good manners. He looked as long as it took to see that she wasn't carrying the razor. *At least she isn't carrying it nowhere visible,* he thought. "Close your duster, ma'am," he said quietly.

"I want the locket. Give it to me," Kitty said firmly, letting the duster fall closed. She held her open palm out.

"I'll give it to you when we see what's going on at the water hole," Sam said.

"But you said I didn't have to go with you back to the water hole," Kitty persisted.

"You don't have to," said the ranger. "But that's where I'm headed, and this locket is going with me." He dropped the locket back into his trouser pocket. "You can suit yourself, whether or not you want to go with us."

Sam turned to the big stallion.

"Wait, Ranger," she said. "You have no right to do this."

"Do what?" Sam asked innocently, swinging up and settling into his saddle, his rifle still in hand. He nudged the stallion over to the other horse and picked up its loose reins.

"Damn it," Kitty said under her breath. "All right, I'll ride along with you as far as the water hole. But I want your word that I can have my locket back when we get there."

"You have my word, ma'am," Sam said. He nodded toward the horse standing nearest to her.

She grumbled under her breath as she took the reins to the horse, but as she started to swing up into the saddle, he said, "What about that empty razor case?"

She gave him a flat stare. "Are you kidding?"

"No, ma'am," Sam said, returning the same flat stare. "I'd feel much better."

She sighed and turned slightly away from him. A hand went somewhere into an inside hem of her duster and came out holding a folded straight razor. "Here, then," she said. "I hope you're satisfied." She held the razor out for him to take.

But without moving the stallion an inch closer, Sam said, "Pitch it to me."

"Pitch it — ?" She caught herself in surprise and said, "You sure are a cautious man, Ranger." She pitched the closed razor.

The ranger caught it. "Yes, ma'am. Cautious to a fault." He looked at the slight smear of blood along the razor's handle, but made no mention of it. Instead he slipped the weapon into its case, put it away and gestured her toward the rocky trail.

"You don't have to be scared of me, Ranger," she said. "I don't bite." She smiled.

"Unless, of course, it's the kind of biting you might happen to like."

"After you, ma'am," he said politely, ignoring her remark. He sat still until she nudged her horse forward. Then he touched his heels to the stallion's sides and rode along behind her, leading the third horse by its reins.

CHAPTER 4

Before the ranger followed Kitty up the last stretch of trail to the water hole, he noted a newly arrived pair of buzzards overhead, circling high, searching the earth below. It occurred to him that the winged scavengers had done well by following the outlaws' trail. It also came to him that either one or both of the men he was after were lying dead somewhere near the water hole. He'd have to be careful that the woman didn't try to make a run for it or try some other trick.

Also seeing the buzzards, Kitty slowed her horse and said over her shoulder, "All right, I suppose I need to tell you that Andy Weeks is dead. You're going to know soon enough."

"What about Trueblood?" Sam asked, noting that the buzzards' circle had centered above the stand of pines.

"He's alive, but I left him afoot. He's madder than hell," said Kitty. She studied the trail ahead warily. "He'll kill me if he gets a chance."

"Stay square with me, ma'am," Sam said quietly, nudging the big stallion up beside her. "I'll see to it he doesn't get the chance."

She paused, slowing her horse. "You have to understand something, Ranger Burrack. What I did, I did in self-defense. It was the only thing that would have stopped what they had in mind."

Sam didn't answer.

"Do you . . . understand, that is?" she asked quietly, studying his face in profile beneath the wide brim of his sombrero.

"Ma'am," Sam said, "it would be best if I see Weeks' body first before I answer." He glanced at her, then back toward the pines lying ahead of them. "I see no signs of struggle on you."

"There was no struggle," Kitty said. "Not yet anyway. I wasn't about to let things get that far along."

They stopped at the edge of the pines, stepped down from their saddles and walked their horses forward. When they reached a spot ten feet from the bloody body lying sprawled and naked on the blanket, Sam let out a breath and pushed up the brim of his sombrero. Dark, dried blood glistened on Weeks' throat and chest. A wide black pool covered the blanket beneath him.

Seeing the look on Sam's face, Kitty said, "I was desperate, Ranger." As she spoke, she looked all around on the ground for her clothes, but couldn't find them. "I knew it was coming and I did what I knew would work." She continued looking for her clothes a moment longer.

"It worked, all right," Sam commented. "This man didn't see what was coming until it was too late."

"Of course not," Kitty said, giving him an incredulous look. "How far do you suppose I'd have gotten if he knew what I was going to do to him?"

Sam didn't reply; he knew she was right. A judge might have a hard time calling it self-defense, her striking the first and only blow. But as to her logic on the matter, he understood, even if he wasn't going to admit it to her. He looked at a blackened, blood-crusted palm that Weeks had used to clutch at his throat for a second. *But only for a second,* he decided, seeing the palm flung out and opened wide. The man had lost blood so fast he hadn't had time to even try to save himself. *Not that it would have done him any good,* Sam noted.

"Can you believe this? The sonsabitch took my clothes and boots," Kitty said with contempt. "Of all the low, spiteful —"

As she fumed and stomped, still looking all around, Sam followed a set of boot prints across the dusty ground until they disappeared into the pines. Leading all three horses, he stopped at a spot where the path plunged almost straight down. *I'll let Trueblood have this stretch of rugged, broken terrain,* he thought. He looked out and down across a rocky stretch of flatland that reached across a wide valley. *Hard tracking through brush and across endless rock,* he thought. Once the outlaw made it onto the flatlands, he could go in any direction, hiding his trail.

But Sam decided he'd follow the outlaw's trail as far as he could. Once he lost him among the difficult terrain, he'd have to postpone the hunt until another time. Right now, he had the woman to deal with. *This must be your lucky day, Delbert Trueblood. . . .* He looked out across the high badlands plain.

"Hey, Ranger," Kitty called down to him from atop the path behind him. "I'm going to wash up a little, get some of this dried, stinking blood off me."

She wasn't asking him; she was telling him. *This is her way of testing me, seeing how far she can push things her way,* he thought. This was how it would be with her the whole trip.

"Go ahead. But you'd better hurry it up," Sam said, turning with the horses and walking back up to the water hole.

When he and the horses topped the path and walked to the edge of the water, he was taken aback to see her standing ankle deep in the water, naked, shameless. The duster lay piled on the rock edge. She made no attempt to hide herself in any manner. She reached down and wet the bandana she'd taken from her wound. Holding it above her shoulder, she squeezed it. Pink, blood-stained water ran down her firm breast, her flat stomach, the rest of her.

She kept a narrow gaze on the ranger, as if inviting him to watch. But he needed no invitation. He wasn't about to look away. Looking away from a woman like this would be a mistake, he knew, no less than turning his back on a male prisoner. No matter what else Kitty Dellaros was — charming, witty, sexy — above all else she was dangerous.

"You know, I'm thinking, Samuel," she said, getting bolder, more familiar with him. "If you'll give me my locket, we can get going our separate ways. The way you said we would."

"Not now, ma'am," Sam said. "This killing changes everything." He gestured toward the body lying on the blanket beneath the circling buzzards. "You're going to have to go back to Wild Wind."

"Killing? It's not a killing," she said. "I told you, it was self-defense. Any court will understand that I had to do it in order to save myself."

"I wish you luck then, ma'am," Sam replied. "But I'm taking you to Wild Wind."

"What about Trueblood?" she asked. "He'll be gone by the time you take me into town and come back out here."

"That's how it looks." Sam had no intention of discussing any more than what was necessary with her. He knew that on foot Trueblood would have no more than a two day start on him. Cutting across the flatlands and back instead of backtracking the high trail they'd been riding would put him back in the hunt soon enough.

"And me? What about me, Ranger?" she asked, trying to sound mistreated in the mix of things.

"What happens to you in Wild Wind is up to the local authority."

"Local authority? Hell, they don't even have a sheriff there," she said. "All they have is Ed Ray. He's not smart enough to feed himself without biting his fingers."

"Ed Ray Richards is the duly elected town selectman," Sam said. He ignored her insult toward the man. "His jurisdiction reaches this far out. It will be his call."

"Damn Ed Ray Richards. . . ." She planted a hand on her cocked hip and stood with her feet spread shoulder-width apart. Her voice fell to a breathy tone. "All right, let's get down to some serious trading here." She smiled at him suggestively. "What have I got here that you just might want?"

"Get yourself washed off," Sam said, ignoring her blatant proposition.

"Oh, I see," she said coyly. "Why bargain with me when you can take what you want anyway."

"You see nothing," said Sam. "Get washed; get dressed. We're leaving."

She let out a breath of resignation. "All right, Ranger. Listen to me. There was no struggle because I told Weeks and True-blood they could both have me. I had to, to keep myself from getting left afoot. But here's what you have to understand. After they got what they wanted from me, they would've had to kill me. After they thought about it, they couldn't have let me live, take a chance on me ever telling Silva what happened."

Sam only stared, expressionless.

She paused, shook her head and continued, spreading her hands in a plea for understanding. "Maybe a judge wouldn't see it this way, but that makes it self-defense in the world I live in. Don't you see?"

"I see," said Sam flatly.

"Then . . . ?" She looked bewildered.

"Get washed; get dressed," he repeated. "I'm taking you back to Wild Wind."

"What if I refuse to go?" she said.

"It won't matter. You're going anyway."

"But if you keep me with you, Ranger, it could draw Silva in," she said, trying any angle. "You do want Silva, don't you?"

Sam didn't answer, even though she might be right. She would no doubt draw Silva out for him, once they were seen together in any of the settlements along the high trails. But he didn't want to have to keep watch on her while they traveled through some of the toughest, most dangerous terrain in the badlands. Besides, there was only one reason she would want to be out here with him, and that was to try to make an escape. Self-defense or not, being in Wild Wind would put a crimp in her plans to meet up with Silva "the Snake." That in itself was good enough reason for Sam to take her to town.

He reached down and picked up the duster and went through it, inspecting pockets and seams for hidden weapons. Feeling her eyes on him, he folded the duster over his forearm and held it for her. She saw the unyielding look on his face, and stopped and dipped water onto her blood-stained forearms and naked breasts.

"I hope you're getting your eyeful, Ranger," she said angrily, "because looking is all you're ever going to do with me."

Again without answering her, the ranger offered quietly, "We'll see what shirts and trousers I might have in my saddlebags when you're finished here. You can't ride to Wild Wind with nothing but skin between you and the saddle."

"Yeah?" she said in defiance. "I've ridden worse."

Sam just looked at her. *I bet you have . . .*, he said to her silently. Then he turned to his saddlebags, keeping her in his peripheral vision.

When he turned back to her, she had stepped out of the water and stood with her forearms closed over her bare breasts. "Here," he said, "give these a try. They're both clean."

She took a folded pair of denim trousers and a rolled-up wool shirt that he held out to her. "Thank you," she said, grateful for the clothes after even a short ride with her bare skin chafing against the saddle leather.

"You're welcome," he said. He stepped back and half turned and looked down across the rocky valley, as she dressed and rolled up the long trouser legs and the long, dangling shirt sleeves.

She looked over to where Weeks' boots stood on the dirt a foot from the blanket edge. "Do you have any spare socks, Ranger Burrack?" she asked, her eyes downcast, as if using up all of her pride.

Sam saw her cut a glance toward Weeks' boots. "I'll see what I've got," he said.

When the woman had put on Weeks' boots, she walked back to the horses, scuffling her feet to keep her oversized foot wear from falling off. Sam held the reins to her horse as she clumsily raised a loose boot into the stirrup and swung up into the saddle. She pushed Weeks' large hat up on her forehead and glanced up at the buzzards, which descended steadily with each wide, slow circle.

"We're keeping someone from their dinner," she remarked.

Sam didn't reply; he backed his stallion a step and gestured her onto the downward trail leading around the water hole.

"But this isn't the way to Wild Wind," she said, a hopeful look coming to her eyes. "You're going on after Delbert."

"I'm following his trail as far as I can," Sam said grudgingly. "Right up until I have to cut south toward Wild Wind."

"Oh," said Kitty, "for a moment there I thought you might have had a change of heart and —"

"You thought wrong," Sam said quietly, cutting her off.

They rode on in silence down the narrow, winding path for the next half hour, until the ranger spotted a line of riders crossing the flatlands below. "Hold it," he said suddenly. "Pull your horse out of sight."

"What is it?" Kitty asked, even as the urgency in his voice caused her to jerk her horse sidelong away from the trail's edge.

"Down there," Sam said, quickly nudging his horse over beside hers and pulling the third horse by its reins. "Step down."

"Why? They can't see me," she said.

"Get out of the saddle," he said, reaching back and pulling his telescope from under his bedroll.

She saw his intense stare and realized that he wanted her out of her saddle so she couldn't try to make a run for it while he checked out the riders. "All right," she said, swinging out of the saddle a second before he did. "There. Satisfied?"

"Stay beside me." He grasped her by the sleeve of her duster and pulled her along with him to a large rock at the edge of the trail. He dropped behind the rock and pulled her down beside him.

"I wasn't going to try anything," she said.

Sam didn't answer. Instead he stretched out the battered field lens and raised it to his eye.

"Who is it?" she asked, noting his expression had turned somber as he scanned each of seven riders.

"Renegades," he said, without taking his eye off the desert-hardened mustangs and their riders. The dusty procession galloped along at an even pace.

"Indians?" Kitty asked. Even as she spoke, she leaned back enough to look around his back toward the big Colt holstered on his right hip.

"Five of them are," he said. "Two of them are Comancheros. They belonged to a trade gang I helped break up last summer."

"So I take it those two have a grudge against you?" she asked.

"Yep," Sam said, still staring at the riders, their faces appearing as close to him as the woman at his side.

"This is great," she said, leaning back even farther, weighing the odds of her being able to reach around and draw the Colt without him knowing it. "Now we've got Apache to worry about."

"Not Apache," Sam corrected her. *"Renegades."*

"What's the difference? They used to be Apache, didn't they?" she said.

"No," he corrected her again. "They used to be Comanche." He watched the leader of the riders bob in the circle of the field lens as he spoke.

"How do you know they *used to be* Comanche?" she asked, straining to see the riders with her naked eyes.

"The one in front is wearing a buffalo headdress," said Sam. "Comanche are the only Indians who wear them. He's not supposed to, being a cast-out."

"A cast-out?" she asked.

"Yes," said Sam. "This bunch was cast out by Quanah Parker himself when they refused to stop fighting a couple of years back."

"You — you know these men?" Kitty asked.

"I know of them," the ranger replied. "The leader's name is Quintos." He stared through the lens at the young, grim-faced rider. Atop the man's head sat a bristly buffalo scalp, horns spiking from either side. "He goes by the plains name of Bloody Wolf."

"Charming . . . ," Kitty said, scooting back and slightly around the ranger, preparing to make a grab for his Colt. "And does Mr. Bloody Wolf also have a grudge against you?" She wanted to keep him talking, distracted. *So far, so good . . .*

"No more than he does against any white man," Sam said.

"Will this keep us from crossing back toward Wild Wind?" she asked, her fingertips inching forward.

"No," Sam said. "We'll be all right as long as we know where they are." Almost without stopping, he continued by saying in the same calm voice, "I wouldn't try that if I were you."

She stopped suddenly, straightened up and dropped her hand onto her lap. "I wasn't *trying anything,* Ranger. Honest."

"Yeah?" Without lowering the lens he replied, "Then why'd you stop?"

Kitty didn't answer; she turned her head and spit dryly. "I've got to have some water," she said. She started to stand and walk toward the horses.

"Stay right where you are," the ranger ordered. He did not reach up and grab her arm, but his stern tone of voice caused her to drop back down instantly, almost as if he had.

"Damn it, Ranger Burrack," she said as she plopped back onto the dirt. "I'm not going to try anything. I'd be a fool to. The least sound I make, those renegades would be on me before I could get halfway across the flatlands."

Sam lowered the lens enough to turn a cold stare toward her. "That wasn't going to stop you from shooting me in the back."

"I wasn't thinking when I did that," said Kitty, recovering quickly. "I'm glad you stopped me. I've had time to think about it. Besides, I wasn't going to shoot you in the back. I'm not that cold-blooded."

"Andy Weeks would have been glad to hear that," Sam replied, collapsing the telescope between his palms. He stood up and reached a hand down to help her rise to her feet.

"Oh," she said, dusting off the seat of her trousers, "so we were getting up to leave; you just wanted to make sure I asked your permission first."

"Yes, something like that," Sam admitted without hesitation. With his naked eyes he caught a glimpse of the riders as they moved out of sight, headed in the same direction he would take to Wild Wind. "From now until we get to town, you do what I say, when I say it."

"I don't follow *orders* well, Ranger. I do better with polite requests," she said.

"No more games, ma'am," Sam said. He gestured in the direction of the renegades. "Now that these boys are in the mix, we might have our hands full trying to stay alive."

"I wouldn't *be here* if you hadn't forced me to come with you," she said with disdain.

"It doesn't matter now," Sam said. "We're here, like it or not." He motioned for her to step up into her saddle while he held her horse's reins. "You know what's out there. From now on, if you try to run, I might not even try to stop you." He swung up into his saddle and handed her horse's reins to her. "Do we understand each other?"

"Yes, we do," she said grudgingly, turning her horse beside his onto the narrow trail.

CHAPTER 5

At the sight of the seven riders, Silva "the Snake" Ceran eased his horse into a dense stand of scrub cedar and sat midtrail, his hand resting on the Winchester lying across his lap. Seeing him, Quintos raised a hand as he reined his own horse to a halt. Behind him the other six did the same, spreading out on either side.

"Six abreast," Silva said under his breath to the three dismounted gunmen he had positioned out of sight among the cedars. "It looks like Mr. Bloody Wolf knows what he's doing."

A half-Mexican gunman named Paco Stazo stood leaning against a large pile of downed cedar and dry bracken, out of sight, his rifle poised and ready. He nodded and continued watching Quintos warily. Two bandoleers of ammunition crisscrossed his broad chest. Across the trail, two other gunmen lay in wait, one of them a former

Methodist minister named Alvin "the Reverend" Prew; the other a wanted killer named Charlie Jenkins.

From one end of the riders spread abreast across the trail, a ragged Comanchero named Mason "Dad" Lafrey rode to the center and stopped at Quintos' side. Lafrey wore a full black beard that covered most of his face, beneath a battered top hat and dirty, fringed deerskin coat.

"It's him, Bloody Wolf," Dad Lafrey said.

"You said he would meet us in Wild Wind," Quintos said, without taking his stare off Silva Ceran, who sat fifteen yards away staring back at him.

"He's a cautious man, Bloody," Lafrey replied. "He must not have wanted anybody knowing his exact whereabouts. You got to respect him for that."

Quintos paused and considered it for a moment. "Yes, it is good that he is cautious. I too am cautious when caution is needed." He tapped the heels of his calf-high moccasins to his mustang's sides and nudged the horse forward slowly.

"I appreciate that. Yes, sir, I do," said Lafrey, trying to placate the solemn renegade.

Watching the renegade ride forward in his buffalo-horn headdress, Charlie Jenkins grinned and whispered to Alvin Prew beside him, "This one is going to be a real huckleberry, Reverend. I'll bet on it."

"Silence, Charlie," the ex-minister demanded. He turned a cold stare to Jenkins, then looked back at Quintos. "I want to observe what kind of man will be riding with us."

A few feet from Silva Ceran, the young renegade stopped his horse and made a quarter turn in Ceran's direction. He looked Ceran up and down with a flat expression.

"All right, now. Here we all are together!" Lafrey said, grinning, trying to sidestep a tense silence before it set in. "All us rough ol' boys gathering up to see what we can —"

"Shut up, Dad, and get on with it," Ceran said, his eyes locked on Quintos as he spoke.

Dad Lafrey fell silent, then backed his horse a step and said in meek tone, "Anyway, Silva . . . this here is Quintos, or Bloody Wolf, if you prefer."

Ceran gave a nod.

"Quintos," said Lafrey, "this is —"

"I know who this is," barked Quintos. To Silva Ceran he said, "I was told you would meet me in Wild Wind."

"This *is* Wild Wind, far as I'm concerned," said Ceran. "What do you think we meant?

We'd meet at a town social, have some cider and pie?" A faint smile stirred on his lips. "Are we going to argue starting right off?"

Quintos let out a breath and looked all around, noting the gunmen on either side of the trail. "No, I join you in order to make money for guns, in order to fight the white eyes. When we have enough money to do this, I will take my men and we will leave. Do we understand each other's words?"

"Yep." Ceran nodded. "I don't care what you and your men do after you leave. While you're riding with me, I only want to know that your men are ready to die for you at the drop of a hat."

Without taking his eyes off of Ceran, Quintos raised a hand in the air and gave a sign with his fingers. "Are my warriors ready to die with me this day?" he called out over his shoulder.

Across the trail behind him four rifles came up and cocked toward Silva Ceran. On either side of the trail, Ceran's men aimed their rifles in return. Ceran didn't so much as flinch; he sat staring at Quintos, calm and steady.

But not Lafrey. "Jesus!" he bellowed, hurling himself from his saddle and scurrying across the rocky trail before he realized no one was firing. His hat flew off when he hit the ground.

Both Ceran and Quintos turned a look of disgust toward the fleeing Comanchero, who stopped crawling and looked back, red-faced, over his shoulder. "Get up, Dad," Ceran said with contempt.

Lafrey rose to his feet with a sheepish look and dusted off his trouser knees and his palms. "I can see right now, both you fellows like strong play. Next time I'll know more what to expect."

All the men on the trail stared at Lafrey until he'd gathered his battered hat and climbed back into his saddle. "Do you need to step into the brush and attend to yourself, Dad?" Ceran asked.

"It is no wonder Comancheros vanish the same way as the buffalo," said Quintos.

Without answering, Lafrey stared away from the two and grumbled under his breath. Back on the trail with the other renegades, Huey Buckles shook his head and breathed in relief. He had come very near to doing the same as Lafrey. *Lucky for me, I was too slow,* he thought, still feeling embarrassed by it.

"Are you ready to ride?" Ceran asked Quintos, the two more at ease with each other.

"Yes, but I will warn you of this," said

Quintos. "There is someone on our trail."

"Oh? How many?" Ceran gave a calm look along the trail.

"I do not know," said Quintos. "But I know they are there. I have felt their eyes on my back throughout the day." He gestured toward the ridges and paths above and behind him.

"Yeah? Why didn't you and your men stop and kill them?" Ceran asked.

Quintos only stared at him.

"Paco," Ceran said toward the gunman standing off the trail to his right, "ride back and bring us the head of whoever's following our friend here."

"*Sí,*" said Paco, stepping up quickly onto the trail, leading his horse behind him.

Ceran stared past Quintos and called out to one of the mounted renegades on the trail behind him, "You, with the bad nose. Go with him. Both of you take care of this business. Meet us farther along the trail."

An Indian with a flat, pinched nose looked to Quintos for direction.

"You heard him, Two Horses," Quintos said to the renegade. "Obey this man's order. He is in charge of us now."

The renegade didn't question Quintos. Instead he rode forward and looked at Paco as the Mexican stepped into his saddle and nudged his horse forward.

As the pair rode away off the trail and through a hillside of brush and rock, the Snake took on a look of satisfaction, liking the way Quintos had handed the authority right over to him.

Reading Ceran's expression, Quintos said, "This is how it must be. There is only one leader. While my warriors and I ride with you, you are that leader."

"Keep that in mind, and you and I are going to get along just fine, Bloody Wolf," said Ceran, nudging his horse closer and slipping his rifle back into his boot.

Paco and Two Horses rode in silence until they reached a covered ridgeline only a short distance above a flatland trail. When they'd dismounted and hidden their horses, the young renegade took a position behind the low bough of a scrub cedar and sat watching the path, almost unblinking, for nearly a half hour. Five yards away, Paco sat watching just as intently, until finally both men watched a single figure round a turn into sight, afoot on the rocky trail.

Two Horses looked over at Paco and drew a long bowie knife from its sheath at the small of his back.

Paco recognized Delbert Trueblood, but

instead of letting the young warrior know that Trueblood was one of their own, he decided to wait. He smiled to himself and nodded for Two Horses to make his move. Two Horses slipped around the rim of brush lining the trail as quietly as a spirit until he loomed above the unsuspecting outlaw, crouched like a mountain cat.

"Hope this doesn't ruin your day, Delbert," Paco said under his breath.

On the rocky trail, Trueblood had just looked back over his shoulder when the renegade let out a loud war cry and sprang down upon him from a rock ledge.

Even caught off guard, Delbert Trueblood managed to throw aside the wiry renegade as the big knife blade slashed across his forehead instead of his throat. "My God!" Trueblood cried out, blood spilling down into his eyes as the renegade hit the ground and shot back onto his feet in a crouch.

Trueblood's hands went up to his bleeding forehead, then reached for his gun. But in his confusion he fumbled and dropped the weapon from his blood-slick fingers, accidentally kicking it several feet away. "Jesus!" he screamed.

Paco winced, but he gave a dark chuckle at the deep blood flowing freely. As the bleeding gunman wiped and clawed at his eyes, the wiry renegade leaped forward again and put two more gashes across his chest, then jumped back.

The helpless gunman screamed, not knowing which wound to clutch first. Blood flew. "I'm part Indian!" Trueblood cried out, as if that information might save him.

Hearing him, Paco stepped out into the open just as the renegade sprang forward again. This time Two Horses grabbed Trueblood by his hair and jerked his head back, exposing his throat. The frightened man sank helpless onto his knees.

"This is getting ugly," Paco said with a cruel grin. Then he called out, "Two Horses, stop! Don't kill him. I know this man."

Two Horses, primed for a kill, caught himself at the final second and settled down. Instead of plunging the knife blade in Trueblood's throat, he let out another bloodcurdling war cry. Trueblood grappled in the air aimlessly with his bloody hands.

"Holy *Madre,*" said Paco, watching as the renegade reversed the knife in his hand and struck the blinded gunman with a solid blow in the middle of his forehead, using the weapon's hard, rounded-brass hilt. A loud *thunk* of metal on bone caused Paco to wince again.

"I said, do not kill him! He is one of us,"

Paco called out. Even as he spoke, he chuckled aloud and walked down to the trail.

The blow of the knife hilt on Trueblood's forehead caused the already addled gunman to fall face-forward onto the dirt. A puff of fine brown trail dust billowed up around him.

"I do not kill him because you say that he is one of us," said Two Horses. "I only knock him out. You must tell him I could have killed him, but I did not." He stared with a questioning look into Paco's dark eyes.

"*Sí*. I'll tell him," said Paco, stooping down over Trueblood. "But I don't think he is going to be happy about it either way." He reached out and turned Trueblood over onto his back and loosened his dusty bandana from around his neck. "He's bleeding like a struck pig."

"Yes, and I would have cut him four more times until he died," Two Horses said matter-of-factly.

"Oh, really?" Paco looked disappointed that he hadn't waited a few moments longer. He shook out the dusty bandana and wadded it into his hand.

"Is — is that you, Paco?" Trueblood said in a halting voice, blinking his bloody eyes.

"*Sí*, it is me, Delbert, your amigo, Paco Stazo," the grinning Mexican said, wiping the wadded-up bandana roughly across the gunman's eyes. "Lucky for you I am here," he said. "This man would have killed you for certain." He helped Trueblood sit up on the dirt and handed him the bandana.

"Then, I — I owe you my life, Paco," Trueblood said, still blinking, trying to see the two men more clearly. He held the bandana against the blood flowing from his split forehead.

"*Sí*, you do owe me your life, Delbert," Paco said, somehow managing to keep a straight face. "But I only do for you what I know you would have done for me, eh? I mean, if it was the other way around?"

"Yeah, yeah, that's right. . . ." Trueblood nodded and fell silent for a moment. Then he said quietly, "I was afraid you still held a grudge against me for me calling you all them hateful names back in —"

"No, no," said Paco, cutting him off. "I forgot about that the minute after it happened." He looked at Two Horses and said, "Help me get our amigo here onto his feet."

"I — I can't stand up yet," Trueblood said as Paco and the renegade pulled him up from the ground.

"Yes, you can," said Paco, holding Trueblood up as he swayed back and forth. "You must be strong and tell yourself that nothing will stop you."

"I'm too dizzy . . . ," said Trueblood.

Ignoring him, Paco gestured for Two Horses to turn the wobbly gunman loose; then he did so himself.

"Whoa!" Paco said, standing back and watching Trueblood fall flat on his face. He looked at Two Horses and shrugged. "We tried to help him. He must be worse off then we thought."

"I will get my horse and carry him on it," the renegade said.

"Yes, you should go do that," said Paco. He reached out with the toe of his boot and poked Trueblood in his ribs. The unconscious gunman grunted, but lay limp and motionless, his forehead bleeding into the dirt. "Some plains riders I know carry a sewing needle for repairing their gear. Do you?" Paco asked.

"I carry such a needle, but it is large, made from the rib of young coyote," Two Horses replied. "It is only used to repair moccasins or saddle leather and other —"

"It will have to do." Paco cut him off with the same slight grin. "Bring it," he said, "along with any rawhide lacing you happen to have with you. We will sew up his wounds and stop the bleeding." He grinned slightly. "I'll hold him down while you do as much stitching as it takes."

"It is good that we do this for him." Two Horses nodded.

"Yes, it is." Staring down at the bloody, unconscious gunman, Paco gave Trueblood another jiggle with his boot toe. Trueblood grunted in pain. "Nothing is too good for our friend here," Paco said.

CHAPTER 6

Darkness had fallen across the badland hills by the time Paco and Two Horses rode back into the clearing among brush and rock where Silva Ceran and the others had made camp. On the perimeters of the camp, three riflemen stood watch, each from a hidden position. As Paco and Two Horses rode in, keeping their animals at a slow walk, Jenkins stepped forward as if out of nowhere.

"Who the hell is this, Paco?" he asked from the shadows, his rifle in hand. He looked up at Trueblood, who sat slumped, riding double behind Two Horses.

"It's Delbert Trueblood," Paco said. "This is who was following Quintos and his men."

"Jesus," said Jenkins, staring at the dark blood and thick rawhide stitches across Trueblood's forehead.

"It is a long story," said Paco, "and I only want to tell it once." He nudged his horse on beside Two Horses until they both stopped a few feet back from a large, glowing fire.

Jenkins walked along beside the riders toward the fire. "Who cut him up so bad?" he asked, staring up at the slumped Trueblood, whose eyes were half closed against the throbbing pain in his tightly stitched forehead and abdomen.

Paco jerked his head toward Two Horses. "The Injun cut him all to hell before I recognized him." Paco spit, and kept himself from grinning. "The poor sonsabitch was trying to find us and got himself mistook."

Two Horses stared straight ahead in silence.

"Damn. I'll say he did," Jenkins commented. "How many times did he cut him?"

Paco stared down at him. "What you don't want to do, Jenkins, is take advantage of my friendly nature. I told you I don't want to have to keep repeating myself, like some kind of damned idiot. I'll tell you when I tell Ceran."

"Tell me what?" said Ceran, standing up from beside the fire and walking over, slinging coffee grounds from his tin cup. A few feet behind him, Quintos also stood and walked forward, toward Two Horses, who sat with the wounded gunman behind him.

Paco and Two Horses stopped their animals a few feet from Ceran. Trueblood swayed in place and muttered painfully under his breath.

Paco continued, saying, "That we found the man who was on Bloody Wolf's trail. It's Delbert Trueblood." As he spoke he reached over, took Trueblood by his shoulder as if to assist him down from behind Two Horses' saddle. But before Trueblood could turn to dismount, Paco gave a yank and turned him loose, letting him fall heavily to the rocky ground.

Trueblood let out a loud grunt.

"Oops," said Paco, straight-faced.

"Jesus," said Jenkins, watching.

"It was a slip," Paco said. He stared down at Trueblood and said, "Are you all right, pal? I hope I didn't save your life out there in order to watch you break your neck."

"I'm . . . all right," Trueblood said haltingly, allowing Jenkins to help him onto his feet.

"You don't look all right," Jenkins commented, taking note of the thick rawhide stitches running the width of his forehead, the same crude stitch work crisscrossing his chest and stomach. "You've been cut all to hell."

"You think . . . I need you to tell me that?" Trueblood said angrily. He jerked his forearm away from Jenkins and looked at Ceran, who stood staring with an air of impatience.

"Where's Kitty Dellaros?" Ceran demanded.

Unsure of how much he should reveal, Trueblood gestured toward the darkness behind them and said, "She's back there, with Andy Weeks. As far as I know."

"With Andy Weeks? As far as you know?" Ceran stared at him curiously, trying to determine if there was any sort of implication being made. He drummed his fingertips on the butt of the big Colt holstered on his hip.

"We — we got split up, Silva," said Trueblood, knowing one false word would get his head shot off. He looked all around, then touched his fingers carefully to the thick rawhide stitches. He said to Ceran in a lowered tone, "Can I . . . get some coffee? Then the two of us can talk somewhere in private."

Before answering Trueblood, Ceran looked up at Paco and Two Horses. "Good work, both of yas," he said. "Now break away. Get yourselves some grub and coffee."

"What about Trueblood being cut all to hell? Are we going to stand for that?"

Jenkins asked Ceran, giving Two Horses a cold, hard stare.

"Get back on lookout," Ceran said to Jenkins.

Seeing an expectant look on Quintos' face, Ceran said quietly, "Your warrior did good."

Quintos nodded in agreement, observing the long, tightly stitched gashes running across Trueblood's head and abdomen. "Two Horses, good warrior," he said. Seeing that Ceran wanted to be left alone with Trueblood, he turned and walked away, around the fire to where his warriors and Comancheros stood watching.

Trueblood held his tongue to keep from issuing a string of curses against Two Horses, although he knew the warrior had only done as he was told by Paco. When the other men saw Ceran give them a questioning look, they turned away. The wounded gunman started straight toward the fire, where a coffeepot sat steaming on a bed of glowing coals. But Ceran gave him a shove, redirected him away from the fire and said, "Start talking. You might not be needing any coffee this night."

Trueblood caught the threat in Ceran's voice as he stumbled out of the glowing light and away from the rest of the men. He fell to the ground and looked up at Ceran, who loomed over him. "Silva, I've done nothing wrong, I swear to God I haven't!"

Ceran's Colt slipped easily from its holster, cocked and leveled toward Trueblood's stitched forehead. "Where's Kitty? Where's Weeks and Wheeler? What went on in Wild Wind?"

"Damn it, Silva, please don't kill me," Trueblood pleaded, his mind still working on how to explain things to the outlaw leader. He cowered with a forearm raised, as if to protect himself. "I don't have nothing but bad news. That's why I didn't want to say it in front of the others. I didn't want to tell you, for fear you'll kill me for just knowing about it."

"Start talking," Ceran repeated, "or it's for sure I *will* kill you. Where's everybody?"

"Okay, Wheeler is dead," Trueblood said. "A lawman rode into Wild Wind and blew him to hell and was gone before the rest of us could do anything to stop him."

"Damn it," said Ceran. His hand eased away from his Colt.

Trueblood breathed a sigh of relief. "We didn't know how many lawmen were there," he lied, "so Weeks and Kitty and me cut out. We got separated in the badlands. I lost my horse when it broke its damned leg."

"Separated? How far out?" Ceran asked.

"I don't know — ten or twelve miles," said Trueblood, feeling better now that it appeared Ceran believed him. With the ranger on their trail, he knew it was a good possibility Kitty had been captured and was on her way out of the badlands in cuffs — better yet, maybe she was shot and killed, he thought. But he would settle for caught and dragged out of the badlands. That would keep Ceran from ever knowing what had happened out there.

"It was Kitty's idea that we split up," Trueblood continued. "She said it's what you would have wanted us to do, so we did. I hope you ain't angry over it."

Without answering right away Ceran considered things. He wasn't too disturbed over Wheeler being killed. In fact, he was glad it happened before they sat down and took their cut of the Poindexter robbery money.

"Are you? Angry, that is." Trueblood ventured, wanting to feel out the explosive gunman, see how much lying he needed to do.

"Before Wheeler died, did you find out anything about the Chicago mining company setting up a place in Wild Wind?" he asked, still without answering Trueblood's question.

"Only what I learned from old Emilio, the cantina owner," said Trueblood. "He said they're raising a building right now to house the valuables. He said it'll be part bank depository, part ore-hauling operation until they can build a rail spur across the badlands."

"Across the badlands — ha," Ceran scoffed. "I have dreamed for something like this my whole thieving life," he chuckled. "When does all this happen?"

"It's happening now," said Trueblood. "The building is being built. There could be silver ore and cash money there almost any time."

"Yeah, there could," Ceran said, getting a wistful look to his eyes as he thought of the possibilities awaiting him. "Did you and Weeks and Wheeler check out what the old man told you before Wheeler got shot, or was you all three too busy chasing whores and drinking whiskey?"

"All right, I ain't going to lie to you, Silva," said Trueblood. "We did get us some whiskey drunk and we was getting our bells rung when the lawmen slipped into Wild Wind on us. But everything the old man told us must be true. I saw enough that I believe him."

For a second, in Ceran's greed he'd almost forgotten about Kitty and Weeks. But then he snapped his stare back to Trueblood. Looking at the thick, reddened stitches on his head and abdomen, he said, "All right. Get yourself some coffee, and grub if you're able to eat. As soon as you're full, get yourself a horse from one of the renegades' spares."

"Where am I going?" Trueblood asked, standing and dusting off his seat.

"We're *all* going," said Ceran. "We're riding back and finding Kitty and Weeks." His eyes riveted onto Trueblood's. "That's not going to raise any problems, is it?"

"No. Hell no," Trueblood said quickly. "The sooner, the better. I want to find them just as bad as you do. I mean, hell, they're two of our own. We got to find them before the law gets to them."

"That's the spirit," said Ceran, studying him closely as he gestured a sweeping arm toward the fire, inviting Trueblood toward the coffeepot.

Jesus. That murdering bitch . . ., Trueblood thought, hoping the ranger had blown Kitty Dellaros' brains out somewhere on the badlands.

The ranger and Kitty Dellaros had taken

the trail that cut across a hill line and a long stretch of flatlands toward Wild Wind. From a cliff ledge inside the hills, Sam lay eyeing the vast, empty flatlands through his telescope before venturing down onto the harsh terrain. Standing off to the side, Kitty Dellaros wet a bandana from a canteen of tepid water and touched it to her hot, dust-streaked face.

"I thought you said we'd outflanked Bloody Wolf and his renegades," she said.

"We did," Sam replied over his shoulder, still scanning with the telescope as he spoke. "But Bloody Wolf's renegades don't have these badlands all to themselves."

"Oh? Who else are we ducking, then?" Kitty asked in a critical tone.

"Let's see . . . ," Sam said, as if giving the matter some serious contemplation. "There's Mexican bandits . . . American bandits. Runaway Apache. *Comadrejas* — desert weasels. A few other assorted saddle tramps, killers, lunatics . . ."

"Well, then," Kitty said cynically, "lucky for them, they won't have to worry about running into Ranger Sam Burrack. Will they?"

"That's right," Sam said, not letting her words get to him. He wasn't going to tell her that he'd spotted a freight wagon sitting with a broken wheel just at the edge of a short, spiky hill line. She would find out once they got there, he decided. "Mount up," he said, collapsing the telescope between his gloved hands.

"When will we be back in Wild Wind?" she asked. "I can't believe it's taking so long going this way." She fanned herself with the wet bandana. "Are you sure you haven't gotten us lost?"

"We'll be there before the day is out," Sam said, not dignifying her question by answering it.

For the past two miles he'd noticed that she'd become more talkative again — more talkative, more taunting and more high-strung. These were traits he'd recognized each time prior to her making another attempt at escape. She had settled down at the sight of the renegades. But now that they no longer posed a threat, and now that the two of them were drawing closer to Wild Wind and closer to the possibility of her freedom being taken from her, he knew she would make some desperate move on him at any time.

"There's no point in me wasting my breath trying to reason with you again, is there?" she asked out of the blue.

Yep, that cinched it, he told himself. She

was about to try something. He'd better be ready for it. Running her options through his mind, he realized there was nothing left for her to do but try to make a hard run for it across the rocky flatlands. She was unarmed; she had learned that she wasn't going to get the drop on him, take him by surprise the way he figured she'd taken down Andy Weeks. Outrunning him was all she had left.

He knew he could catch her easy enough. The horse she was riding was no contest for Black Pot. But there was more to consider. This was rugged terrain. He didn't want to risk injuring the stallion in a race across treacherous ground.

"We'd be foolish to wear these animals out and have to walk the last miles into town," he said quietly.

"What?" she asked, looking around at him quickly, his quiet tone of voice having caught her by surprise. She watched him draw his Winchester from its saddle boot and prop it up on his thigh.

"Even with the renegades behind us, we'd be in trouble if they happened back this way and came upon us afoot," he said. "So, keep it in mind that I'm not going to chase you." He levered a round into the rifle chamber, making sure she heard it.

"For God's sake, Ranger," she said. "Is that all you think about — me trying to escape?" She gave him a feigned look of shock and disgust. Her real shock was that he seemed to have just then read her mind. She had been on the verge of nailing her oversized boot heels to the horse's sides and making a run for it. Now she realized it would be useless. And he was right: this was no place to be on winded or injured horses. *Damn. Now what?* She asked herself, looking all around as if in defeat.

Would he actually shoot me? She wondered. He hadn't offered her a close enough look inside him to allow her to know what he might or might not do. She prided herself on reading men. But this one was not an easy study. This one didn't play along enough to let himself be seen. *Damn it to hell. . . .*

Sam had drawn Black Pot back a step behind her, keeping a close watch on her until he saw her slump ever so slightly in her saddle. *The move was genuine,* he told himself. She had considered her chances, then changed her mind. Maybe she was starting to understand that he was not out here to either play or be played with — only to do a job.

CHAPTER 7

On the flatlands, the freight wagon lay partly hidden in a stand of scrub juniper and saguaro cactus at the foot of the short hill line. But Sam knew where it sat, and as they came to the crest of a low rise and the wagon came into view, Kitty stopped her horse and sat staring until the ranger stopped beside her.

"What have we here?" she asked, seeing no one in sight in or around the wagon. Looking around at the ranger, she noted his lack of surprise. "Did you see this sitting here from atop the ridge?"

The ranger didn't reply. Instead he said in a guarded tone, "Keep moving."

"Yes, sir," she replied, her voice sharp with resentment.

Leading the spare horse by its reins, Sam nudged the Appaloosa forward at a walk, Kitty right beside him. When they were only a few yards from the wagon, they stopped again and sat quietly for a moment.

"Hello, the wagon," Sam called out, looking in among the sprawl of cactus and juniper scattered along the base of the hills.

"Can't you see there's nobody here, Ranger?" Kitty said, sounding impatient.

"Step down," Sam ordered.

In frustration she let out a puff of breath and swung down from her saddle. The ranger followed suit, and they led the horses forward, Sam with the Winchester still in hand. "Stay here," he said as they both stopped twenty feet from the wagon. He gave her a look of warning. "Don't forget what I said about not chasing you down."

"I won't," Kitty said. She stood with her reins in her hand and watched him walk over to the wagon and look down into the open bed.

In the wagon bed Sam flipped back a canvas cover and looked closely at a pile of silver ore. "What is it?" Kitty called out.

The ranger looked all around again, knowing that no one would abandon a valuable load under ordinary circumstances. "It's silver," he said.

"Really? How much?" Kitty asked.

"I don't know; quite a bit," he said. He walked to the team of horses hitched to the wagon, and felt the muzzle and the mane of

90

the one on the right. The animal's mane felt dry, its muzzle cool.

Walking back to the rear of the wagon, he stooped down beside the broken wheel and saw where someone had started to remove it from its axle, but had stopped halfway through the task. He ran a gloved finger through a dark streak of blood on the oak wheel hub and inspected it closely. *An injury? Maybe,* he thought.

"What is it, Ranger?" Kitty called out.

He straightened and looked back down at the ore. Running a hand over a chunk of stone the size of a melon, he said, "Bring your horse over here and tie it. I'm going to change this wheel and take this load on into —"

"Take your hand out of the wagon bed or lose it," a voice from the shelter of a saguaro cactus said, cutting him off.

Sam froze for a second, his ears searching for the direction of the voice. Then he raised his hand from the ore and started turning toward the cactus.

"Nice and easy," the voice said. "This scatter gun has a hair trigger."

"No harm intended," the ranger said, raising both hands chest high, knowing that in doing so, the badge on his chest would be visible from behind the lapel of his riding duster. The badge could be either a blessing or a curse, depending on who was standing behind the cactus.

"I spotted the wagon from the ridges a while ago," he said. "I rode down to take a look."

"Is that a territory ranger badge?" the voice asked.

"Yes," Sam replied, knowing it was time to see where he stood. "Who's asking?"

"My name's Longworth," said the voice, as a young man around Sam's own age stepped into view, a double-barrel shotgun resting over his raised left forearm. "Clayton Longworth," he added. "I'm a detective with Western Railways Transportation." His right hand held the shotgun, his finger on the trigger. But his left hand was wrapped in a bloody bundle of burlap.

"You've hurt your hand?" Sam called out, realizing now where the blood on the wheel hub had come from.

"But I can still handle a gun," the young man replied. "Stay where you are until I get a better look at that badge." He walked forward. To Kitty he said, "Do like he told you, ma'am. Bring your horse on over here and hitch it to the back of the wagon."

Thinking quickly, Kitty said, "Mister, this man is not who he says he is. He's holding me against my will. Make him drop the rifle and let me go. If you'll let me ride away from here, I promise that if we ever run into each other somewhere, someday, I'll make sure you get —"

"Bring your horse over and hitch it, lady," the young man said in a stronger tone of voice. "I'm hurt, and I've got no time to waste on you."

Damn it! Kitty cursed to herself. Jerking the horse by it reins, she led it over to the back of the wagon and hitched it. "There. Everybody happy?" she said.

Clayton Longworth stopped a few feet away and lowered the shotgun upon getting a better look at the badge on the ranger's chest. Sam noted the black, sweat-soaked linen suit jacket, the loosened black string necktie, the white but soiled shirt with a stiff clip on collar.

"Clayton Longworth, I'm Arizona Ranger Samuel Burrack," he said. "Before you listen to anything she tries to tell you . . . this woman is in my custody until we arrive at Wild Wind."

"I understand, Ranger Burrack," said Longworth, with a look of relief on his pained face. "I know you are who you say you are. I recognize you by the sombrero and the Appaloosa stallion." He gestured a

93

nod toward Black Pot standing nearby, then said, "I am mighty glad you come along when you did."

"What happened to your hand, Detective?" Sam asked.

Longworth gave him a long strange look as he leaned back against the open wagon bed and held his bandaged hand before him. Seeing a curious expression come to the ranger's face, he said, "Forgive me for staring, Ranger Burrack, but you're the first person who has ever called me *Detective* — the first lawman anyway."

"Oh?" Sam said curiously. "How long have you been a detective?"

"I've been a detective almost a year now. But most of that time I've been in Chicago," said Longworth, "doing what we call detail work, same as I've been doing here."

"Details need doing too," Sam said.

"Yeah, that's how I figure it," said Longworth. "But most of the lawmen I've had occasion to work with have had a hard time considering me a detective, owing to my age, I suspect." He looked the ranger up and down, as if to emphasize their closeness in age.

Sam gave a wince as he looked at the young detective's mashed and broken left hand. White bone and tendon stuck out from split and blackened flesh beneath the edge of the bloodstained bandage. "How'd this happen?" he asked.

"The jack slipped and pinned my hand between the hub and the wheel," said Longworth. "I had a hard time pulling it out."

"I can see you did," said Sam, noting the heavy wagon jack lying in the dirt.

"Next time I'll use a rock and a long lever," said Longworth. "I never should have trusted a wagon jack. Newfangled inventions never work for me like they should."

Sam only nodded as he inspected the mashed hand closely.

"What do you say, Ranger?" Longworth asked. "Am I going to lose it?"

"You've banged it up awfully bad," Sam replied, knowing the man wanted to hear something encouraging. "But it's going to take a doctor to say whether or not you'll lose it."

"I was getting ready to unhitch a horse from the wagon and ride back to Wild Wind when I saw the two of you in the distance," said Longworth. He relaxed a little in spite of the pain running from his mashed hand up the length of his arm. "First I had to get this ore unloaded and hidden somewhere."

"Unload the wagon first?" Kitty cut in, staring at him in disbelief. "You must be out of your head."

The ranger saw the sweaty white sheen on the young man's face and realized that Kitty was closer to being right than she realized. It was taking everything the young detective had had to keep from passing out.

The ranger gave Kitty a look and gestured toward the horses. "Why don't you get a canteen? Give him a drink; then we'll wash this hand off, take a better look and bandage it up good before we head to town."

Clayton Longworth sat staring blankly, but managed to say, "Obliged, Ranger. I could use a swig of water, or something even stronger if you've anything on hand."

"Water is the strongest thing I've got," Sam said. He looked at the big wagon jack lying in the dirt, and at the spare wagon wheel lying beside it. "When we get you bandaged up, I'll see if I can get this spare wheel on. It'll save us having to unload all this ore and come back for it."

"I'm in your debt, Ranger Burrack," Longworth said. Sam noted that his voice had begun to sound distant and shallow. He suspected that any minute the young detective would fall into unconsciousness.

"Take it easy, Detective," Sam said. "I'll see to it everything gets done the way you want it." He looked back along the distant hills. "We saw a band of renegades on the high trail. The sooner we get out of here, the better."

"Will they be coming this way?" Longworth asked. "If they are, I can still shoot, Ranger. I can handle my end of things."

"I'm sure you can, Detective," said Sam. "I doubt we'll be running into them. I just wanted you to know."

At first light, Ceran, Bloody Wolf and their men had ridden in the same direction up into the hills that the ranger and Kitty Dellaros had taken down to the flatlands. But the band of outlaws had ridden different paths. Ceran did not realize it until he stood looking out from atop the same high ridge Sam had stood on the day before.

"Whoever it is, damned if we didn't pass them somewhere," he said almost to himself, staring out through a pair of binoculars he had used to follow the winding double strips of wagon wheels and the upturned dirt of hoofprints across the dusty flatlands. Lowering the binoculars, he looked back down at the two sets of big boot prints and the hoofprints on the ground at his feet. "I can't make heads or tails of it," he added, shaking his head.

"Yeah, bad luck for us," Trueblood said,

feeling relieved that they had managed to not catch up to Kitty Dellaros, if indeed her horse's hoofprints was one of the sets on the ground. Ceran saying *heads or tails* brought back the image of the coin toss between him and Weeks. *Jesus, what a stupid thing to do . . .*

Seeing Trueblood's troubled expression, Ceran studied his face closely, looking for any signs of deception. He had just started to say something when Quintos called out, "Here comes Little Tongue. He brings something in a bag."

"Little Tongue," Ceran said under his breath, watching the scout ride into sight on the rocky trail. He shook his head again. "Christ, where do they get these names?"

Trueblood just stared at Silva Ceran, not knowing what to say.

"Come on, Delbert. Stick close to me," Ceran said, stepping back from the edge of the cliff and walking toward the approaching rider. "I don't want you out of my sight until I figure what's going on."

"Silva, please," said Trueblood, "you've got to believe me. . . ." He let his words trail, watching the scout stop ahead of them and pitch a grass sack to the ground at Bloody Wolf's feet.

"What the hell is this?" Silva said, quickening his pace toward Quintos.

When the two arrived, Quintos had stooped down, grabbed the grass sack by two bottom corners, turned it upside down and shaken out the contents. Trueblood stopped cold as Weeks' pale, bloodless head rolled across the ground toward him. "Holy God!" he said.

Ceran also came to halt. But he stuck out a boot and clamped it down onto the rolling head and held it in place while he stared down at the turned-up eyes and sharply severed neck, just beneath the wide, bloodless gash left by Kitty's razor.

Looking up at the mounted scout, he said, "You better tell me quick-like that this is how you found him." He gripped the butt of the big Colt on his hip.

Little Tongue sat staring, expressionless.

"This is how he found him," Quintos interceded on behalf of the scout.

"Hold on, Bloody Wolf," said Ceran. He continued to stare at the scout. "Doesn't this man talk?"

"He talks, but you do not want to hear it," Quintos said. "He was born with a tongue that is too small for his mouth. His words sound like the squawking of a strange bird. It is better that I sign with him and speak his words for him."

"I see. . . ." Ceran tried to imagine what the Indian's voice must sound like. But he quickly shook the thought from his mind and said to Quintos, "All right, what happened out there? Why did he only bring back my man's head?"

Little Tongue made sign with Quintos. Then Quintos turned to Ceran and said, "The buzzards, wolves and coyotes had taken their turn at the body. Little Tongue brought back only the head because it was easier to do so. It is the cut throat that shows what happened to the man."

"I see," Ceran said quietly. He rolled the head back and forth an inch under his boot for a better look.

"It is plain that his throat was cut," Quintos said.

"Yeah, it is," Ceran agreed, feeling Trueblood's eyes upon him. Both of them knew that Kitty Dellaros carried just the right kind of instrument for such a clean, slick cutting job.

Ceran avoided Trueblood's eyes for the moment and asked Little Tongue, "Was this man dressed or undressed when you found him?"

Little Tongue only stared back at him blankly. A tense silence set in among the men. Finally Ceran said, "I want an answer."

Little Tongue turned to Quintos and made more signs while Ceran watched impatiently.

"He wore nothing," Quintos said without hesitation when the two were finished making signs. "Not even his drawers or his boots."

"Buck naked, huh?" said Ceran. He turned an enraged stare to Trueblood. "Delbert, if you're keeping something from me, now's the time to spill it." He tapped his fingers on his gun butt.

"Silva, I swear to God," said Trueblood, "I'm not keeping anything from you." He quickly crossed his heart and said, "That's the gospel truth."

Ceran stared at him for a moment longer, then said to everyone, "Mount up. We're going to backtrack all the way to Weeks' body and see where everybody went from there."

"What about the wagon tracks?" Paco asked.

"Whoever it is, they're headed for Wild Wind," said Ceran. "We know where to find them." He turned as the men reached for their horses. "So long, Weeks," he said, "you shifty sonsabitch. I don't know what you was up to" — he gave the head a long kick and sent it flying out off the edge of the cliff

— "but by hell, I'll find out." He turned a harsh glare at Trueblood. "You ride at my side, Delbert. I want to be able to reach out and know you're there at all times."

"Yeah," Paco said, with a slight grin turned toward Trueblood. "In a few days I will pull those annoying stitches out for you, and you will feel much better, eh?"

"Paco," Ceran cut in, "I want you to pick yourself one of Bloody's men to go with you and follow those wagon tracks into Wild Wind. Lie low there and keep an eye on things until I get there."

"Right," said Paco. He looked at Huey Buckles and said, "You, *Comanchero.* Come on. You're riding with me."

Buckles grinned and asked Quintos, "Any problem if we rob something while we're there?"

Quintos only stared blankly at him.

Buckles turned to Ceran for an answer.

"Keep your nose clean, Buckles," Ceran warned. "Do what Paco tells you. Both of you keep an ear open for how things are coming along with the rail spur."

Trueblood wished he was riding with Paco — anything to get out from under Ceran's thumb. But that wasn't going to happen. He sighed and turned to the horse he'd chosen from among Quintos' string of spare mustangs. Without another word to anyone, he stepped up into a battered, wood-framed cavalry saddle and let out a long breath. He didn't know how he'd ever get off of the spot he was on.

■ ■ ■ ■

PART 2

■ ■ ■ ■

CHAPTER 8

Sitting beside Kitty, who drove the big, lumbering freight wagon, Clayton Longworth had drifted off to sleep. He awakened with a start when he realized his head had fallen onto Kitty's shoulder. "Begging your pardon, ma'am," Longworth said, straightening quickly on the wagon seat and batting his eyes. He looked all around. "I didn't mean to fall asleep. It won't happen again."

"I don't mind, Detective," Kitty said. "You can lay your head on my shoulder any time." She gave him a coy look and continued guiding the team of horses.

Riding beside the wagon, leading Kitty's horse and the spare, Sam said to Longworth, "We let you sleep, hoping it would take your mind off the pain in your hand. We'll be coming into Wild Wind in another couple of miles."

"Obliged, Ranger," said Longworth, holding his swollen, bandaged hand on his lap.

"It helped some, but I need to stay awake. I'm still on the job. I need to keep my wits about me."

"Why?" asked Kitty. "Don't you trust the ranger here with your load of rocks?"

"I trust the ranger, ma'am," Longworth offered. "But I'm paid to watch over these samples, and that's what I've got to do." As he spoke he looked up at the ranger.

"I understand," Sam nodded.

"Anyway, I need to have my wits about me. I've got a lot to do when we get to town." He nodded at the load of ore behind him in the wagon bed. "As soon as I get my hand fixed up, these samples have to be crated up and ready to ship out to the mining office."

"Silver samples, huh?" Sam glanced back at the pile of rough, jagged-edged rock.

"Yep," said Longworth. "Western Railways is considering buying interests in the mining companies up here. They want to know the silver is worth what it's going to cost to build a rail spur all the way out to Wild Wind. My job is to send whatever it takes to help them make that decision."

"That's the *detail* work you were talking about?" Sam asked.

"That's part of it, for now anyway," said Longworth, looking embarrassed by the question. "I know it's not gun work, but it's my job. I do it the best I can."

"No offence intended, Detective," Sam said.

"None taken," Longworth replied, staring ahead as the wagon rocked and swayed along the rocky trail. After thinking about it, he said, "I expect there will be plenty of gun work here, once the rail crew gets to town and the tinhorns and thieves follow the smell of money. But that'll be the new sheriff's concern, not mine."

Looking over at the young detective, Sam said, "Sounds like gun work is your only interest."

"It is," the young detective said with no hesitation. "The Longworths of Virginia are known for making their living carrying a gun. My father was a town sheriff in Virginia hill country until the day he died. I have four brothers. Every one of them makes their living carrying a gun." He paused, then said, "You could say gun work is expected of me."

Kitty gave him a sidelong glance and said with a smile, "You certainly look strong enough and capable enough to uphold the law, Detective Longworth. Or may I call you Clayton?"

Here we go . . . , Sam thought to himself,

knowing the woman had shifted her focus away from him and onto the young detective. He hoped Longworth saw what she was doing. If he didn't, Sam told himself, he would never make it in this business. He gazed ahead at a rise of dust looming like a dark halo above the town of Wild Wind.

A half hour later, the wagon rolled into town and came to a parallel stop in front of a newly constructed building. "This is Wild Wind's new sheriff's office, and Western Railways' mining offices," Clayton Longworth said, gesturing his good hand toward the two-story clapboard frame.

"Law and commerce under the same roof," Sam said.

"There's nothing unusual about that. Is there, Ranger?" Longworth asked.

"No," Sam said, "nothing new about it at all."

"Allow me, ma'am," said Longworth, pulling the brake handle back for Kitty with his good hand.

"Well, thank you, Clayton," Kitty said. "It's good to find a gentleman of manners." She shot Sam a flat look as she spoke.

As soon as Longworth set the brake, he stepped down from the wagon seat, his bandaged left hand cradled against his chest. "Well, Ranger Burrack, aside from these unfortunate circumstances, it's been good to meet you."

"Likewise, Detective Longworth," Sam said, touching the brim of his sombrero. He swung down from his saddle, rifle in hand. Seeing that the detective was having a hard time keeping the pain in his hand from showing on his face, he said, "Why don't you go on and get your hand looked after? I'll make myself at home here."

"My hand will have to wait long enough for me to show you both inside, Ranger," Longworth said, well-mannered to a fault. "Anyway, the doctor's office is just next door." He nodded toward a smaller building only a few yards away along a plank boardwalk.

"*Ahem,*" said Kitty, attempting to draw Longworth's attention to her as she stood up from the seat. "May a lady get a hand? Or, did I speak too soon about gentlemen and manners?" Again she gave Sam a look.

"Why, certainly you may have a hand, ma'am," said Longworth. He reached up with his good hand and assisted her down from the wagon.

Sam watched as he spun the reins around an iron hitch rail out in front of the new building.

"After you, ma'am," Longworth said,

gesturing Kitty ahead of him to the door of the sheriff's office. To Sam he said, "Wild Wind doesn't have a sheriff right now. But Western Railways will be sponsoring an election for one before long."

"Sponsoring an election?" Sam asked, as the two walked inside ahead of him.

"Yes," said Longworth, not catching any skepticism in the ranger's words. "Western Railways is good about that sort of thing. They believe in helping the community they do business in any way they can."

"For now, I suppose Ed Ray Richards is still handling matters of the law here?" Sam asked.

"That's right," said Longworth. He stopped and gestured through an open door toward a row of three cells along the rear wall. In one cell, two pairs of eyes stared out through the shadows. "The cell on the right doesn't yet have a lock on it yet."

Kitty eyed the cells with a look of disgust. "You're not putting me into one of those cages," she said.

"No, I'm not," said Sam. "That'll be up to Ed Ray when he gets here."

"Hey, lady!" a voice chuckled from the only cell in use. "You can come in here with us, if you're scared of being alone."

"Shut up back there," said Longworth. To

Kitty he said, "Pay them no mind, ma'am. They're the Cullen brothers. They're here awaiting a territory judge." He raised his voice for the two prisoners' benefit. "They'll most likely be off to prison soon enough."

Kitty gave Longworth a look of desperation. "Can you do something to help me, Detective? I don't belong in a cell."

Longworth shook his head apologetically. "Ma'am, this is the ranger's call." He looked at Sam. "I'll be getting on over to the doctor now. As soon as Ed Ray sees the wagon out front, he'll be heading this way."

"You do that," Sam replied. "We'll be fine here till he arrives."

"Tell Ed Ray to bring us some damn food," one of the Cullen brothers heckled from the cell.

"And some damn whiskey," the other brother said with a chuckle.

As Longworth turned and left, closing the door behind him, Kitty looked up at the ranger and said, "Sam, please don't put me back there in a cell."

It was her first attempt at calling him by his first name. He ignored it. "I'm not putting you in a cell," Sam said. "I'm not even going to hold you here any longer than it takes for Ed Ray to get here. It's up to him what he does with you."

"But you could tell him that what I did was in self-defense," she said, grasping his forearm.

"I'll tell him what I saw," Sam replied. "Ed Ray will have to take it from there and do what he thinks best."

"Well," she said, "thanks for not putting me in a cell, at least." She stepped back and sat down on the end of a wooden bench attached to the wall. "Suppose I can get a cup of coffee? Or is that asking too much?" She nodded toward a battered coffeepot sitting atop a potbellied woodstove in the corner.

Sam stepped over to the stove, picked up a coffee mug, inspected it and filled it with hot coffee. "This looks strong enough to float a pistol."

"That's how I like it," Kitty said, taking the mug and cupping it between her hands.

Sam saw a look in her eyes that alerted him, and he took a step back. "Don't even think of doing anything with that coffee besides drinking it."

"Jesus, Ranger," Kitty replied, "I've never seen a man so suspicious in my life. I wasn't thinking about throwing it on you."

"Good," said Sam, but he'd seen the look on her face change again. It told him he'd been right. She'd thought about throwing the hot coffee on him and making a dash for the door. Now she'd abandoned the idea, seeing that he was on to her.

Kitty blew on the coffee, sipped it, then set the mug on the bench beside her. "You're right," she said. "It is a little too stout for my taste."

"I thought it might be," the ranger said. He retrieved her mug and pitched the coffee into a waste bucket. He set the cup down on a table and started to turn when he heard five rapid blasts of gunfire coming from the direction of the cantina.

"Damn. *Somebody's* bell got rung!" one of the prisoners called out from the cell.

Sam's eyes went to Kitty.

"Go!" she said, seeing that would be his natural response. "Don't worry. I'll be right here — I promise!" she said quickly. "You trust me to not —"

Her words stopped abruptly as she saw one handcuff go around her wrist and the other snap around the arm of the bench.

"Damn it to hell," she said under her breath, watching the ranger go out the door.

A dark chuckle came from the cell. "Ain't he just the berries, that ranger pal of yours?" said a voice.

"Shut up, idiot," Kitty snapped back at the Cullen brothers, who stood at the bars, staring out at her.

The brothers gave each other looks of feigned shock. "Damn, Cadden!" said Price Cullen. "Did you hear what she called you?" He looked stunned. "An *idiot,* of all things."

"She didn't call me that, brother," said Cadden Cullen. "She was talking to you." He turned his eyes from his brother and stared out at Kitty. "If a woman called me that, she'd be bound to have a spanking coming first chance I got."

"Would she sure enough?" said Price Cullen.

"Oh, indeed, she would," said Cadden, a dark, wistful look coming to his eyes. "A bare-handed spanking on her warm, naked buttocks," he cooed. "I'd make sure she felt every —"

"You should live so long, you drooling idiot," Kitty snapped.

"Whoa!" said Price in a shocked tone. "Now she's upped it from a regular idiot to a droo—"

"I heard her," said Cadden. He stared coldly at Kitty and said, "You've got a dirty mouth toward the only two people who can bust you out of here."

Kitty looked back at the cell and eyed them up and down with distaste. "Yeah, right, you two hand-pumping fools," she said with scorn.

"Whoa!" Price repeated. "She *was* talking to you that time, Cadden."

"Oh yeah, she's got a spanking coming for sure," Cadden said.

Kitty took a deep breath and collected herself. "Do either of you idiots know who you're talking to? Who I ride with?"

The brothers looked at each other. "Why no, I expect we do not," said Price with a bemused smile. "Why don't you just tell us?"

CHAPTER 9

The ranger ran the length of the dirt street to the Belleza Grande Cantina. Then he came to a halt, his Colt in one hand, his rifle in the other, watching Ed Ray Richards stagger out onto the boardwalk. "I've got . . . it under control . . . ," Richards said, blood spilling from his lips, his hands pressed to three bleeding wounds on his chest.

No sooner had the wounded man spoken than another gunshot exploded inside the cantina. The bullet struck the townsman in his back and hurled him forward. He staggered off the boardwalk and into the street. Sam crouched and moved forward. Along the street, townsfolk who'd ventured out to investigate the gunshots now took cover inside shops and open doorways.

Hearing someone run up behind him, Sam gave a quick look over his shoulder and saw Clayton Longworth coming to halt at the end of his run from the doctor's office.

"I've got you covered, Ranger," Longworth said, half crouching, his Colt in hand. The ranger saw the swollen, injured left hand hanging limp at the detective's side. The doctor had been unwrapping the wounded hand when the shots rang out. The young detective had wasted no time running toward the sound of trouble, Sam noted to himself as he motioned him toward the other side of the cantina. Sam moved forward.

"Watch the door to the alley," Sam said over his shoulder.

"Got it," Longworth said, hurrying away in a crouch, his attention never leaving the doors of the cantina.

The ranger hurried up and stopped beside the open doorway as another gunshot exploded and a bullet whistled past him, out along the empty street.

"I'll kill any son of a bitch that comes through the door!" a drunken voice called out from the bar. "I'm going to hang anyway!"

"Who's in there?" Sam asked, buying time, looking for a way to get control of the situation. "Why are you going to hang?"

"Harry Ginpole," said the drunken voice. "Who's asking?"

"I'm Arizona Ranger Samuel Burrack,"

Sam called inside. He recognized the name Harry Ginpole. It was another of Silva Ceran's gang of thieves. Peeping around the door frame, Sam saw the half-naked body of Ramona, the young whore, lying lifeless in a pool of blood. *Oh no . . .* He pictured her smiling face from only a few days earlier. "Is the woman dead, Ginpole?"

"Oh yeah, she's dead, Ranger," said the drunken gunman. "One bullet straight through the noggin. Damn shame, though. I didn't mean to kill her. I wasn't even shooting at her. She just got in the way."

He was talking instead of firing. *Good . . .*

"What about Ed Ray Richards?" Sam asked. "Did you mean to kill him?"

"Yes and no," said Ginpole. "He pulled a gun and started asking me questions like he was some kind of damn lawman. So I shot him once, you know, just to shut him up and back him down."

"Yes, I understand," Sam said, looking back and forth along the floor of the cantina.

"But he still wouldn't shut up, and he wouldn't back down. Instead he shot me in the gut. So I shot him some more," said Ginpole, "until the damn fool finally turned and walked away. He dropped his gun on the floor."

"Then you shot him in the back," Sam said.

"Yeah, that's right," said the drunken outlaw. "I wish I hadn't done that." He paused again, then said, "Anyway, he's dead, and so is this little dove. I feel bad about her."

Looking in, Sam could see the gun hanging in the big man's hand. His other gripped his bloody lower belly.

"There's a doctor here, Ginpole," Sam said. "Come on out. We'll get you patched up."

"Uh-uh," said Ginpole. "Patched up for what? So I can get my neck stretched? I'm not coming out there. I'm going to stand here and drink till I'm bled out. I ain't swinging in front of a crowd, letting them see me soil my britches, the way ole Hadden Cooper did in Leadville."

"You might not hang, Ginpole," Sam said. "You might go to prison. Learn to make leather goods."

"Wouldn't that be fun," the wounded gunman said with sarcasm.

Sam straightened up. He'd heard a total of six shots, so he knew now was his chance. He stepped warily inside the cantina. The gunman stood sweating, staring at him from the bar. *Did he manage to reload?* Sam wondered. He raised a cautious hand toward him.

"Easy, Ginpole," he said. He slowly stepped forward across the floor, toward Ramona's body. "I've got to see if this girl is alive. I can't let her bleed out just because *you* want to."

"I told you, I shot her in the head, Ranger," Ginpole said. "Damn. You as stupid as Richards was?"

"I've got to check," Sam said quietly. But as he stooped slightly and saw both the entrance and exit wound on the girl's head, he let out a sigh and stood back up.

"I told you," said Ginpole. "Now get out 'fore I put this last bullet in your gullet."

Last bullet? Sam didn't think so. He ignored the threat, knowing that he had the man now. He held his big Colt cocked and half raised toward him. He'd counted six shots, and Ginpole hadn't reloaded. If he had, he wouldn't have mentioned the last bullet. He was holding an empty gun and trying to bluff his way along. That was all right. For now Sam wanted to learn whatever he could about the man Ginpole rode with.

"You must have come here to meet up with Trueblood, Weeks, Wheeler and the woman," Sam said matter-of-factly. "I know you were all supposed to get with Ceran and collect your part of the Poindexter job."

Ginpole stared at him through a glistening sheen of sweat. "How the hell did you know that?"

"Weeks is dead, Trueblood is on the run and Kitty Dellaros is over in the new jail right now, handcuffed to a bench. She told me what's going on."

"Shit," said Ginpole. "Kitty never told a lawman nothing in her life."

"You think she's wanting to learn to make leather goods?" Sam asked. He let the question lie for a moment, then said, "Of course, if she's lying to me, I'll see to it she turns old behind bars."

Ginpole gripped his belly tighter and winced as pain radiated upward through his chest. Then he let out a breath and said, "Hell, all right, she's not lying to you. We come to meet here to look the town over . . . then find Ceran and get our money."

The gunman swayed and almost fell before he caught himself on the bar edge. Sam nodded and pushed further. "It's hard to believe Kitty took part in the robbery."

"I never said she took part in it," replied Ginpole.

"Are you saying she had nothing to do with the robbery?" Sam asked. "If she wasn't in on it, why would she have any money coming?"

"Money comes for lots of reasons," said Ginpole. "I'm not saying no more about it, Ranger." He raised his pistol and dropped it onto the bar top. On the side wall, Sam watched the door to the alley open a crack, then slowly open more, enough for Clayton Longworth to slip inside the shadowy cantina.

"It's all right, Ginpole," Sam said, seeing a look of fear come upon the gunman's sweaty face. "He's a lawman. He's with me."

"That doesn't . . . buy him much in my book," Ginpole said, his halting voice growing weaker.

With his gun out and aimed, Longworth stepped sidelong around the body of the girl on the floor. He glanced down at her, than stared at Ginpole with an expression of pure rage in his eyes. "Where's the owner, old Emilio?"

"He's dead too," said Ginpole. "He's lying behind the bar."

The words took Sam aback. He started to walk quickly around behind the bar to check on Emilio. Seeing him make the sudden move, the fading gunman shouted, "Stay where you are!" He reached a bloody hand toward the pistol on the bar top.

Sam stopped, but it was too late.

As the wounded outlaw reached for the gun, Longworth wasted no time. His Colt bucked twice in his hand, and Harry Ginpole jerked straight up, poker stiff for a second. Then he fell forward, dead on the floor, his gun in his bloody hand.

Sam stopped and gave Longworth a questioning look.

"He went for his gun," the detective said.

Sam didn't reply. Instead he went around behind the bar and stooped down beside the old cantina owner. Seeing that Emilio was dead, Sam closed his eyes, stood up and walked back around to where Longworth stood over Ginpole's sprawled body.

"I thought he was going to start shooting, Ranger. I swear I did," Longworth said.

"Did you count the shots?" Sam asked. He reached down and took Ginpole's gun from his bloody fingers.

"What?" Longworth asked, his crushed, swollen hand hanging at his side.

"When the shooting started, did you count the number of shots fired?" Sam asked.

"I — I think I counted five, then another one when he shot Ed Ray in the back. Six," he said.

"You figure he had time to reload?"

"What are you telling me, Ranger?" Longworth stared at him.

Holding Ginpole's gun in way that kept Longworth from seeing it, Sam said, "Nothing. Forget it. Go get your hand taken care of."

"Wait, Ranger. Let me see his gun," said Longworth.

"Go on back to the doctor's," said Sam.

"Not until I —" Longworth's words were cut short as a burly red-bearded man in a black pin-striped suit walked in and stopped with a shotgun in the crook of his arm.

"What the blazes is going on here?" the man barked. He stared hard at Longworth, as if that was where he wanted the answer to come from.

"Mr. Bell," said Longworth, "I didn't know you were in town." He straightened as if he'd been called to attention.

"That's because you failed to check the hotel desk for any messages. Didn't you, Longworth?" the man asked almost accusingly.

"Sir, I only returned to town a few minutes ago," said Longworth. "I haven't yet been to the hotel. I stopped first at the doctor's office."

"I saw the wagon out front of the new sheriff's office," said the red-bearded man.

"I'm glad to see you were able to bring the ore samples we need." He only glanced at Longworth's crushed hand. Then he looked at the ranger and said, "I'm Hansen Bell. And who are you, young man?"

"Excuse me, Mr. Bell," said Longworth, cutting in to make an introduction. "This is Arizona Territory Ranger Samuel Burrack."

"Oh?" Hansen Bell looked the ranger up and down, eyeing the badge on his chest. "I daresay, I have heard of you, sir."

"Ranger Burrack, this is my superior, Mr. Hansen Bell, head of security and investigations with Western Railways."

"A pleasure, Ranger," Bell said gruffly. Without waiting for a reply from either of the two young men, Bell looked all around at the blood and the body on the floor and said, "I heard the shots. What went on here, Ranger Burrack?" His question sounded more like a demand.

The ranger ignored the question. "Why don't we get Detective Longworth over to the doctor's office? His hand is in bad shape. We can talk there."

"I prefer to talk right here, sir," Bell insisted, planting his feet. "Is that a problem?"

"No problem at all, Mr. Bell," said Sam. "Talk all you want. When you're finished, you'll find us at the doctor's office."

Bell saw he wasn't going to get anywhere bullying the ranger. He offered a tight smile. "Forgive me, Ranger." As if in afterthought, he said, "You too, Detective Longworth. To the doctor's office we go."

He gestured them both toward the open door as townsmen ventured in off of the boardwalk and looked all around. "All this excitement has made me cross and irritated." He looked at Longworth's hand as if just noticing its condition. "What happened to your hand, Detective?" he asked, his countenance more sedate, friendlier as they stepped out onto the boardwalk and down onto the dirt street, where three men lifted Ed Ray Richards' body and carried it away.

Bell stopped for only second and pulled his derby from his head in respect for the dead townsman. "Poor bastard," he said. With a turn of his wrist he placed his hat back atop his head and walked on.

Once inside the doctor's office, Sam and Hansen Bell stood, hats in hand, and watched a white-haired doctor escort Longworth back into a treatment room. As the doctor closed an oak door between the two rooms, Sam and Bell heard him say to Longworth, "Run out of here like that again, and you better hope this hand can fix itself."

"Sorry, Dr. Ford," said Longworth as the door closed.

Sam turned to Bell and began explaining everything that had gone on, including the fact that he had Kitty Dellaros handcuffed to the wooden bench next door. "I'd hoped that Harry Ginpole might slip up and tell me she was involved in the Poindexter robbery. But he didn't."

Bell lowered his voice and asked, "Who says he didn't?"

"I say he didn't," Sam said, not liking what the man was suggesting.

"Come, now," said Bell. "We both know she rides with Ceran — for God's sake, she's his strumpet. The judge knows it too. She was there when that robbery occurred. There is absolutely no doubt of it, *Burrack.*" His voice had gotten more demanding as he spoke.

"There may be no *doubt,* but there is no hard *proof* either, *Bell,*" Sam said in an even tone. "There's only suspicion. I won't change anything Ginpole told me just to get her railroaded."

"If you don't think she's guilty, why'd you even bring her here?" Bell asked.

"I had a body lying with its throat cut

inside Wild Wind's jurisdiction," Sam said. "It was my job to bring her in, to tell Ed Ray what I saw and turn her over to him. Now that Ed Ray Richards is dead, I have to turn her loose or haul her around with me. I'm still on the trail of Delbert Trueblood, and I'm still hunting for Ceran and his men."

"Don't worry, Ranger Burrack," Bell said. "I'll be taking custody of her, for questioning on both the murder of this Andrew Weeks and on the robbery of the Poindexter mine payroll."

"I'm afraid I can't turn her over to you, Mr. Bell," said Sam. "I can only turn her over to someone in the official capacity of upholding the law in Wild Wind and its surrounding jurisdiction."

"I understand, Ranger. And that would be me," Bell said firmly. "Only yesterday, Ed Ray Richards and the other two town selectmen signed over the power of office to Western Railways Transportation until such time as a proper election for sheriff can be held."

"You have papers to that effect?" Sam asked.

"Of course," said Bell, his hand going inside his lapel as he spoke and producing a folded document. He handed the document to the ranger, who opened and read it silently.

"Will that be sufficient, Ranger Burrack?" Bell asked coolly.

Satisfied, Sam folded the document and handed it back to Bell. "Yes, it will," he said. "But I want to tell you that I have no proof of Kitty Dellaros participating in the Poindexter robbery. As to the killing of Andy Weeks, it'll be hard to prove it wasn't self-defense."

"Be that as it may," said Bell, "Territory Judge Lawrence Olin will be through here in less than two weeks. It will be his call. Meanwhile I have no intention of allowing that woman out of Wild Wind, or even out of my sight." He jammed the folded document back inside his lapel and stared closely at the ranger. "You said Ginpole told you he was to meet her and the others here, to *look the town over?*"

"That's what he said," Sam replied.

"That can only mean Ceran is waiting and biding his time. As soon as he sees large amounts of revenue coming into Wild Wind, he and his thieves and murderers will set upon this town like vultures."

"That's the way I see it," Sam agreed.

"Then it's all settled," said Bell. "I'm taking her off your hands."

Sam nodded. If this was the way Wild Wind wanted to handle its law work, he was not the one to argue the point. Thinking about Kitty Dellaros' locket, which he still carried in his pocket, he said to Bell, "I'm walking next door and checking on Kitty before I leave. I'll leave her razor in the bottom desk drawer for evidence if you need it."

"Before you leave?" said Bell. "But you just got here."

"I told you, I'm still tracking Trueblood," he said, turning to the door.

"I'll be right along behind you," said Bell. "I want to see this woman myself."

CHAPTER 10

Kitty Dellaros looked up as the ranger walked in through the front door. "Well, Ranger," Kitty said, eyeing Sam up and down, "I see you've made it back in one piece."

"Who got their bell rung, Ranger?" Price Cullen called out from the cell on the back wall.

Ignoring the prisoner's question, Sam reached into his trouser pocket, pulled the locket and held it out toward Kitty's free hand. "Here. I didn't forget," he said. "I always keep my word."

"Thanks for giving it back to me, Ranger," said Kitty. "I wouldn't have let you get away without reminding you." She took the cheap tin locket, checked it and put it away. "I'll give you back your clothes as soon as I get some of my own." She looked at him closely and asked in her playful way, "No chance of me getting my razor, huh?"

"None in the world," said Sam. "It's going in a drawer here, as evidence. There's no hurry on the clothes. I'm going to be leaving here real soon."

"Oh?" said Kitty. "Did Ed Ray say he's going to keep me here?"

"Here's some bad news for you, Kitty. Your friend Harry Ginpole is lying dead over in the cantina. He killed Ed Ray."

"Ginpole . . ." Kitty appeared to consider the name. "I'm afraid I never had the pleasure."

"Don't lie to me, Kitty," said Sam. "He told me he was here to meet you and the other three."

"Oh?" Kitty said. "And what else did this Mr. Ginpole have to say?"

"Stop it," said Sam, "or I won't even talk to you about him."

"I can't say I'm real broken up about Ed Ray," Kitty said. She let out a breath and started to say something more. But before she could, Hansen Bell walked through the door and stood in front of her.

Sam gestured toward the big man. "Kitty, this is Detective Chief Hansen Bell. He's Detective Longworth's superior."

"Oh," said Kitty, trying to warm up to Bell right away, "are we going to get to be friends, Detective Chief Hansen Bell?"

"No, we're not," Bell said flatly.

"In that case, Ranger," she said to Sam in a playful tone, "I refuse to stay here. Unlock these cuffs and take me away from here."

Bell made no attempt at recognizing her sense of humor. He pounced right away. Leaning down close to her face, he said in a threatening tone, "Listen to me, you little tramp. Your party is over. Ed Ray is dead. He was a good man, and one of *your* outlaw pals killed him. You're in *my* custody now." He thumped his thick thumb on his chest. "You do not want to trifle around and play games with me. I will tolerate none of it!"

"Where did they dig up this sack of pig fodder?" Kitty snapped back, leaning into his face with the same scornful, threatening look.

"Where?" Bell said in his rage. "I'll tell you where I'm from." He thrust his face only an inch from hers. "I'm from a place where we sweep scum like you into a pile and burn it."

But Kitty did not give an inch.

"Get him out of my face, Ranger," she said, her voice the low growl of a wild cat.

"Ease up, Bell," Sam said, seeing from the look on the woman's face that at any second she would go for the man's eyes with her nails. Sam took the stocky man by his shoulder to pull him back.

But Bell didn't listen. He rounded his thick shoulder away from the ranger and said only inches from Kitty's face, "Don't look to the ranger for help. You belong to me now. What I do is strictly up to —"

"Oh-hhh!" said Price Cullen, seeing Bell stagger back a step as Kitty's nails made a gash across his face just below his eyes.

"She got him good!" said Cadden Cullen, laughing aloud at the sight of a big man like Bell cowering back, crouching, a hand pressed to his bearded face.

"Why, you little harlot," Bell said through clenched teeth. He drew back an open palm to slap her across the face, but as he started to swing, Sam stepped in between the two. He grabbed Bell's wrist and stood facing Bell as closely as the detective had faced Kitty.

"You're not going to hit her. Put it out of your mind," Sam said in a lowered but unyielding voice.

Bell resisted the ranger's grip, but only for moment. Then, reading the look on the ranger's face, he eased up. "All right . . . all right. I lost my head." He lowered his hand as the ranger released his grip on his thick wrist. "I'm okay now."

"See that you are," the ranger cautioned

him, still keeping himself planted between Kitty and the burly red-bearded detective.

Stepping back, Bell pulled a white handkerchief from his coat and touched it to two bloody cuts across his cheek and the bridge of his nose. "Some of these whores have nails like knife blades."

Sam thought about the razor he'd taken from Kitty and reminded himself just how lucky Bell had been that the razor wasn't still hidden among her clothing.

"I'm not a whore, mister," Kitty said coolly. "If I were, a pig like you couldn't afford me."

She grinned smugly. The ranger could tell she had Bell where she wanted him. He had cooled Bell down and kept him from losing his temper. *Now she knows she can taunt him all she likes,* Sam thought. She knew he wouldn't lose his head again. If he did, so what?

Sam stared at her, seeing the confident look in her eyes, knowing that she was counting on him not to let Bell manhandle her. They had both shown her enough to let her see that she could play them one against the other. *A game she is good at,* Sam told himself.

"I don't like leaving her here with you, Bell," Sam said.

"Be that as it may, Ranger," said Bell. "I have the authority." He dabbed at the cuts. "But you needn't worry. I'm not going to harm her."

The Ranger wasn't going to say it right now, but it wasn't Bell that he was concerned about. He'd seen what Kitty could do both with a razor and without. He saw Kitty's smug grin turn to a subtle smile, as if she knew what he'd just thought.

"I promise I'll be good, Ranger," she said. She crossed one knee over the other. "But if you really wanted to, you could get the two of us a room. You could keep me in your custody until the judge arrives. You could do that, couldn't you?"

"Holy God!" shouted Price Cullen. "Can he really do that?"

"If he can, *I* want to be a ranger!" Cadden Cullen joined in.

Bell pointed a thick finger toward the cell. "You two, that's enough out of you. Shut up, or you'll get no grub come meal time."

"Damn, that's harsh and inhuman treatment, don't you think, brother?" Cadden said to Price in a lowered voice.

"Yes, I think so," Price replied in the same lowered tone. "But what do I know? I'm just an outlaw."

Ignoring the Cullens, Sam said to Bell, "If

I thought you were going to abuse this office, I'd go to the selectmen —"

"You do that, Ranger," said Bell, cutting him off. "I have Western Railways standing ready to pump investment money into this town. Who do you think they'll side with — you and the territorial law, or big business?" He gave Sam a grin. "Let's not kid each other. This town belongs to Western Railways. Go do your job, Burrack. Leave me to do mine."

Sam didn't reply. He knew Bell was right. Wild Wind wasn't going to do anything to upset Western Railways and hurt the town's chances to prosper, especially not after having signed over the documents that put the company in charge of the law until after an election.

"Well, there went my idea," Kitty said to Sam with a sigh. "I had hoped we could become close friends, you and I." She gave him a suggestive look. "A hotel room, a nice, hot bath . . . dinner brought up to us."

"Afraid not, Kitty," Sam said, "I'm leaving here. Come morning. I still have Trueblood's trail to follow." Sam realized that even as she spoke to him, her message was directed in part to Hansen Bell, to annoy him, to entice him, to get whatever response she could from him.

"Oh . . ." She sounded disappointed. "Another time, maybe?"

"It's not likely," said Sam.

"I'll take you up on it, ma'am," Cadden Cullen said from his cell.

Sam said to Bell, "I'm going next door to see how Longworth's hand is before I leave."

"When he's finished with the doctor, have him come on over here," said Bell. "We've still got lots to do."

"What about me?" Kitty asked playfully. "Whatever is to become of little ol' me?"

Bell looked down at her. "You're going into a cell, that's what."

"You're not really going to put me back there, are you?" Kitty asked.

"That's right," said Bell, taking the key to the handcuffs that Sam had given him earlier.

"Please don't put me there," she said. "I know we got off on the wrong foot. But I don't deserve to be treated this way."

From the cell, both Price and Cadden Cullen laughed under their breath. "Why didn't we think of saying that, brother?" Cadden said to Price in a lowered tone. "Maybe we could have avoided this whole thing."

"Yes, you do deserve it," Bell said to Kitty. "Now on your feet. He turned the key in the cuff and loosened her wrist from the bench arm.

As he opened the door to leave, Sam heard the two talking. He had an idea that Kitty Dellaros wasn't as horrified as she pretended to be about going into a cell.

As soon as the ranger was gone, Bell directed Kitty toward the cells and followed a foot behind her as she walked there slowly. He gave here a slight shove as she hesitated against getting into the cell next to the Cullen brothers, who hung on the bars, leering out at her.

"Must I be in this cell next to these two?" Kitty asked.

"Yes, you must," Bell said smugly. "The other cell doesn't have its lock installed yet."

"What's wrong with being next to us?" Price Cullen asked in a feigned hurt voice. "We won't bite."

"Not much anyway," said Cadden, grinning, licking the corner of his upper lip like a dog.

"Both of you, settle down," said Bell. "If I have trouble out of you, it'll be tomorrow morning before you get anything to stuff into your gullets."

"Sorry, Chief Bell," said Price Cullen. "Where is Detective Longworth anyway? I hope he didn't get his bell rung, did he?"

"No, he didn't. But he crushed his hand with a wagon jack," said Bell. "He's getting it fixed right now."

"Well, bless his heart," said Cadden. "You tell him we'll remember him in our evening devotionals."

"Yeah, I'll tell him," Bell said sarcastically. He locked the door on Kitty's cell with the twist of a large key on a brass ring.

"Speaking of stuffing our gullets," said Price. "Is it just me, or has someone at the restaurant forgotten to bring us anything to eat?"

Bell took out a pocket watch, flipped it open and checked the time. "I expect all the shooting commotion at the cantina has Shelly and the restaurant folks thrown off schedule. I'll go see."

"Obliged, Chief," said Cadden, eyeing Kitty through the bars dividing the two cells. "I don't know about Price here, but I could eat anything that's off its hooves."

"Me too," said Price. He also eyed Kitty through the bars. "It wouldn't even have to be all the way off its hooves."

Cadden gave a short, dark laugh, the two leering at the woman, who had sat down on the edge of a cot and crossed her arms as if to protect herself from the world. "If I just had something to suck or nibble on till we get —"

"*Shut up,* both of you!" Kitty sobbed, sounding near hysteria. She turned sideways, flung herself facedown onto the cot and said in a muffled voice into the thin mattress, "Detective, please don't leave me back here with these two."

Bell kept himself from giving a thin, cruel grin. "I thought you'd be right at home here. After all, these are your kind of people."

As Kitty sobbed into her cot and the Cullen brothers stood watching her through the bars, Bell turned, walked to a far wall and hung the brass ring on a wall peg.

"I'll go see abut Shelly bringing that food over," he said over his shoulder to no one in particular. "Try not to upset the *lady* while I'm gone." He unfastened his gun belt and hung it on the wall beside the key.

The Cullen brothers stood watching Kitty sob into the cot until the front door closed behind Bell. The thud of the man's boots could be heard across the boardwalk, then stopped as he stepped down into the street. The two looked at each other and grinned.

"He's gone," Price said through the bars into Kitty's cell.

"Good," said Kitty. She raised her dry-

143

eyed face from the cot and walked over to the bars. "Now go on with what you were saying about Western Railways' big-money shipment coming here."

The three outlaws huddled at the bars standing between them. "You misunderstood," said Cadden Cullen. "The money's not coming here. It's already here."

"Where?" said Kitty, getting more and more interested, since the three had started talking about it before the ranger and Bell had came in and interrupted them.

"If we knew that, we'd already be rich men and gone the hell away from here," said Price.

"Oh . . ." Kitty looked discouraged.

"But we know it's here somewhere. It's hidden in a wagon," said Cadden.

"What makes you so cocksure?" Kitty asked.

"We snuck into the livery barn and watched them load the wagon in Cottonwood," said Price. "While the guard was asleep, Cadden crawled under the rig and filed a cross on a rear wheel band."

"Yep." Cadden grinned. "I marked it good. We followed it all the way across the badlands, just watching that X in the dirt."

"But in the middle of the night the wagon disappeared right outside of Wild Wind," said Price. "That's when we come into town and got caught breaking into the livery barn. We confessed to being there trying to steal horses. But it was the money wagon we were looking for."

Kitty considered things, then said, "It disappeared, huh?"

"Somewhere in the night," said Price.

Cadden said, "The next morning we found an empty camp. We started following the wagon tracks, but they went up into some rock and we lost sight of them."

"Smart thinking on somebody's part," said Kitty. "Is Bell that smart?"

"He's not smart enough to find the socks on his feet," said Cadden. "Clayton Longworth might be, but he's too young. Nobody at Western Railways is going to tell him anything."

"I doubt that anybody even told him the money was coming," said Price. "The fact is, the money is either lying somewhere on that wagon, or else it was taken into the new bank building up the street."

"Which ain't very likely," said Cadden. "The building is not finished yet, and the way banks have been getting robbed, Western Railways wouldn't risk putting it there."

"Even if they did," said Price, "if we were partnered with a bunch like you ride with, we could sweep through here, rob the bank and turn this town upside down till we come up with that money wagon."

"Either way," said Cadden, "we'd ride out of here with that money."

"You did right telling me," said Kitty. "This is something that's too big for just the two of you."

"That's what we figured," said Cadden. He reached out and placed his hand over Kitty's hand on one of the bars between them. "And hey, all that catcalling we did before we realized who you are . . . That was nothing."

"I know that," said Kitty. She didn't try to move her hand from beneath his. Instead, she reached her other hand through the bars and smoothed his hair back off his forehead. "We all do what we have to do to make ends meet."

"Hey, what about me?" said Price, looking jealous. He moved in closer, his hand also wrapped around a bar.

"Come on, now," said Kitty. She laid her other hand over his and rubbed her thumb back and forth. "I've always got something warm waiting for a couple of handsome, strapping men like you."

"What about Silva Ceran?" Price asked, feeling a hot surge inside him at just the feel of her thumb moving back and forth on his skin.

"He's not here," said Kitty. "You two are."

"Jesus . . . we sure are," Cadden said with bated breath.

"Now, let me ask you fellas," said Kitty. "What have you got in mind to get us out of this cage?"

"Oh, that's the easy part," said Price, clearly aroused by her slow-moving thumb.

"Take a guess," Cadden said.

Kitty looked all around. Seeing the key on the brass ring across the room, she said, "You have a string or something that you're going to pitch over and —"

"God, no," said Cadden, cutting her off. "But you're close. The whole idea is to get *that* key off *that* wall, and get it over here to where it will do us some good." He looked at Price and asked, "Why didn't you think of that string idea?"

Price shrugged. "I *did* think of it, but we didn't have any string. Anyhow, I like our way better."

"Which is . . . ?" Kitty let her question trail.

"You think about it a while; see what you come up with." Cadden winked.

"I don't like guessing games," Kitty said, her hands still on theirs, but her thumb not moving, the warmth and feel seeming to change.

"Oh, you don't?" Cadden smiled. "You could've fooled us, with what we were watching a while ago with you, Bell and that ranger."

At the sound of the front door opening the three turned quickly, their hands dropping from the bars. They stepped back from the bars as a dark-haired young woman and a small boy walked in, each carrying a dinner tray.

"*Yoo-hooo,* everybody," said the woman, walking ahead of the boy. "Supper's here. Sorry it's late."

"We'll talk later," Cadden whispered to Kitty as the woman and child walked back toward the cells.

At the Cullen brothers' cell, the woman set the tray inside the wide upper feed slot in the barred door. At the bottom of the barred door, another slot had been built to accommodate a waste bucket. The boy walked over to Kitty's cell and slid the tray in to her. "My, my, Miss Shelly Linde," Cadden Cullen said to the dark-haired woman, "you look lovely, as usual."

CHAPTER 11

Inside the doctor's office, the ranger looked down at Longworth, who still sat across from the white-haired old doctor. His crushed hand seemed better, having been stretched, pressed and manipulated back into its normal shape. The exposed tendons were back beneath the skin, where they belonged. The skin had been stitched together over them. The swelling appeared to have gone down a little, the ranger thought.

"Feeling better, Detective?" Sam asked.

"Huh," said the doctor before Longworth could answer for himself. "The dang fool refused any laudanum for the pain. He wouldn't even drink whiskey."

Sam looked at Longworth's pained and red-rimmed eyes. He shook his head and said, "You asked me on the trail if I had any whiskey."

"That was on the way here," Longworth said. "I wanted it for the pain." He held his breath as the doctor pushed the hooked needle through the skin of his hand. But he managed to put the pain aside and say, "You heard Bell. We've got lots of work to do here. I can't be drinking. I need my wits about me."

"You've got no business working this evening, not with this hand in this kind of shape," said the doctor, drawing the stitch snug, tying it and clipping it with a small pair of scissors. "I'm starting to think you're a little touched in the head, Detective," he added, getting ready to make another plunge with the hooked stitching needle.

"No, Doctor, I'm not touched," said Longworth. "I've got a job to do and I'm going to do the best I can at it."

"There's nothing you're going to do tonight that can't wait until tomorrow," said the doctor, making another stitch. "You won't be able to use this hand for a while, even to go to the jake."

Longworth gave another slice of breath, then relaxed and said, "Chief Bell says we need to get some things done. He's the boss."

"You should tell *Chief Bell* to go pile sand up his ass," the old doctor said matter-of-factly. "Get yourself an honorable job clerking or something."

"Railway detective *is* an honorable job," Longworth insisted.

"Yeah, sure it is," said the old doctor wryly. He clipped the stitch and started to make another plunge with the needle.

"Anyway, I'm leaving, Detective," Sam cut in. "I wanted to check on you first."

"Ranger, I know I've said it already, but I'm obliged to you for all you've done for me," Longworth said. "If there was time, I'd buy you dinner."

"Next time I'm through Wild Wind, I'll hold you to it," Sam said. "But I'm eating on the trail tonight, before Trueblood's trail gets too cold to follow."

"Best of luck to you, Ranger," said Longworth. He reached his right hand around to shake hands. But the doctor gave him a jerk and said, "Hold still, man! I came dang near sewing your hand to the table."

Outside, in the long shadows of dusk, Paco Stazo and Huey Buckles rode onto the dirt street from the north. They watched as a man stuck a torch to the oil pots sitting on either front edge of the cantina, but not to the ones sitting directly out front. They both noticed that no music resounded down the empty street to greet them.

"I'm betting this has something to do with

the gunshots we heard earlier," Paco said to Buckles under his breath.

Buckles looked around with his head bowed slightly, moving only his eyes. "I don't like it," he replied. "I say we turn around now, and tell Silva —"

"Turn tail if you want to," Paco Stazo said, cutting him off. "I came to see what's gong on here. That's what I intend to do."

"Hell, me too," said Buckles, having a fast change of heart. "You didn't let me finish what I was saying."

"Oh . . . ?" Paco gave him a skeptical stare. "Then finish."

"Never mind now. It don't matter," said Buckles with a shrug, looking away as they rode on to the Belleza Grande Cantina.

The two climbed down from their horses and spun the reins around an iron hitch rail, noting that theirs were the only mounts there. "This ain't natural," said Buckles, sounding wary and unsure of himself.

"Neither is riding into a town and not having whiskey to drink," Paco said, nodding toward the closed door and the cantina's dark interior through a dusty window.

"My God — it's closed?" said Buckles as if his eyes could not comprehend such a thing.

"We'll see," said Paco. He stepped onto

the boardwalk and to the closed door as the pot lighter walked along the boardwalk with his flaming torch. "Hey you, mister," Paco said in an agitated tone of voice, "why is the Belleza Grande closed?"

"Death," the old man said without stopping.

"Death? Whose death?" Paco demanded.

"Owner's," the man said. He shuffled along.

"Damn it, stop him," Paco said to Buckles.

Buckles grabbed the man by the back of his coat. The man turned toward him, the torch coming so close to Buckles' face that he felt his eyebrows crackle and fry. "Jesus!" he said. "You've singed me like a chicken!"

"Sorry," the old man said in a flat tone. "Don't stand so close."

Buckles felt like beating him in the face, but the looming torch held him back.

"What happened to the owner?" Paco asked. He raised a finger in warning. "Do not give me another short answer, or we will nail your tongue to this door."

The old man looked at the rough cantina door as if trying to visualize such an occurrence. He cleared his throat. "A gunman named Harry Ginpole shot him in the head. He shot a young whore and a town selectman. Then a ranger and a detective killed him."

"A territory ranger and a railroad detective, both in town at the same time? They killed Harry Ginpole?" said Paco, looking all around cautiously, as if the ranger and the detective might be lurking in the shadows.

"That's right," said the old pot lighter. "The same ranger was through here last week. Killed another bad egg, a road agent by the name of Wheeler." He looked back and forth between the two. "It's been a busy time here in Wild Wind."

"Road agent . . . ," said Paco with a smile, not caring much that Wheeler was dead. "That is a name I have not heard in a long while."

"Yeah," said Buckles, "that's an old one."

The old man continued. "Today the ranger brought the detective in with a broken hand. He had a woman prisoner. The detective was getting his hand fixed when Harry Ginpole started his killing."

"A woman prisoner, you say?" Paco asked, getting more interested. "What did she look like, this woman? She is pretty, yes?"

"They're all pretty, far as I'm concerned," the old man said.

"But this one, did she have nice, *you*

know. . . ." He cupped his gloved hands at his chest and jiggled them up and down.

"They all have nice, *you know* . . . as far as I'm concerned," the old man said.

"Where is this woman prisoner?" Paco asked.

"Where do you suppose she would be?" the old man said flatly. When he saw the dark look come over Paco's face, he pointed his torch toward the new jail and sheriff's office down the empty street.

Paco and Buckles looked just in time to see the single rider in the silver-gray sombrero ride out of sight into the darkness toward the badlands trail. "I'll be double damned and salted," said Huey Buckles.

"Is that the ranger?" Paco asked, squinting at the darkness.

"Yep," said Buckles, "that's him — the one who killed Junior Lake and his pa. He always wears a gray sombrero. Right, old man?"

"So the story goes," the old man said. For the first time he looked the two up and down. "Say, you fellows aren't road agents yourselves, are you?"

"Road agents . . . I like that," Paco chuckled again. "Hold your torch over here so I can see."

"See what?" the old man asked.

"See where to kick this door in," said Paco. "A *road agent* does not ride this far and not get something to drink." He drew his Colt, pointed it at the old man and wagged it toward the locked door.

From the boardwalk out in front of the restaurant three blocks away, Bell had heard a crash come from the cantina. He stepped into the street for a better look and saw the light of the torch flicker through the dusty front window. *What the hell?* Feeling his bare hip where his holstered Colt should be, he started to turn and go to the sheriff's office and get the big gun. But then he reminded himself that whoever it was inside the Belleza Grande, he shouldn't need a gun to roust them out. He walked on with determination along the darkened street.

Inside the cantina, Paco and Huey Buckles stood at the bar with a bottle of whiskey and two shot glasses between them. Standing beside them, the old pot lighter held the torch up for them to see by. Even as Paco filled two glasses for Buckles and himself, he kept his gun trained on the old man.

"I don't know that it's a good idea, us being in here when there's railroad lawmen in town," Buckles said. But his concern didn't keep him from upending the shot glass to his dry lips and draining it.

"We saw the ranger leave, Huey," said Paco. "Railway detectives don't give a damn about a man opening a cantina to get himself a cut or two of whiskey." He tipped his shot glass as if in salute, then tossed back his drink in one gulp.

"I hope you're right," said Buckles, grinning as he refilled both glasses.

Turning to the old man, Paco asked, "What is your name, old one?"

"Merlin Fletcher," said the torch holder. "Most folks call me Gabby." Holding the torch in one hand, he laid his other hand on the bar and gestured toward the bottle. "Suppose I said could take myself a swig? Holding this thing cocked up like this builds a thirst."

"Get Mr. Fletcher a glass, Huey," said Paco, staring at the old man with a harsh grin.

While Buckles snagged a shot glass from a stack along the inside edge of the bar, out front, Bell eased up onto the boardwalk and peeped in through the dusty window. He watched the ragged Comanchero pour a glass of whiskey and stand it in front of Gabby Fletcher. He took note of the pistol in the Mexican's hand, its barrel aimed loosely in Gabby's direction.

"Sonsabitches," he growled to himself.

As he slid the filled shot glass closer to his waiting fingertips, Paco said to the old man, "Tell me, Gabby Fletcher — how are things going here? I mean, with Western Railways setting up an office, a rail spur and such."

"Going well," said the old man. He picked up the glass, tossed back half its contents and let out a whiskey hiss.

"Good, good. That is good to hear," said Paco, eyeing the old man with scrutiny. He leaned in closer and asked privately, "And what of the money? Has Western Railways sent in any money?"

"Money? What kind of money?" The old man raised the glass, drained it, set it down and pushed it back toward the bottle with a bony fingertip.

"Oh, you are cagey as a fox. You are, my friend," Paco laughed under his breath. He refilled the shot glass and shoved it back over to Fletcher, who let the torch sag a little as he relaxed in a whiskey glow. "I am talking about *operating* money. Big money. The kind of money it takes for a company to buy silver from the hill mines and transport it out of these badlands."

"Oh, that money," Fletcher said. He appeared to put some thought into the matter. "I recall hearing that some money come

158

into Wild Wind a while back. I can't say how much it was or —"

"That'll do, Gabby," Bell interrupted. He stood inside the open doorway amid broken planks that had flown off the frame when Paco put his big boot to the thick oak door. "One man should never discuss another man's money. That's the way I was raised to believe in Nebraska."

Paco and Buckles spun toward the big railway detective chief. Both stood with their guns pointing at him. But upon seeing that the man was unarmed, Paco let his gun slump and said, "Ah, Nebraska. Tell me, did they ever find out where they are?"

Bell let the insult slide past him. "This cantina is closed," he said. "Not that it would have meant much to you two scarecrows."

"Scarecrows?" Paco looked himself and Buckles up and down. Then he looked back at Bell with a wizened grin. Raising a finger for emphasis he said, "You know what? I don't think you come here to be sociable, my friend."

"You're smarter than you look *half-breed,*" said Bell, glaring at the two. "Gabby, get yourself out of the way. This is a matter for the law."

"The law?" Paco mused. "I do not see a

badge on you, my friend. In fact, I do not even see a gun."

"I don't have a badge," said Bell. He patted the lapel of his coat. "I have a letter."

"A letter?" said Paco, cocking the Colt in his hand. "You are a very brave man or an idiot, coming here with no badge, no gun." His brow furrowed; he shook his head. "Just a letter?"

"That's right. A letter," said Bell. "It tells everybody that Western Railways Transportation is now the law in Wild Wind." As he spoke, he looked around at the debris on the floor at his feet. "As far as a gun, I've got one in the sheriff's office." He stepped forward, bent over and picked up a three-foot-long oak plank. He hefted it in his broad hands and inspected it.

"In the sheriff's office?" said Paco, dismissing the plank as a threat. His smile melted into a serious look. "But, *senor,* we have ours right here, as you can see." He wagged his gun, as if the stocky, red-bearded detective hadn't yet noticed it.

"Jesus, look out!" Buckles shouted, seeing the detective suddenly charge forward like a raging buffalo, head down, gripping the plank like a baseball bat.

Paco fired his already cocked and aimed pistol. But just as he fired, Bell zigzagged quickly, swinging the rough, hard plank. The whistling plank smacked the gun from Paco's hand as it fired wildly into the ceiling. The gun flew across the cantina before it ever hit the floor. The second swing slapped Paco across his face with a sickening sound. He spun along the bar edge as Gabby Fletcher jumped back out of his way, his torch flickering in hand.

Buckles was stunned and frozen in place by the speed and fierceness of Bell's attack. Before he could react, Bell's plank slapped him sideways to the floor. His gun flew from his hand. Both outlaws lay prone and helpless. But not for long. Although addled from the blow to his face, Paco managed to shake his head clear and scramble along the dirty floor. Bell gave chase, swatting him with the plank as if he were a roach.

Behind Bell, Buckles recovered quickly in spite of his throbbing jaw and the insistent ringing in his ears. While Bell swatted Paco, Buckles hurled himself forward atop Bell's broad shoulders in an attempt to bring the man down.

"Hang on, Huey!" Paco shouted, coming to his feet, snatching a knife from his boot well.

Bell's plank flew from his hand.

Buckles hung on, but it was like riding an

enraged grizzly. Bell slung him back and forth as if he were a rag doll, growling loudly, reaching back over his shoulders and clawing at the outlaw's eyes.

"Kill him, Paco!" Buckles shouted, seeing the flash of steal in the half-breed's hand.

But Bell saw the big knife too. As Paco made a killing lunge at his chest, Bell spun quickly, putting Buckles between himself and the big blade. Paco couldn't stop himself from sinking the blade deep into Buckles' haunch. Gabby Fletcher stood watching raptly, a shot glass raised halfway to his lips, his torch still in his hand, casting an eerie, flickering glow over the melee.

With the screech of a wounded mountain cat, Buckles fell to the floor, clutching the hilt of the big knife sticking out of his bloody rear.

With the knife gone, Paco reached for a chair. Bell saw the chair swing into the air above Paco's head. He snatched the torch from Fletcher's hand and swung it back and forth at the half-breed. "Come on, outlaw! I'll burn you to the ground!"

Paco backed away; he'd had enough. But as he dropped the chair and headed out the door at a run, Bell turned and looked down at the crawling, screaming Huey Buckles. "Take this, Comanchero!" he said. He jammed the fiery torch down on Buckles' bloody behind.

Buckles screamed loud and long. He scrambled to his feet on his way out the door, both hands slapping at the flames licking from his trouser seat up to the back of his ragged shirt.

"And don't come back!" Bell shouted out onto the dark street as the two hurried into their saddles and beat a retreat out of town. Turning to Fletcher, Bell said, "What did you tell them, Gabby?"

"Nothing," said the old man.

No sooner had the two outlaws cut off the main street, out of the light of the oil pots lining the streets, than Longworth came running, rifle in hand. "Chief Bell," he said, "are you all right?"

Bell brushed a hand along his coat sleeve. "I'm fine, Detective. Those two will think twice before they ever ride back into Wild Wind."

CHAPTER 12

No sooner had the two outlaws ridden out of town into the darkness than they stopped alongside a thin creek and dropped from their saddles. "I can't go on like this," Buckles moaned. He limped out into the shallow creek and squatted down, letting the cool water run across his bloody, scorched behind. "I need a doctor, bad."

"Yes, I see you do," said Paco, "and we will get you to one."

Buckles stopped moaning and looked at him in the purple light of a half-moon. "We will?"

"Yes, we will," said Paco, staring back toward town, a trickle of blood running down his swollen jaw.

"Where?" Buckles asked.

"In Wild Wind," said Paco.

"Ride back there? Are you out of your mind?" Buckles asked. "We don't even have guns. They're both lying back there on the cantina floor."

"Yes, they are. And I am not leaving this shit hole without my Colt," said Paco.

Buckles watched him pull a sawed-off shotgun from under the bedroll behind his saddle.

"Nobody treats me this way and lives to tell about it," Paco said with a slight lisp, owing to his swollen jaw. He broke open the shotgun and checked it. Seeing both barrels loaded, he clicked it shut. "I am a man. I will live like one or I will die like one."

Buckles thought about it as the water took some of the sting out of his burning rear end. "Hell, I hear you," he said. "Count me in." He dipped cold water with his cupped hand and held it to his jaw.

Back in Wild Wind, Longworth gathered the two Colts from the floor of the cantina with his good hand and stuffed each of them down into his belt. From the open doorway he stared out into the darkness in the direction the two outlaws had taken out of town.

"I hope you're right, Chief Bell," he said, "about them not coming back."

"Oh, I'm right. You can count on it, Detective," said Bell. He stood beside Longworth and squared his broad shoulders. Gabby Fletcher stood to the side and watched, his torch still in hand. "Saddle trash like those two — they'll go off and lick their wounds. They'll vow to each other that they're coming back. They'll make bold threats between themselves. But they won't show their faces here. Trust me on this."

Longworth was doubtful, but he kept his doubts to himself. "You know more about these kinds of men than I do, Chief."

"That's right, I do," Bell said immodestly. "What it comes down to is, they're cowards . . . men like these." He gave a confident smile. "Truth be told, I almost wish they would come back. I've still got some bark on."

As the two stood watching, the waitress from the restaurant walked back across the street toward the sheriff's office. "There goes Shelly to get the dishes. I best go help her out some," said Longworth.

"No, wait here," said Bell. "The feed and waste slots in these new cells make it easy for anybody to take care of prisoners." He grinned. "Unless you're interested in *helping her out* some other way. I've seen the way you look at her."

Longworth felt embarrassed. "No, Chief, it's strictly business for me. We've got too much going on here for me to take on a romantic interest in a woman."

"Whatever you say, Detective," said Bell.

"She is a little on the homely side, I have to admit." He took out a cigar and stuck it in his mouth. "As to this town, I've got it under control."

"Yes, sir. I understand," said Longworth.

"I know I demand a lot of the so-called *physical* work from you. But it's me who takes care of the most important work, the thinking and planning. I keep it all laid out nice and proper, right up here." He tapped a finger to the side of his head. "I hope you're paying attention to everything I'm teaching you." He took out a long match, struck it and lit his cigar.

"I am, Chief. Most certainly," said Longworth.

"That's good, Detective," said Bell, blowing out a stream of gray smoke. "You need to learn all you can from me as quickly as possible. You never know when you'll be called upon to run the show." He looked around. "And there is no better learning place than here, in town like this. This is still a frontier town — not even a telegraph office yet. Of course, now that Western Railways is invested here that's all forthcoming."

"Yes, sir," said Longworth, gazing away into the darkness.

"But be on your toes. Responsibility could

be thrust upon you all at once, at any time," said Bell. "You could wake up one morning and find yourself in charge, with lives depending on you." He stared at the contemplative young man. "Would you be ready to shoulder such a responsibility?"

Longworth looked gravely concerned at the prospect of such an occurrence. "I can only hope that I would be, Chief," he said.

Bell looked down the street at the wagon of ore samples. "Why don't you put the wagon away for tonight? We'll get the samples ready to ship first thing in the morning. I'm retiring early this evening. Don't let anyone disturb me unless it's awfully damned important."

"Whatever you say, Chief," said Longworth, relieved that his throbbing hand would have a night off after he completed the chore with the horses and wagon.

Longworth drove the wagon around to the town livery barn, where he pulled the wagon into a side shed, unhitched the team and led the horses out. He locked the shed doors behind him. Inside the livery barn he grained, watered and rubbed down the team of horses with his good hand. Over an hour had passed by the time he'd finished attending to the horses and led them into separate stalls.

On his way back to the sheriff's office he saw the waitress walking away from the closed restaurant with a shawl thrown around her shoulders. The two acknowledged each other with a cordial exchange and continued on their separate ways. Once inside the office, Longworth walked back and checked on the prisoners.

"How's the hand, Detective?" Price Cullen asked as Longworth stepped close to the bars, carrying two folded wool blankets over his forearm. His bandaged hand stuck out from beneath them. A dimly lit lantern hung from his good hand.

"Sore," Longworth said. He held the blankets over to the feed slot for Price to take. "This is to hang on the bars between the cells for when you need privacy."

"Privacy?" Price said. He grinned as he reached and pulled the top blanket in through the slot and looked it over.

"You know," said Longworth, nodding toward Kitty in the other cell and lowering his voice almost to a whisper. "When you need to relieve yourselves."

"Why, hell," said Price, "we're not bashful if she's not."

"I am, though," Kitty said, hearing them

169

talk through the bars. She stood up walked over to where Longworth stood. "I'll take that other blanket, Detective," she said.

"Why?" said Price. "You've got nothing me and Cadden haven't seen before."

"What you and your brother saw was most likely a doe sheep." Kitty glared at him and said to Longworth, "I hope you're going to be here tonight on watch, Detective. I don't trust these two turds even with steel bars between us."

Price gave her a nasty grin. "That's no way to talk to your fellow convicts."

"I'll be on watch all night, ma'am," Longworth said to Kitty. To Price he said, "Hang the blanket up and act civil. Maybe it'll make things go better for you with the judge."

Cadden ventured forward to the bars and said, "Hold on, Detective. Are you saying you'll put in a good word for us?"

"I'm saying I'll tell the judge whether or not you've been good prisoners while you were here," said Longworth.

"And you think it might help?" Price asked, taking on a more serious demeanor.

"It couldn't hurt, could it?" said Longworth.

"You're right," Cadden said, "it couldn't hurt." He looked at his brother, then back at Longworth. "All right, from now on, no more fooling around. We're going to be so quiet you won't hardly know we're here."

Longworth gave him a questioning look.

"Brother Cadden means it, Detective," Price said with feigned sincerity. "So do I."

"I hope you mean it," Longworth said. He turned and gave a quick glance toward the brass-ringed cell key hanging behind Bell's gun belt. Then he walked back out front to the desk. The three prisoners looked at one another through stripes in the shadowy, moonlit darkness. Cadden winked. "Good night, Detective Longworth," he called out in a respectful tone of voice.

Next door, an hour later, in the living quarters behind his office, Dr. Martin Ford awoke with a start to the sound of a gun butt rapping soundly on his back door.

"Who the blazes is it?" he called out as his feet swung off of the bed and found their way into his battered leather house slippers.

"Please, Doc, open up. It's an emergency," Huey Buckles called out painfully, his pain both real and intense.

"All right, then," the old doctor grumbled. "Don't beat my door down." He struck a match and lit a candle sitting on a stand beside his bed. He stood up with a grunt, candleholder in hand, and walked over and unlatched the rear door. Opening the door a crack, he peeped out bleary-eyed and said, "What are you doing coming to the back door, this hour of the night?"

"I — I couldn't come to the front, Doctor," Buckles said, "for fear someone would see me like this." He cocked his backside around for the doctor to see. "I'm in a wretched condition."

"Good Lord, man. You surely are," said the doctor, seeing the seat of his trousers burned away, bits of blackened cloth clinging to the blistered, peeling flesh. He saw blackened blood gathered and crusted atop the stab wound. "Get in here. Damned if it doesn't hurt just looking at you."

Once inside, the old doctor closed the back door and said, "Follow me."

In the treatment room, he set down the candle, raised the globe of an oil lamp, lit the lamp and adjusted the wick up for optimum light. "Drop your trousers and sit down — no, *lean down* over that table."

The doctor picked up a pair of thick spectacles from beside the oil lamp and strung them behind his ears. When Buckles had gotten into position over the table, his burnt trousers down around his ankles, the doctor leaned in for a closer inspection.

Shaking his head, he straightened up and said, "Before we get started here, are you one of the fellows Detective Bell found breaking into the cantina this evening? I heard the ruckus."

"I am," said Buckles. "But you've got to believe me, Doc. We had no idea it was closed down. We were what you might call ignorant of circumstances."

"Ignorant of circumstances," the old doctor repeated, shaking his head. "I've got to remember that one."

"You're still going to fix me up, aren't you?" Buckles asked.

"Yep, I'll fix you up. From what I'm seeing here, it looks like Detective Chief Bell must've taught you whatever lesson you needed to learn."

"You won't tell him about me being here, will you, Doc?" Buckles asked.

"What difference would it make if I did?" the doctor asked. As he talked, he stepped over to a desk and took a bottle of whiskey from a lower drawer. He uncorked it and handed it to Buckles.

"None, except I don't want you to," said Buckles. He took the bottle and turned back a long, deep drink.

"All right, then. I won't," the old doctor said, reaching out for the bottle, wondering if he would have to pry it from the wounded man's hand.

Something in the doctor's voice told Buckles he was lying. But before he could do anything to make sure the old doctor didn't tell, Buckles had to get his wounds tended to.

"Thanks, Doc," he said, letting go of the bottle. "I never needed a drink so bad in my life."

"You needed it more than you know," said the doctor. "This is going to hurt some."

Buckles let out a whiskey breath and said, "Have at it, Doc."

For most of an hour, the doctor plucked burnt cloth and bits of charcoal from the outlaw's behind. He cleaned and swabbed both the knife wound and the burn, smeared a heavy layer of ointment over the entire area and bandaged it with a thick layer of white gauze cloth. When he'd finished working on the wounds, he took a blue bottle of laudanum from a desk drawer and handed it to him. "Start taking this when the ointment starts drying up and the pain comes back."

"Obliged, Doc," said Buckles, stepping into a pair of worn-out pin-striped trousers the doctor had rummaged up for him to wear. He pulled the trousers up, buttoned them and swung his empty gun belt around his waist. "Now, about what we were saying."

"About what?" the doctor said, taking off the spectacles and pushing the sleeves of his nightshirt back down his forearms.

"You know about what," Buckles said. "About you keeping your mouth shut." He reached over on a table laid out with sharp surgical instruments and closed his hand around the handle of a bone chopping knife.

"Wait, mister," said the doctor. "I said I wouldn't tell him anything. I meant it. I wasn't lying."

"The thing is, we'll never know," said Buckles.

Chapter 13

When Huey Buckles left the doctor's office he took a swig of laudanum from the blue bottle. He capped it and put it away, feeling a soothing numbness run down his throat and through his chest as the medicine worked its way down. By the time he'd reached the alley running behind the darkened Belleza Grande Cantina, the pain in his rear end had subsided. A warm, furry glow seemed to surround him. He found himself grinning for no reason.

"There you are," said Paco in a lowered voice, "it's about time." He looked the smiling man up and down in the moonlight. "Did your doctor take care of you?"

"Oh yes. I'm better already," Buckles said. "Where's our horses?" He looked all around, but he didn't see the two animals standing only a few feet away in the moonlight.

"Never mind the horses," said Paco. He

held up a worn wicker basket filled with bottles of whiskey. "Look what I took from inside, to make up for all the trouble we've gone through."

"Good thinking," said Buckles, seeming relaxed, unhurried, more sociable than Paco remembered ever seeing him.

Paco chuckled proudly. "It has taken us two tries to do it, but finally we have what we came after: information and whiskey." He jigged the basket of whiskey on his arm.

"Damn right we did," said Buckles, feeling as if he stood atop a wispy cloud.

"Did you take care of the doctor?" Paco asked.

"Oh yes," said Buckles, the easy smile still on his face.

"Then you are ready to go?" Paco asked.

"Ready, able and willing," said Buckles. "What about the woman, Kitty. The one in jail?"

"We'll see about her on our way out of town," said Paco. "If she is in the jail, we'll break her out. But first things first."

They took their horses' reins and led the animals around the side of the cantina and out to the front corner, looking onto the dirt street. Gazing across the street at the hotel, Paco gestured upward and said, "The son of a bitch we want is staying right there in the corner room."

"How do you know?" Buckles was still alert enough to ask, but his head had begun to nod a little beneath the laudanum's powerful grip.

"I watched him stand on the balcony up there and smoke a cigar while you were getting your wounds attended to," Paco said.

"Good enough for me," said Buckles, his head bobbing a little, his eyelids drooping, "let's go."

"Wait," said Paco. "Look at you. I don't want you falling asleep. This is serious business."

"I'm all right," Buckles insisted.

"Yes, you are all right," Paco said. "You are all right to stand here and hold the horses." He pressed his reins into Buckles' hand and hung the basket handles around his saddle horn. Then he crept away along the edge of the buildings lining the street, out of sight, until he stepped up onto the porch of the hotel.

In the lobby, at the hotel desk, he stared over at a night clerk until he satisfied himself that the young man was fast asleep. After a few silent seconds had passed he eased over to the stairs and walked up them quietly.

Inside the room, Chief Detective Bell awoke to a rapping on his door much like the sound that had earlier awakened the ill-fated Dr. Ford. As consciousness came to him, he sat up on the side of his bed and rubbed his face and said, "Who is it?"

"The clerk," said Paco, disguising his voice to a higher pitch, to what he thought a clerk's voice might sound like.

Bell sat for a moment, then said, "Who? The clerk? What do you want?" Even as he spoke he looked at the corner bedpost for his gun belt before realizing he'd left it hanging on the peg at the sheriff's office.

"I have a message for you," said Paco. "It can't wait until morning."

A Winchester rifle leaned against the wall beside the bed, but Bell didn't bother picking it up. "Damn it," he growled. He stood up, walked to the door and took the handle in his broad hand. "This better be good," he said, pulling the door open.

Paco's grim but smiling face met him in the darkened doorway. "Good for me," he said. "But not so much for you."

An orange-blue flash filled the doorway. The first blast from the double barrel slammed Bell backward across the room, his feet barely skimming the floor's wool rug. Before his bloody body could settle and fall, the second shot hit him, slinging more blood and body matter in all directions.

From his position on the street below, Buckles saw the balcony doors crash open in the moonlight. "My God, that's pretty!" he said dreamily, watching the balcony rail break away as Bell hurtled through it. In the moonlight, the effects of the laudanum made the detective's body and the spray of broken glass look like some sort of an angel flying through a burst of glittering stardust.

At the sheriff's office, Longworth woke at the sound of the two shotgun blasts. He started to bolt straight up from the desk chair where he'd been sleeping, but the bite of a hard steel gun barrel atop his head sent him sprawling back down.

"Damn, Cadden," said Price Cullen. "You hit him too hard. We're going to have to carry him to the cell."

"We don't have to carry him anywhere," said Kitty. She hurriedly opened drawer after drawer, looking for the razor the ranger said he'd left there as evidence.

"What are you looking for?" Price asked her.

"My razor, so I can cut his throat," said Kitty, rummaging frantically.

Price and Cadden looked at each other. "Let's drag this knocked-out sumbitch to a cell," said Cadden. "This is going to be worse than cutting his throat, when Bell sees he let us get away."

"Whatever we do with him, let's get it done," said Price, Bell's gun belt hanging over his shoulder. He looked off through the dusty front window. "What do you think the shotgun blasts were about?"

"Probably just some bastard decided he'd been married long enough," said Cadden. He reached over with Bell's revolver and shoved it down into the holster hanging from Price's shoulder.

As the two picked up Longworth by his arms and his boots, Kitty stopped searching for the razor and hurried to the gun rack on the wall. "Whatever those shotgun blasts were about, we better be getting out of here pronto. Bell is probably headed this way right now."

The two brothers hurriedly carried the knocked-out detective into the cell, hand-cuffed his wrists through the bars and tied a bandana around his mouth. "Pull his pants down," said Price with a dark chuckle.

"Why?" Cadden asked.

"Just for the hell of it," said Price.

"Why not, then?" said Cadden. They both laughed, unbuttoned the helpless detective's trousers and jerked them down around his boots.

"Pull his pecker out," said Price.

"You pull it out," said Cadden. "I ain't touching his pecker."

"Yeah, forget that," said Price.

They left the cell and locked it behind them. Instead of hanging the key back on the peg, Cadden slipped the brass ring around his wrist. "I'm making this a keepsake," he said.

As they came out of the cell, Kitty had killed the light of a dim oil lantern in the front window. She immediately shoved rifles and ammunition into their hands and shooed them out the back door, into the alley. Without a word they ran in a crouch to the livery barn, gathered three horses and began saddling them.

"Where do we start looking for the money?" Kitty asked as she slung a saddle up over a dun gelding.

The brothers looked at each other. "At the bank. Where else?" Cadden said with a shrug.

"You said the bank is still under construction," Kitty snapped back at him.

"That's right," said Cadden. "But they could already have a safe built into the wall."

"If it's not there," said Price, "we try the new express office, or the —"

"Jesus!" Kitty cut him off. "We don't have all night to look for this money. How do we know it's even here yet?"

"We don't," said Price. He grinned. "But that's the sort of stuff that makes life interesting."

"Okay," said Kitty, "we look in the places where it might be. But we do it fast. I don't want to land back in jail. If we don't find it, we cut out and find Silva and his men."

"Sounds first rate to us," said Cadden, leading his horse out the livery door, a loaded rifle in hand.

Following him, Price veered to the side and looked through a crack in the shed door where Longworth had parked the wagon loaded with its load of sample ore. "Hey, what have we here?" he said in whisper. The wagon sat barely visible in the grainy purple moonlight.

Kitty stepped over beside them and peeped through another crack. Seeing the chunks of rock in the wagon bed she said to Price, "Forget it. That's the silver ore samples Longworth had when we found him hauling out on the badlands."

"Hell, those rocks have got silver running through them," said Price. "They've got some value to them, don't they?"

"Yeah, they've got value," Kitty replied impatiently. "About two or three hundred dollars for that whole load, the way it sits.

You want to hitch it up and drive it out of here tonight, with the detectives and the townsmen on our behinds?"

"Damn it, Price, let's go," said Cadden, hearing the two of them whisper back and forth. "We've got our sights on some *real* money for a change. Don't be wasting time on a bunch of rocks."

On the street, the sound of the two shotgun blasts brought townsfolk to their windows and doorways for a curious look toward the hotel. Upon seeing the body crumpled in the dirt amid pieces of broken wood railing and shards of glass, many ventured out in nightshirts and hastily grabbed clothing. "It's Detective Chief Bell! He's dead!" one man called out, bending over the body with a lantern in one hand, a shotgun in the other.

"Yes, it is him. The pig," Paco chuckled under his breath, watching from a darkened alley. He grinned at Buckles, who stood right beside him. "He better be dead, with all the iron I put in his belly."

Buckles chuckled too, his eyes half closed in his dreamy laudanum haze. "Is it me," he said, "or did the lights go out at the sheriff's office?"

Paco looked back at the office three blocks

away and saw the blackened window, where a light had been shining dimly only a moment ago. "You're right, it's out," he said with a note of suspicion in his voice. The two had hoped to gun down whoever came running from the office at the sound of the shotgun blasts. Now their ambush plan appeared to have gone amiss.

"Let's go see what's wrong," said Buckles. He took an unsteady step forward, but Paco grabbed him by the back of his coat.

"Are you crazy, Huey?" he whispered. "It must be a trap." He turned, pulling his horse by its reins. "Come on, we've seen enough. We're getting out of here."

"What about the woman?" Buckles asked with a thick tongue.

"We have done all we can do here," said Paco. "Come on. Hurry up, before we end up fighting for our lives in this shit hole."

On the street a voice called out, "Where the hell is that young detective?"

"Yeah, where is he?" another voice said as Paco Stazo and Huey Buckles slipped away along a shadowy alleyway leading to a trail out of town.

"Nobody could sleep through that kind of noise," said a woman.

"Look, the light is out at the sheriff's office," said another townsman.

185

"Where is our selectman, Tyler?" the woman cried out in a near frantic voice. "Somebody needs to get to the sheriff's office and see if that young detective is dead or alive."

"I'm right here, Margaret," said Paul Tyler, an elderly selectman with a completely bald head and a thick, white walrus mustache. He came running up, pulling a suspender onto his shoulder, an army Colt in his thin, bony hand. "I'm going right now and see what's happened to young Longworth." He looked all around.

"Should we wake Doc Ford?" said another man. "Just in case we need him?"

"I'm surprised he's not already here," said another man.

"It's not like Dr. Ford to sleep through gunfire," Margaret Bratcher called out, her voice quivering, still near hysteria. "Something bad has happened — something terrible, I fear!"

"Now, Margaret, calm down," said Tyler. He gazed through the darkness, first toward the doctor's office, then toward the darkened sheriff's office, as if still expecting Detective Longworth to come bolting out at any second.

"Well, Tyler?" a townsman asked after a moment of pause. "Are you going to do something or not?"

"Yeah," said Tyler, giving up on Long-worth. "The ones of you with firearms, follow me. We're going to get to the bottom of this."

"I'll get the Doc," said Gabby Fletcher, who stood, using his blackened torch as a walking stick.

"Obliged, Gabby," said selectman Tyler. "Send him out here to Bell's body. He'll find me at the sheriff's office if he needs me." He turned quickly to the other towns-men as Fletcher hurried ahead of them to the doctor's office.

"Gentlemen, follow me," Tyler said, his Colt army revolver raised, as if for emphasis.

CHAPTER 14

Inside the locked cell, Clayton Longworth began coming to as the Cullen brothers snapped the cuffs around his wrists and tied the bandana around his mouth. His head pounded with pain. As soon as the three outlaws were out the back door, his first re-action was to tug and pull and thrash wildly at his cuffs, realizing the futility of it even as he did so. He gave up with sigh of resigna-tion.

Hoping to free his mouth and try to sum-mon help, he tried rubbing the bandana off against his shoulder, but it held fast. Finally, long after he knew the Cullens and Kitty Dellaros had left town, he stood slumped at the bars, staring out at the dark front window, preparing himself to face his hu-miliation. Only as the front door opened did he happen to look down and see that his trousers were around his ankles. "Oh no . . ." He moaned under his breath.

The first townsman through the door was Paul Tyler, who stepped into the center of the room with his army Colt raised in one hand and a brightly glowing lantern in the other.

"Where's the young detective?" a townsman asked, venturing in behind him, carrying a rifle.

At the sight of the open gun rack, the empty rifle slots inside and the spilled ammunition on the floor, Tyler said with a worried expression, "There appears to have been a jailbreak here."

"Boy, I'll say," the townsman added, seeing all the desk drawers flung open where Kitty had rummaged through them, looking for her razor. "Somebody was hunting for something, sure enough."

From his cell Clayton Longworth made a loud wailing sound behind the bandana. Tyler looked back and saw him in the outer glow of the lantern. "Oh, my goodness. Look back there," he said, bringing the gathering townsmen's attention toward the cuffed and helpless detective.

"Damn!" said another man. "That's what I call *caught with your britches down.*"

Longworth lowered his eyes in shame, wishing it was over. He dreaded seeing Hansen Bell when he arrived, and hoped the townsmen would set him free before that happened.

"Where's the key?" Tyler asked, seeing it missing from its place on the wall peg. His gaze went to the town blacksmith, a wiry little man named Hilliard Porter.

"How the hell do I know?" Porter asked. "I don't keep track of this place."

"I just figured since you're the one building the cells, you might — Oh, never mind," said Tyler, stopping himself.

Longworth could only make a grunting sound, trying to roll his eyes downward in a gesture to get the selectman to take off the bandana.

"Take his gag off," said Porter to the excited selectman. "Maybe he'll tell us."

"Oh, right," said Tyler. He clamped the army Colt under his arm, reached in through the bars, loosened the bandana and pulled it off.

Longworth spit wet lint from his lips. "I don't know what they did with the cell key. But there's a handcuff key in my trouser pocket here." He swung his legs around to the bars. "Hurry. I want these cuffs off my wrists, and I want my trousers up."

"I understand," said Tyler. He looked embarrassed for the helpless detective as he stooped down and ran his hand through the bars and into the lowered trousers and found the small key.

"How did this happen, Detective?" Tyler asked as he straightened up and stuck the key into the cuffs.

"I — I don't know," said Longworth. "A gunshot woke me up. I saw the Cullens standing over me. How they got out of the cells, for the life of me, I don't know." The cuffs came off of his wrists, and he touched the welt on his forehead. "One of them must have hit me in the head and knocked me cold." He spit more lint from his lips.

"Somebody get him some water," Tyler ordered.

Longworth wasted no time reaching down and pulling up his trousers and buttoning them, in spite of the sharp throbbing pain in his head. "Where's Chief Bell?" he asked, still dreading having to face the man, but needing to get some guidance on what to do next.

"Chief Bell . . ." Tyler stared at him grimly. A hush fell over the townsmen. "I'm afraid Chief Detective Bell is dead," Tyler said quietly. "He was murdered in his hotel room."

"Oh no," said Longworth, rubbing his wrists. "Were those the gunshots I heard?"

"Yes, they were," said Tyler, taking a dipper of water a townsman handed him and passing it in through the bars to the thirsty detective. "He must not have known what hit him, if that is any comfort."

"My gosh . . . ," said the young detective, lowering the dipper from his lips. He shook his head. Then he said to Tyler, "Have everybody look around. The key has to be here somewhere."

"No," said Porter. "They took it with them, I'll wager." He felt of the square iron lock casing in the barred door, sizing up the job before breaking into the cell. "I'll be most of the night getting you out of there, Detective," he surmised, even as the men searched all around for the key.

"Then let's get started, Mr. Porter," said Longworth. "The quicker you can get me out of here, the quicker I can get on their trail."

"Let me through!" Gabby Fletcher said, elbowing his way through the townsmen back toward the cells. He stopped in front of Tyler, gasping for breath, his face ashen in fright. "Dr. Ford is dead too!" he said. "I found him lying in his own blood. His throat's chopped so deep, his head's nearly off."

"Oh, my God, Detective!" Tyler said to Longworth. "What have these monsters done to us? What on earth are you going to do?"

"What's he going to do? What can he do?" said one of the townsmen. "Nothing he does can bring back poor Doc Ford." The man turned from Tyler to the rest of the townsmen. "This is what we get for following these selectmen's advice and talking in Western Railways to administer the law for us."

Longworth stood looking shocked, dumfounded and helpless. *I have no answer,* he told himself. He couldn't even get out of his own jail.

Ten miles from Wild Wind, after a hard ride across the flatlands and up onto a steep hill trail, Kitty and the Cullen brothers stopped for a few minutes to rest their horses and drink water from a thin runoff stream. Upset and grumbling under his breath, Cadden sipped a mouthful of cool water from his cupped hand. He swished the water around and spit it back out.

"I say we should have stayed and looked for it longer," he said. He and his brother, Price, had been bickering about searching for the money ever since they'd left Wild Wind.

Kitty sighed and turned her eyes upward

as if praying for patience. "Christ, we turned the place upside down before we left. If there's money there, Longworth and Bell did a damn good job hiding it. Far as I can see, neither one of them are all that smart."

"We gave up too easy," Cadden said. "We should have stayed and kept looking."

"Brother, if you keep it up with your grousing, I'll be forced to box your jaws," said Price.

"You won't be boxing my jaws, Price," answered Cadden. He sprang to his feet. "I've put up with you thinking you know everything long enough —"

"Hold it. Shut up," said Kitty with urgency in her voice. She stood with her ear turned to the trail behind them. "Hear that? Did you hear it?" she said, her voice dropping to a hushed tone.

The two fell silent and listened alongside her. "I heard it," said Cadden.

"Yeah, me too," said Price.

"Horses . . . ," Kitty said.

"Yep, horses," said Price.

"Coming this way," said Cadden.

"Sounds like they're coming fast," said Price.

"I've never seen a town get a posse together this quick in my life."

"You have now," said Kitty. She reached

down and picked her rifle off the ground where he'd laid it. "Get above the trail on the moonlight side. As fast as they're coming, they'll ride right into our gunfire," she said. "We'll pick out their eyes in this darkness."

"How does she know so much about ambushing?" Cadden asked Price in a whisper.

"I don't know," said Price, "but she's right." He grabbed his horse's reins and began leading the animal away from the runoff stream.

"Get out of sight, Cadden," Kitty said. The three climbed up above the trail and took position on a rock-strewn hillside.

After a moment of listening and hearing nothing, Cadden said in a whisper, "They've stopped."

"Just long enough to get down and make sure they're still following our tracks," Price whispered in reply. The three sat frozen, listening intently.

"Maybe we ought to try to make a run for it," Cadden said, the tension getting to him first.

Kitty remained cool and calm. "And risk breaking a horse's leg on these rock trails? No, thanks. I've done that, and I didn't like it one bit. If anybody breaks a horse's leg, let it be these jakes." She cradled her rifle in her arm and sat quietly, her finger in place on the trigger.

Less than a mile back, Huey Buckles stood up in the middle of the rocky trail, brushed himself off and staggered in place. He'd been nodding, half asleep in the saddle, and let his horse ride right out from under him. Luckily he'd managed to flip backward, and landed facedown on his stomach instead of his wounded rear end.

"That won't happen again," he said in a thick voice, as Paco Stazo circled back to him.

"It better not happen again," said Paco. "If it does, you must save us both the trouble and shoot yourself. You're no good to either of us if you can't sit your horse." He stared at the wounded outlaw, the Winchester he'd taken from Bell's room in hand. "Do we understand each other?"

"Yes, we do," said Buckles. "It's not my fault. It's this laudanum I'm taking." Buckles tried a friendly chuckle. "It's got me cross-eyed crazy."

"Then get rid of it," Paco said flatly. He had the wicker basket full of whiskey bottles hanging from his saddle horn.

"I can't yet," Buckles said. "I need it for this pain in my rump." He tried another drug-induced chuckle. "Maybe if I cut it down some with some more whiskey."

But Paco didn't share his attempt at humor. "You are causing me a pain in the rump," he said. "I can't leave you behind and allow a posse to get their hands on you. So either stay the saddle, or I must shoot you and drag you off the trail."

"Boy, you are just all heart, Paco," Buckles grumbled.

"I am in a heartless business," said Paco.

"Yeah, we both are," said Buckles. "But how would you feel, traveling on an ass like this?" Taking hold of his saddle horn, he turned his bandaged rear end toward Paco in the moonlight before stepping up into his saddle. He said, "Look at it! Go on, look at it."

"I don't want to look at your ass, Buckles," Paco said, knowing if the man didn't settle down and get his senses about him, he'd have to shoot him. "Get in your saddle and let's get going. A Wild Wind posse will be on us any time now."

Buckles struggled to get a grip on his wavering senses. "All right," he said. He swung up onto the saddle, but overshot it and landed with a grunt in the dirt on the other side of the horse.

Jesus . . . Paco stepped his horse around

and stood it over Buckles as he cocked the hammer on the Winchester and took aim.

The deadly metallic click seemed to sober Buckles momentarily. "Wait! Damn it, don't shoot! Give me one more chance! You don't want to fire that gun anyway up here. It's a dead giveaway!"

Paco knew he was right about the gunshot. He took a deep breath and let it out. "On your feet, Huey," he said, uncocking the rifle. "Get back in your saddle, and this time stay in it."

Mounted, the two rode on, putting their horses into an even pace along the rocky trail. Moments later as they rounded a bend, a rifle shot exploded overhead. Paco heard the bullet thump into the hard ground near his horse's hooves. He nailed his spurs to his mount's sides and raced off the trail into brush and rock, Buckles managing to stick right beside him. Bullets whistled past them, thumping into the hard earth and ricocheting off rock.

In a second, Paco was out of his saddle and firing back, the Winchester bucking round after round in his gloved hands. Buckles hit the ground beside him, a Remington he'd taken from the doctor's desk in his hand. But having only six shots and no spare ammunition, he held his fire and scanned the hillside.

"There's more than one up there," he said. "That's for sure."

"I have seen barrel flashes from three different positions," Paco said. Above them on the other side of the trail, the rifles had stopped for a moment. Paco held his fire too.

"What I don't get is, how'd they manage to circle around and get ahead of us?" said Buckles.

"There is no way they could," said Paco. He stared at Buckles in the purple moonlight and considered it. "You, up there — who are you?" he called out across the dark, empty trail to the three on the hillside.

"You know damned well who we are," Kitty called back to him. "Following us here is going to get you all killed."

"Kitty?" Paco shouted.

Instead of a reply, a shot exploded, aimed toward the sound of his voice. Paco and Buckles both scooted along the ground, pulling their horses by the reins. "Kitty, don't shoot," Paco called out. "It is I, Paco Stazo!"

"The hell it is," Kitty shouted, not recognizing the half-breed's voice. "Pour it on them," she said sidelong to the Cullens.

Bullets whistled past Paco and Buckles.

One grazed Paco's shoulder. "Damn you!" he shouted, convinced it was Kitty's bullet, but also knowing that a bullet from her rifle would leave him no less dead than if it were a bullet coming from a stranger. The hillside blossomed with flashes of blue-orange fire. Paco returned fire madly.

CHAPTER 15

The ranger ate a late dinner of jerked elk, hoecake and coffee, then continued on after dark. He followed the trail back halfway across the flatlands, eventually reaching the spot where he'd stopped tracking Delbert Trueblood and instead detoured to Wild Wind to leave Kitty Dellaros for the town law to deal with. It was an easy flatlands trail, and he'd made good time in the moonlight. But he stopped the big Appaloosa when rifle fire resounded in the distance, and drew his eyes to the blinking bursts of fire along the black line of jagged hills.

Staring off at the sight and sound of the raging gun battle, he patted a gloved hand on the stallion's withers and said, "What do you think, Black Pot, huh? Should we check it out?"

The big Appaloosa understood only the sound of his name. But upon hearing it, he shook his mane, blew out a breath and sawed his big head up and down.

"Yeah, me too," the ranger said quietly, still gazing off toward the flashes of gunfire. He turned the stallion and rode off at a quickened pace across the flatlands, straight to the black hill line where the battle continued to rage with no sign of letup.

An hour later, the ranger rode up off the flatlands and ascended a narrow, rocky trail that cut his time sharply. Still, it was nearing daylight in the east as he heard two pistol shots followed by a return round of rifle fire. "Maybe it's starting to wind down after all," he said to the stallion, nudging it upward, closer toward the sound of gunfire.

On the rocks, Paco lay pinned beneath his dead horse, which had taken a bullet and collapsed atop him an hour earlier. Paco had struggled to free himself, but the saddle had him snared and he could neither loosen it nor his legs from beneath the weight of the animal.

"Crazy bitch!" he cried, his voice gravelly from shouting throughout the night over the pounding of rifle fire. He would have made a run for it long ago had the horse not fallen atop him. He felt as if his leg might be broken. Dark blood was smeared across his face and clotted in his eyebrows from a bullet graze on his head.

"What's the use?" said Buckles. "She's probably half deaf from all the gunfire." He sat holding the empty Remington in one hand, his six precious bullets long since spent. His free hand was pressed to a bad shoulder wound that had already cost him a great deal of blood. The whiskey and the laudanum, however, left him cloaked in a warm, fuzzy glow.

"Yeah, what's the use . . . ," Paco repeated to himself in defeat. "I'm saving two bullets. One is for her when and *if* she ever decides to come down here. The other I will use on myself, if I cannot get out from under this horse."

"I — I would help you if I could," said Buckles, barely able to speak from the loss of blood and the effects of booze and narcotics. "But I'm too weak . . . to do any big pulling." Beside him on the ground sat the wicker basket. Drained whiskey bottles were strewn all around it, and the empty blue laudanum bottle lay broken in the dirt.

"Just shut your drunken mouth, Huey," said Paco in disgust, "or I will use *her* bullet on you."

Up on the hillside, Kitty looked past one dead horse and one badly wounded one that nickered pitifully from its spot on the bloody ground. Next to the two animals sat Price Cullen, sprawled back against a rock, slumped, his head bowed onto his bloody chest.

"Price, shut that horse up," she said. "Put it out of its misery."

"Jesus," said Cadden, lying at Kitty's feet among the rock and brush, "I'm afraid he's dead."

"Then go see," said Kitty. "If he is, see if he's got any bullets left. And shut that poor horse up."

Cadden, himself wounded in the forearm and above his left knee, crawled over to Price and shook his shoulder gently. "Wake up, brother. Are you all right?"

"I'm . . . all right, brother . . . but I've been dreaming that I'm dying," mumbled Price, and unleashed a wet, bloody cough. He shook his head. "I don't know . . . which is worse: the nightmare I had, or the one I've woke up to."

"I know," said Cadden. "We're horseless. Are you able to walk out of here once I get you onto your feet?"

"I might be," said Price, "if these . . . sons-abitches will stop shooting at me."

"It's been a while since I heard the rifle," said Cadden. "I'm thinking they're out of bullets."

"But so am I," said Price. He managed to shake his head again. "We've been here . . . shooting all night. It ain't got no better."

"Sit tight, brother," said Cadden. "I'm going to tell her this is enough. We've got to get out of here, some way."

He crawled back to Kitty and said, "He's empty. How are you fixed?"

"I'm down to my last few shots," said Kitty. "I'm not counting; it's bad luck."

"Bad luck?" said Cadden in disbelief. "You've had us counting our rounds all night."

"And look at the two of you," Kitty said. "You're both shot all to hell, and your horses are down."

"Jesus," spat Cadden. "You mean to tell me we've been counting rounds and you've been holding off, putting all the bad luck onto us?"

"Not all," Kitty said, "I'm hit too."

Before Cadden could answer, the ranger's voice called out from a few yards above them, "Drop the rifle, Kitty. You've been at it all night. It's time to put this thing to rest."

Kitty swung the rifle toward him, but she stopped suddenly. The ranger's own rifle was cocked, leveled and waiting. "All right, Sam. You win." She let her rifle fall from her hands and raised her tired arms as high as the bloody wound in her upper shoulder would allow.

"It's Ranger Burrack to you," Sam said, stepping down toward her and Cadden Cullen.

"All right . . . Ranger Burrack, it is," she said with resignation.

"Tell your posse not to shoot, that we give up, Ranger," Cadden said.

Sam stood over the two. He kicked Kitty's rifle out of reach, stooped down and picked up the Colt lying beside Cadden Cullen. "That's not my posse," he said. He gestured Cadden toward his brother Price. "Go help him over here. Go for a gun, and it'll save me having to take you back to town."

"That's a hell of a cavalier attitude," said Cadden, but he rose and limped over to where Price sat slumped and drooling.

"It's not your posse, Ranger?" Kitty asked.

"No, ma'am," said the ranger. "I had no idea you and the Cullens even broke jail. I heard the shooting while crossing the flatlands last night. I came to take a look-see."

"If it's not a posse from Wild Wind, who the hell is it?" she asked.

"I don't know," said Sam. "Why don't we ask?" He stepped away from Kitty and without revealing himself to the gunmen

206

below, he called down over the rocky narrow trail, "This is Arizona Ranger Sam Burrack. Who's down there? Detective Longworth, Chief Bell, is that you?"

"Hell no," Paco Stazo called back in a dry, raspy voice. "It is not the law down here. It is I, Paco Stazo and Huey Buckles. I have been trying to tell her this all fucking night long. The crazy bitch would not listen to me!"

"Oh, Christ . . . ," said Kitty. She shook her bowed head and said, "It really is Paco Stazo. . . ."

"Well, now that we know who everybody is," Sam said to Kitty. He called down to Paco and Buckles, "Stand up, both of you. Walk into sight with your hands raised."

"I cannot do this for you, Ranger," said Paco, "I have a dead horse lying atop me. If not for this horse I would have fled from this madness long before now."

"What about you, Huey Buckles?" said the ranger. "Any dead horses lying on you?"

Huey actually looked himself up and down as if to make sure before he answered. "No," he said drunkenly. "None that I know of."

Sam gave Kitty a faint, wry grin. "None that he knows of," he said. "Sounds like all of you had a hard night." He gestured her up onto her feet and cuffed her hands in front of her.

"Am I the only one you're going to cuff, Ranger?" she asked.

"Yep," said Sam.

"Does that mean I'm the only one you don't trust?" she asked pointedly.

Sam didn't answer. He looked at the Cullens and realized they weren't going anywhere on their own. "All right, now. Are the three of you able to walk down to the trail?"

At midmorning the weary, wounded band of prisoners walked off the hill trail onto the flatlands. The ranger led Black Pot, who carried Price Cullens, the only one of the five who could not walk. The wicker basket of whiskey bottles hung from Black Pot's saddle horn. In front of the ranger, the other four limped and staggered along. Cadden Cullen used a piece of twisted scrub cedar as a walking stick; Huey Buckles kept a hand on his rear to keep the dirty, ragged bandage in place beneath his seatless trousers.

Kitty and Paco Stazo had bickered back and forth since dawn. "How was I supposed to know it was you?" she said to the half-breed, who limped along painfully, staring straight ahead, refusing to look at her.

"How would you know it was me?" Paco asked. "How about this? I said most clearly, 'It is I, Paco Stazo!' Did that tell you anything?"

"You know what I mean, Paco," said Kitty. "Under these circumstances you couldn't expect me to just throw down my rifle and say, 'Oh, it's Paco!' Now, could you?"

"I could expect you to at least investigate and make sure of *who* it was," Paco said. "Instead of firing as if you'd lost your mind."

"Keep it down out there," the ranger cautioned the two.

"Lucky for me, I was already wounded," Buckles said to Cadden Cullen, "or I'd be in one hell of a shape right now."

"What happened to your behind anyway?" Cadden asked, limping along beside him.

"I was stabbed and set afire," Buckles said.

"Jesus," said Cadden. He craned his head back and took a look at the bandage showing through the missing seat of Buckles' trousers. "You smell like burnt hair."

"I expect I do," Buckles replied. "I'm noticing it more as the whiskey and laudanum wears off."

"Hold up, everybody," said the ranger, seeing Longworth and a group of townsmen riding up out of the sage and cactus. "It looks like a posse from Wild Wind."

"It's about damn time," Cadden whispered under his breath to Buckles. "I've been so glad to see a law posse in my life."

"Not me," said Buckles, sober enough to remember what he'd done to the doctor, and what he and Paco had done to the detective. "Instead of burning, my ass is going to be swinging from a rope."

Longworth and the six townsmen riding with him slowed their horses to a walk and formed a half circle around the prisoners. Longworth himself rode forward, stopped and looked down at the ranger.

"I don't know how you did it, Ranger Burrack," he said, pushing up his hat brim, "but I'm glad you caught all these murdering dogs."

Murdering dogs . . . ? Kitty gave Paco a glance; he turned away from her. She looked back at Cadden Cullen. He shrugged. He had no idea what the detective was talking about.

Selectman Tyler called out to the ranger, "It looks like they put up quite a struggle, but you managed to thrash them soundly, eh, Ranger?"

"No," Sam replied, "I haven't fired a shot. There are two groups here. They did all this to each other."

"Two groups?" said Longworth. He looked the five wounded prisoners over. "I had decided the three who broke jail had these others helping them. You mean to tell me that's not the case?"

"Apparently not," said Sam. "These three were shooting it out with these two. Each of them thought the other was the law." He nodded toward the prisoners who were afoot. "As you can see, they beat each other up pretty good."

"Good Lord," said Tyler, looking bemused as he and the others rode forward and gathered around the ranger, staring at the prisoners as if they were remnants of some ragged circus parade. "The irony is that they killed the one man they will all need once we get back to Wild Wind."

Sam looked at Longworth for an answer.

"Doc Ford," Longworth explained. "One of them cut his throat so deep they almost cut his head off."

Sam started to look at Kitty, but caught himself. He thought about her razor, which he'd put in a desk drawer as evidence. He had no definite reason to suspect that she'd used it on the doctor, and he knew this was not the time or place to make any guesses. The townsmen were still reeling from the events of the night before; he could see it in their eyes.

"They killed Chief Bell too," said Longworth. "It was a bloody night in Wild Wind." He scanned the dirty, blood-streaked faces of the five prisoners, not allowing himself to show the rage he harbored for them.

But Sam saw it. And he understood what the young detective was going through. "But it's over now," he said quietly.

Longworth continued to stare intently from one face to the next. The five saw that they were on dangerous ground with the detective and his posse. "They knocked me out, Ranger," Longworth said, the resentment in his voice apparent.

"I understand," said Sam.

"They locked me in my own jail and pulled my britches down," he said. "They ransacked the town, burgled the cantina. Killed the doctor, killed Chief Bell — the man sent to report back on my *progress* here." He continued staring and shook his head. "They left me cuffed and gagged, locked in *my own jail,* with my britches down," he repeated.

"You said that," Sam offered quietly. To get things back on task, he said, "We need to share horses with them. If we don't it'll take all day to get them back to Wild Wind."

"*My own jail,* Ranger." Longworth turned his gaze from the prisoners to the ranger.

"We'll talk more back in town," Sam said.

"Lynch 'em," said a tough-looking livestock broker named Fred Elliot. He stepped his horse in closer. "I'm not sharing my horse with any of this trash."

Sam looked up at him. "What did you say?"

"I said, I'm not sharing my horse with any —"

"No, before that," Sam said.

"I said lynch —"

Sam grabbed Elliot's shin with both hands and hurled him upward off his saddle. As the man hit the ground, Sam was around the horse and upon him, his Colt out of the holster. The barrel made a wide swipe and left a welt on the man's forehead. The big man crumbled, senseless, flat on his back.

"My God, Ranger!" said Longworth.

Sam stood half crouched, his Colt still in hand, glaring at the rest of the townsmen, who had drawn back in shock.

"Does everybody here understand my position on *lynching?*" he said, glaring from face to face. The townsmen sat stunned, staring down at him from their saddles. "I don't even want to hear the word *said,* not even in a whisper."

"Easy, Ranger," Longworth said, his voice cautious. To the townsmen he said, "You all heard him. Let's get doubled up and get back to town before this sun bakes all our brains."

"Oh, goody," Kitty said, "I'm riding with the ranger."

"No, you're not," Sam said, slipping his Colt back into its holster. "You're riding with him." He reached down, dragged the slowly awakening townsman to his feet and helped him stand wobbling in one spot. "Get in the saddle, Kitty. I'll help him up behind you."

"What about these," Kitty asked, showing him her cuffed wrists.

"Make do," Sam said. He helped her and the wobbling Fred Elliot onto the horse. Then he swung up onto Black Pot's back behind the saddle, and behind Price Cullen, who sat slumped, barely conscious. "Don't bleed on me, Price," he said, taking the reins around the sweaty, bloody outlaw. "I don't like this any more than you do."

PART 3

CHAPTER 16

The townsmen took turns sharing their horses with the prisoners in order to keep all of the animals equally rested. Halfway back to Wild Wind the ranger and Longworth shifted Cullen and Stazo over to ride with two of the townsmen and dropped back together in a position that allowed them to see prisoners and townsmen at all times. The townsmen were not happy about riding double. But they all managed to keep their mouths shut about it after what the ranger had done to one of their own.

"The one thing I can't get figured out," said Longworth, the two having discussed the jailbreak and the murders for the past half hour, "is how they managed to get the key off the wall."

Sam asked, "You found no string, no scrapings across the floor, where they might have snagged the key and dragged it over to them?"

"No, nothing," said Longworth. "I checked. *Believe me,* the whole time the blacksmith was getting me out of that cell, I had a good long look at the floor." His face reddened in humiliation just thinking about it.

"You hadn't gone into the cell earlier for anything?" Sam asked.

"No," said Longworth. "With these new cells you seldom have to go inside them. There's a tray slot built into the bars on the door for passing food through. There's a small slot at the floor level just big enough to fit a short bucket for waste."

"So, you didn't go inside when you fed them their supper?" Sam asked.

"No," said Longworth. "In fact, with these food slots, we have a waitress from the restaurant come deliver their food; then she comes back later to take the trays away." He considered it for a moment, then as if dismissing any doubts, he said to Sam, "But she had nothing to do with this. The townsfolk will tell you, Shelly has been waiting tables in Wild Wind since she was fourteen years old. Anyway, I saw the key on the wall after she'd left for the night."

Since she was fourteen . . . Sam considered it silently.

Longworth looked him up and down. "Do

you suppose we'll have any more talk about, *you know . . . ,*" he said, leery of even saying the word himself.

"You mean, lynching?" Sam said, lowering his voice a little.

"Yeah," said Longworth. "Do you suppose it's all done with? I hope so."

"No, it's not over," said Sam. "Putting a pistol barrel to that man's head only stopped it for a while. As soon as we get back to town and everybody has time to get a drink or two of whiskey and think things over, the talk will start again."

"I suppose you're right," Longworth said. "I wouldn't have guessed Fred Elliot saying such a thing. He's a quiet fellow; tends to his business and keeps to himself."

"Maybe he learned a lesson," said Sam. "But be prepared for somebody to bring it up again. Wild Wind is hurting. They've lost their town doctor. Doc Ford was a good man, from what I know of him. I don't blame them for wanting to hang whoever killed him. But it's for the judge to decide when he gets here."

"I know," said Longworth. "I'm glad you're here in that regard. It might be hard to get them to listen to a paid detective who works for Western Railways. You represent

Arizona Territory. That means more to them."

"I know it does," said Sam. "It shouldn't, but it does. So I'm going to be sticking close until the judge gets to town."

"I'm glad to hear you say that, Ranger." Longworth sounded relieved. "I've never dealt with a town wanting to hang somebody, vigilante style."

"We'll be all right," said Sam. He wasn't about to admit that neither had he. "Being young doesn't make us wrong. After all, we represent the law." As he nudged Black Pot forward to go check on Price Cullen, who sat slumped against a townsman's back, he said quietly, "We'll keep our heads cool and Colts handy."

"Yeah, that's what I say," said Longworth, not wanting to appear weak or worried.

When Sam rode up beside Price Cullen and started to shake him gently by his shoulder, the wounded outlaw's eyes opened slightly. "I'm awake, Ranger," Price said in a weakened voice. "I ain't dead yet. . . ."

"That's good," said Sam, "I don't want anybody dying on us."

"Is that . . . an order?" Price Cullen asked, one hand gripping his bandaged chest. His eyes closed as his head crept forward and rested against the townsman's bloodstained back.

"Yes, that's an order," Sam said. He asked the townsman, a realty speculator named Thurman Parks, "How are you holding up, mister?"

Parks, recalling the way the ranger had turned on Fred Elliot so quickly, wasn't about to complain, even though Price had bled all over the back of his shirt and down onto his bedroll. "Oh, I'm fine, Ranger. Can't wait to get home and get out of these clothes, but otherwise fine and dandy."

"You can tell Western Railways they owe you for the shirt," Sam said.

"No, sir, Ranger. I wouldn't dream of it," Parks said quickly. "I'm here doing my part for Wild Wind."

"That's the spirit," Sam said, and nudged Black Pot forward.

When he passed Cadden Cullen, the outlaw looked at him from behind a townsman and asked, "Is my brother going to be all right, Ranger?"

"If we get him to town and get him treated," Sam replied.

"Yeah, but don't forget, we no longer have a doctor in Wild Wind," the townsman said sarcastically over his shoulder. Seeing the stoic look on the ranger's face, the man uickly added, "Although we do have a damn fine horse doctor. I expect he can dress a wound as well as the next fellow."

Sam nodded and rode away.

"Look at him," Kitty said under her breath to Fred Elliot, who was now in the saddle with her riding behind him. "He thinks he's the cock of the walk. After what he did to you, he should be ashamed to hold his head up." She had looped her cuffed hands up over his head and lowered them into his lap earlier. She had stroked his crotch moments earlier, but she'd gotten no response from him.

She tried again. This time as her hands worked expertly on him through his trousers, she cooed near his ear, "I hope you're feeling better, Fred. Is there anything I can do for you?"

Elliot didn't answer. He stared straight ahead, unmoved by her.

"I mean, anything at all?" she whispered, tilting her face in a way to make sure her warm breath caressed his ear and neck. Her cuffed hands worked more intently.

"No, ma'am, there's not," Elliot said flatly. The ranger's gun barrel had left a purple welt across his forehead.

"There's not? Are you sure?" she whispered.

"I'm sure," Elliot said over his shoulder.

"What's wrong? Is it your head?" she asked.

"My head hurts, but that's not it, ma'am," he said quietly. "I have no use for women."

"You *have no use for women?* Oh!" she said, catching herself in surprise as she got his message. Her hands fell limp.

"I never have," Elliot said.

She raised her cuffed hands up over his head and dropped them into her lap. "Just my luck, I roped a gelding," she said half aloud.

When the posse and the prisoners arrived in Wild Wind, the town citizenry turned out and met them on the wide dirt street. "By God, sirs! They've caught those murdering dogs!" shouted a man wearing muttonchop sideburns and a long, handlebar mustache. Sam and Longworth lagged back a few feet and observed the prisoners. They allowed the townsmen to line their horses along the iron hitch rail and step down, before they both ventured forward and stepped down themselves, rifles in hand.

"The shape these gunmen are in, I doubt if there's much chance of them trying to make a break for it," said Longworth.

Sam eyed Kitty Dellaros and remembered

how severely she had cut Andy Weeks' throat. "You never know what a person is apt to do just to keep himself free and on the run."

Longworth nodded in agreement.

"As soon as we get them behind bars, we'll get some length of chain and locks to wrap around the doors, since we don't know where the key is or how they got out last time." He gave Longworth a look.

"I'll get right on it, first thing," said Longworth.

Standing on the boardwalk, awaiting the ranger and Longworth, Paco Stazo looked all around at the angry faces gathered and said in a guarded voice to Cadden Cullen, standing beside him, "Look at them. To them this is like having a circus come to town." He made only a trace of a grin.

But the grin was enough to infuriate one woman, Margaret Bratcher, who had been in the street the night before when Bell lay murdered in the dirt. "Wipe that smile off your filthy face, you murdering, rotten snake!" she bellowed. She ran forward onto the boardwalk, spit in Paco's face and slapped at him. Paco raised an arm to shield himself.

"Let's stop it, Detective," said Sam, "before it gets out of control."

"Right," said Longworth, the two of them already starting forward. "I'll get her; you get the prisoners inside."

Sam hurried in between the townswoman and the line of wounded prisoners, getting there just in time as Kitty leaned toward the shouting Margaret Bratcher and said, "And you can go straight to hell, you pig-licking bitch!"

"Whoa! Hey, that's enough, Kitty," said the ranger, standing in front of Kitty, blocking her view if not her cursing. "Open the door. Let's get inside," he said to Cadden Cullen.

Cadden did as he was told, and the prisoners began filing in off the boardwalk. As they left the street, Kitty gave the townswoman an obscene gesture with her middle finger.

"I want to watch you hang, you filthy outlaw's harlot!" the townswoman railed back at Kitty. "I want to see your eyes pop out and watch you soil yourself before your neck sna—"

"Come on, ma'am," said Longworth. "Let the ranger take these people inside. The judge will see to it they get what they deserve."

"Oh, will he?" said the woman. "I seriously wonder. He's gone easy on women before."

"He's gone easy on men too," said a townsman named Joe Clancy, standing nearby. "Sometimes he sends murderers like this to prison instead of stretching their necks for them."

"We all know how to keep that from happening, don't we?" said another townsman, one who had not ridden with Longworth's posse and witnessed what the ranger did to Fred Elliot. "We string them up, right here and now!"

Longworth looked around nervously to see what the ranger was going to do. He breathed a sigh of relief when he saw the ranger step inside the office behind the last of the prisoners.

"Be thankful the ranger didn't hear that," Longworth said, keeping his voice down. "I'm going to pretend like I didn't hear it either." He turned and walked inside the sheriff's office and closed the door.

Clancy noticed the hushed trepidation fall over the townsmen who'd ridden in with Longworth. "What?" he said with a shrug. "It's true, ain't it? It's what we're all thinking ought to be done. Am I right?"

Fred Elliot stepped in close to him and said under his breath, "Being right can get you the same thing it got me, if you're not careful, Clancy." He raised his hat high enough to the give the man a good look at the long purple welt across his forehead.

"Damn," said Clancy. "The ranger did that to you? All you did was exercise your right to free speech?"

"Keep talking, Joe," said another townsman. "That ranger will have your freedom of speech talking through a broken jaw."

Clancy settled down and took a cautious look at the closed door to the sheriff's office. "Maybe we can't talk here, but Mama Jean has opened the cantina. We can talk there. That's for damn sure."

The townsmen began walking away from the sheriff's office toward the Belleza Grande. From the cantina doorway, a newly arrived gunman named Chug Doherty grinned and said to a gunman named Vernon Reese, who stood beside him, "Now they're all coming here. Think we ought to cut out, go find Ceran and tell him we saw his man Paco and his gal Kitty drug off to jail?"

"In a few minutes, Chug," said Reese. "I want to hear what they've got to say first."

"Think we ought to break Paco and the whore out of jail?" asked Chug.

"Hell no," said Reese. "She ain't my

whore, and Paco Stazo ain't my right-hand man."

"What do you want to do, then?" Chug asked.

Reese grinned. "I want to have another drink and hear what these men have to say. Then we'll take the word to Silva Ceran. After that he can do as he damn well wants about it."

CHAPTER 17

As soon as Clancy, Selectman Tyler, Fred Elliot and the rest of the townsmen filed into the cantina and spread out along the bar, Vernon Reese said to all of them, "Damn, gentlemen, I can't believe my eyes, what I just saw out there."

Elliot and Clancy looked at him.

"I just saw the law taking sides with a bunch of saddle trash against the town's respectable citizens," said Reese. "Somebody tell me it ain't so."

"I wish I could tell you that, mister," Elliot said bitterly, "but I'd be lying." He gestured to Mama Jean, a large, half-Mexican, half-Irish woman who had worked for the deceased owner over the years. "A bottle and some glasses, Mama," he said. "There'll be some big whiskey drunk here today."

"This wouldn't be happening in Texas, Mr. Doherty," Reese said to Chug, who stood beside him. He made sure he spoke loud enough for the others to hear them.

"I expect I know that well enough, Mr. Reese," Chug replied in an equally audible voice.

Mama Jean stood a newly opened bottle of rye in front of Fred Elliot. Elliot filled a glass and slid the bottle of whiskey along the bar to the others. He took off his hat and dropped it atop the bar and gently touched his bruised forehead.

"I take it you gentlemen are from Texas, then," he said to Reese and Doherty.

"You take it correctly, sir," said Reese, tipping a shot glass toward Elliot.

Standing on the other side of Elliot, Joe Clancy cut in and said, "Here's something else you wouldn't see in Texas." He gestured toward the purple welt across Elliot's forehead.

"My goodness," said Reese. "One of those criminals put it on you, I expect?" he asked Elliot.

"Hell no," said Clancy.

Elliot said, "One of our own lawmen did this." He again touched the welt as he raised his filled glass to his lips. "This was done by none other than an Arizona ranger named Samuel Burrack."

"Ouch!" said Reese. "This kinda makes

me wonder whose side he's on."

"Don't think I haven't seriously pondered that myself, all the way back to town," said Elliot. "All I did was mention *lynching* those murdering dogs. This is what it got me." Upon saying the word, he cut a guarded glance toward the door, lest the ranger walk up and hear him.

"Well, that's nothing but plumb crazy," said Reese, enjoying himself. "A man has a right to say what suits him in this great nation of ours."

"That's what I thought too," said Elliot. "But I was wrong. Just saying the word will get a man beaten like a dog."

"I'll say it," Reese declared boldly. "Lynching, lynching, *lynching.* I dare any damned territory ranger to try calling me down for it." He raised his shot glass toward the townsmen. "Boys, this is America. We've got our rights spelled out for us *in writing.* Freedom of speech is one of the main ones."

"By God, this man is right," said Clancy, inspired by the stranger — and by his second shot of rye. "I'll say it too. *Lynching!*" He raised his shot glass. "A lynching is what it's going to take to bring this town its share of justice."

"Lynching!" the townsmen along the bar shouted as one, all their glasses raised.

"And here's to Doc Ford. God bless him," someone added.

"And God bless Texas!" said Reese.

"Hear, hear!" said Doherty.

"And God bless America!" Elliot added.

In the sheriff's office, the ranger and Longworth let the waitress, Shelly Linde, inside and closed and locked the front door behind her. Longworth stood at the door with her.

"I saw all of you riding into town, Detective," she said to him. "I came to see how I can help you." She looked around the room and back at the cells, where the ranger had already led the prisoners. The Cullens occupied the first cell, Paco and Buckles the second, and Kitty Dellaros the third. The cell doors were closed but not locked. "It was terrible — I mean, the jailbreak and all."

Sam watched her eyes as she looked from face to face among the prisoners in their cells. He also checked the faces of the prisoners, all of them staring at the young woman, except for Cadden Cullen, who sat intently looking down at his wounded leg.

What have we here? the ranger asked himself, looking back and forth between the prisoners and the young woman.

"That's kind of you, Miss Shelly," said

Detective Longworth. "But these men have already broke jail and killed the doctor and Chief Bell. I can't risk having you around them. They're not to be trusted."

"Not even long enough for me to take each of them a dipper of water from a bucket?" the woman persisted quietly. "I'll be careful, Detective. And I'll have the two of you watching over me."

"Well . . ." Longworth let his answer stall as he slid a glance to the ranger for approval.

Sam gave a slight nod.

Longworth looked at the dusty, battered prisoners. "All right," he said to Shelly Linde. "Bring them some water. But don't let your guard down, not even for a second, with these men."

"Or the woman," Sam said to Shelly, seeing Kitty Dellaros staring appraisingly at the young waitress from the bars of her cell.

"I won't let my guard down, Ranger," Shelly said to Sam. To Longworth she said, "Thank you, Detective. I'll go fetch a bucket and start watering them right now."

When she'd turned and left, Sam opened the door a crack and looked down the street toward the Belleza Grande Cantina. Through the cantina's open doors he could see that the place was crowded. *But it's not a festive crowd,* he told himself. There was no music, no laughter resounding along the dirt street.

He pulled the door shut and locked it. Turning back to Longworth, he asked just between the two of them, "Are you and the young lady together?"

"Together?" Longworth appeared taken by surprise that the ranger would ask him such a thing. "No. I haven't had time for any social occasions since I've arrived here —"

"But I can see you have eyes for her," Sam said bluntly, cutting him off rather than hearing his awkward denial.

Longworth stared at him.

Sam asked in an even quieter voice, "Do you think she might have had a hand in the Cullens and Kitty breaking out of jail?"

"No," Longworth said, his voice rigid. Sam could tell he had to struggle to keep from bristling at the question. "The time I've been here, I've known Shelly Linde to be an upright young woman, Ranger. I have to say, I don't appreciate you even asking that kind of question."

Oh yes, Longworth has eyes for her, the ranger told himself. He decided to walk softly on the matter, for now anyway. "Detective, asking these kinds of questions

234

comes with pinning tin on our chests," Sam said. "I ask because I have to, not because I want to."

"I understand," said Longworth, cooling down quickly and letting out a tense breath. "The answer is no," he said in a calmer tone. "I'd stake my life on it."

Careful . . . , the ranger cautioned him silently, but decided not to press the issue. "Then I'm glad I asked you now and got the question out of the way," Sam said. He glanced toward the cells, then back to the detective. "It's a fact they got their hands on the key some way."

"I know they did," Longworth said with resolve, "but it wasn't from Shelly Linde. I think it was from those two." He glared at Paco Stazo and Huey Buckles.

Sam made no comment. He walked back toward the three cells. Longworth followed him to the empty peg on the wall where the key had hung. With a nod in the direction of the cantina, he said, "Anyway, shouldn't our main concern right now be what they're getting fueled up to do over at the cantina?"

Sam stood looking at the cells, at the battered, bruised, sweat-streaked faces staring back at him. "We know what they're going to do," he said. "They're going to get drunk enough to come over here and demand we give them the prisoners." He stared grimly from face to face. "We need to find out *who done what,* in case we have to give them somebody to hang."

Longworth stood stunned by the ranger's words; so did the prisoners. But after a dead silence, Cadden Cullen chuckled a little and said, "Nice try, Ranger."

"Shut up, Cullen. This ain't funny," said Huey Buckles, knowing that he and Paco were the two with the most to worry about.

"Yes, it is," said Cadden. "Can't you tell he's bluffing? He's not giving anybody over to a lynch mob. He just figured we'd let something go if we thought it might keep us from a lynching." He grinned and stared hard at the ranger. "I say we tell him nothing. He's a lawman — let him sort things out. That's his job."

"Why don't you both keep your mouths shut," Paco said, seeing what the ranger was doing. "It does not matter what we say. We will be lynched in the street, or we will all hang when the judge is finished with us." He stared at Sam with a wizened expression. "Eh, Ranger?"

Sam stared stone-faced. Cadden Cullen didn't know it, but his attitude alone had just told the ranger a lot. So had Buckles, by the way he'd reacted. But Sam's main question was still the cell key. He'd already decided Shelly Linde had given the key to the Cullens. But why had she done it? And where was it now?

When Shelly Linde returned, she went from cell to cell, dipping water from a bucket and handing it to the prisoners through the bars. Sam stood back watching, checking the look on her face and Cadden Cullen's as she gave him the dipper.

"My, my, Miss Shelly Linde," Cadden purred. For a moment, the ranger thought he detected a trace of a sly grin. "You look as lovely as ever."

Shelly took a step back from his cell, even though the iron bars stood between them, and both the ranger and Longworth were close at hand. Sam took note of her action and continued observing.

"Oh, did I scare you, young lady?" Cadden asked quietly, not realizing the ranger was catching every word, every gesture. "I wouldn't scare you for the world," he cooed. "No, ma'am . . ."

Shelly looked down. *In shame?* The ranger's eyes narrowed as she took the dipper from him and walked to the next cell.

But before he could give the matter more thought, the ranger and Longworth turned to the front door as a hard rapping sounded from the other side of it.

"I've got it," said Longworth, stepping over to the door, rifle in hand. He opened the thick oak door a crack, then wide enough for Hilliard Porter, the town blacksmith, to walk through.

"Men, I don't mean to be an alarmist," said the blacksmith, walking quickly back to the cells with three lengths of thick chain draped around his shoulders. "But there's some awfully *ugly talk* going on at the Belleza Grande." He raised the three chains and dropped them to the floor. On the end of each length he hooked a thick brass padlock with its key sticking out from the keyhole in its center.

"Obliged," said the ranger. "We've been expecting some *ugly talk*." He and Longworth stooped down beside the blacksmith. Each of them picked up a length of chain.

"Who's the one heading it up?" Longworth asked, standing with his chain and walking to the cell where Paco and Buckles stood watching, listening intently to what the blacksmith had to say.

"Clancy and Elliot," said the blacksmith, also standing, going to the next cell. "I believe they would have drank it out of their system had it not been for a couple of strangers who happened to be there."

"Just happened to be there, huh?" Sam said, almost to himself. He stepped forward and wrapped the length of chain around the bars of Kitty's cell door, fastening it to the iron doorframe. "What'd these *strangers* look like?" he asked, hooking the brass lock, shutting it, testing it, and taking the key from it while Kitty stood looking on, holding the water dipper in her hand. Shelly Linde stood back with the water bucket while the ranger completed his work.

"Oh, these two look like just what they are," said Porter. "They're straight-up border trash." He stared hard at Paco and Buckles as he tested his lock and took the key from it. He stepped over and handed the key to Longworth. "I notched each key, one, two and three notches, for which cell it goes to," he said. "So you won't have to fumble around if you have to open up in a hurry."

"Obliged," said Longworth, taking the key from Porter, and the one from Sam as well.

"I sent my boy out to bring back Doc Stanton," said Porter. "He's treating a sick buggy mare a few miles out of town."

"Obliged again," said Sam.

"Yeah, that's thoughtful of you, Blacksmith," Cadden Cullen said with a nasty smile. Sam noted that he slid a guarded glance over to Shelly Linde as he spoke.

"Don't talk to me, you murdering sons-abitches," Porter erupted. "Far as I'm concerned, lynching is too good for yas. But the law is the law, and like any civilized man, I live by it."

"*Lynching?* Uh-oh, Ranger, you heard him. He said that word," said Cadden. "Ain't you going to bust his head for him, the way you did the livestock broker?"

The wiry blacksmith gave the ranger a quick worried look.

"No. He said it with the right attitude," Sam replied, more for the blacksmith's sake than for Cadden Cullen's.

As Kitty handed Shelly the dipper, Kitty saw the others looking away from her cell toward Cadden Cullen, and she made her move. She grasped Shelly's hand and held it firmly as she leaned in close to her through the bars. "I know what you did," she whispered almost into Shelly's ear.

Shelly looked shocked; her face turned ashen. She tried to jerk her hand free without the others noticing, but Kitty held it firmly, wearing a deceptively sweet smile. "Don't worry. It'll stay our little secret. You help me, and I'll help you."

This time Shelly did pull her hand free,

but only because Kitty released it as the ranger looked back around toward the two.

"Thank you, young lady," Kitty said in a normal tone of voice. "I needed that." She ran a hand across her wet lips. *Did the ranger hear anything, see anything?* She wondered, staring at him. If he had, his eyes weren't about to reveal it. *I've learned that much about him,* she told herself.

Shelly Linde backed away from the cells. Sam saw the tremble in her hand as she hooked the dipper on the bucket's edge. "I'll go fetch some more water and heat it up for Doc Stanton when he gets here. I'll find some bandages too."

Longworth stepped over closer to her and said in a soft voice, "Miss Shelly, I hope someday soon you'll allow me to thank you properly for all your help." As he spoke he guided her farther away from the cells. "I hope you'll accompany me to dinner some evening?" he asked.

"Oh, my . . ." Shelly paused and stood looking at him in silence for a moment. Finally she said, "Why, yes, Detective Longworth. I would be most pleased to dine with you."

With the three cells padlocked, Sam cut in for a second and said to Longworth, "I'm going to walk to the cantina and see what's

241

going on there."

Longworth turned from Shelly and said, "I — I'll go with you, just in case —"

"No," said the ranger before Longworth finished his words. He knew the detective was more interested in talking to the young lady than in a cantina full of angry drunks. "We need you right here, keeping an eye on things. I'll be all right."

"What're you going to do?" Longworth asked.

"Just straighten things out a little," Sam said quietly.

"I need to go get that water started," Shelly said, sounding harried. She walked to the door.

The ranger walked with her, opened the door for her and said, "After you, Miss Shelly." Then he gave Longworth a look and followed her out the door, onto the board-walk.

CHAPTER 18

The ranger walked alongside Shelly on her way to the restaurant. Halfway there he said to her in a gentle tone, "I know you gave the Cullens the key, Miss Shelly."

They both walked on in silence for the next few yards, until the young woman stopped and broke into tears. "What's going to happen to me, Ranger?" she asked in a shaky, frightened voice. "I didn't mean for anything like this to happen. He promised me they would slip out of the jail, leave town and never come back."

"*He* being Cadden Cullen?" Sam asked.

"Yes, Cadden made me do it." She stopped and corrected herself. "No, he didn't make me do it. I'm the one to blame. But he was going to tell everybody about me if I didn't help get him and his brother out of Wild Wind," she said. "But I swear to you, Ranger Burrack, I never thought they would kill anybody." She buried her face in her hands and sobbed out of control. "I don't think I can live with myself knowing I caused all this."

"Take it easy, Miss Shelly," Sam said. "I'm not sure the Cullens killed anybody."

"You-You're not?" Shelly asked.

"No, I'm not," said Sam. "It's going to take some time to sort out what happened here, but I've got a hunch the Cullens and Kitty Dellaros made their break and got out of here. I think Paco Stazo and Huey Buckles did all the killing. I'm not saying that the other three wouldn't have killed anybody who got in their way if it came to it. I'm just saying I don't think they did."

"But I still did a terrible thing," Shelly said. She continued to cry.

Sam looked all around and saw eyes turn toward them. Rather than talk on the public street, he guided her into the doorway of a boarded-up shop and said, "All right, now. Take a deep breath and settle yourself down. You're going to have to tell me everything."

"You're right, Ranger," she said. "I gave Cadden Cullen the key to the cells when I took their dinner to them. He and Kitty unlocked their cells. I hung the key on the wall peg when I came back and got their empty plates."

Sam looked at her closely as he considered what she'd told him. "That's why Longworth saw the key hanging there before he went to sleep in the office," he said.

"Yes," said Shelly. "The key was hanging there, but the cells were already unlocked."

"Longworth failed to shake the doors before he went to sleep," Sam said aloud to himself. "Had he done that, the whole mess would have never happened."

"What? Shake the doors?" Shelly asked, having no idea what he was talking about.

"Nothing," Sam said, realizing it no longer mattered. What was done was done; no amount of reconsidering would change anything. He shook his head. "Go on," he said to the young woman.

"He — Cadden Cullen, that is — promised me they wouldn't hurt anyone," she said.

"A promise from a man like Cadden Cullen isn't worth the air it's written on," Sam offered.

"I realized that now," said Shelly. "Maybe I even realized it then. But I was desperate. I made myself believe his word was good." She shook her head.

"You were desperate?" Sam asked.

But she didn't answer him. Instead she said, "Still, I would never have agreed to do it if I thought it might have gotten anybody killed." She trembled a little. "Just think: if Clayton had awakened when they were on their way out the door. . . ." She sobbed into her hands at the thought of what might have happened.

"What do you mean you were *desperate?*" Sam asked, pulling her hands down from her face, forcing her to continue on.

"*Desperate* to get him out of my life," Shelly said. "I would have done just about anything to get Cadden Cullen out of Wild Wind and away from me," she said, sniffling, collecting herself. "Now it appears I've only made matters worse."

"Why? What's between you two?" Sam asked. "What's this outlaw holding over you?"

Shelly just stared at him for a moment, reluctant to say any more.

"Are the Cullen brothers kin of yours?" Sam asked, familiar with the strength of blood ties, and what it could force a person into doing.

"No, Ranger, they are no kin of mine," Shelly said. "I have no kin, none of any kind."

"Was Cadden Cullen your lover? Your beau?" Sam asked bluntly, pursuing the matter relentlessly.

"No, he was not my lover," Shelly replied just as bluntly. "He was my customer. I was a whore before I came to Wild Wind. Cadden Cullen knew it. He knew because I *did it* with him for money. He threatened to tell everybody here if I didn't help him get out of jail and out of town."

"Your customer . . ." Sam pondered the information for a moment, then said, "But I was told you were only fourteen when you started working at the restaurant."

"Yes, I was," she said, staring into his eyes. "I was fourteen years old when I bargained my way onto a freight wagon headed here from Abilene. Before that I was a whore in Abilene. I belonged to a whoremaster named Rowan Garrity. He bought me from the conductor of an orphan train that was taking me to Abilene."

Sam studied her eyes, and knew she was telling the truth. "The conductor sold you to this fellow Rowan Garrity?" he asked quietly, keeping the rage from showing in his voice.

"Yes," said Shelly. "I was twelve. For a year Garrity kept me for special customers who paid extra for a young girl like me. But when I turned thirteen he turned me out into his brothel like all his other whores. I made up my mind to escape as soon as I could. Almost a year later, I did just that . . . and I made it all the way here to Wild Wind."

"How long ago was that?" Sam asked, working out her story in his mind.

"It's been seven years," she said. "I found work at the restaurant. The owners, Bart and Rosemary Tinkens, are good to me. They trust me to watch their son, little Tommy." She had stopped crying for a moment, but now fresh tears welled in her eyes. "I thought my past was behind me. I had a good life here — hard but good. Respectable, you know?"

"I know," Sam said quietly.

"One night I went to take food to the jail to some new prisoners there," she said, "and it all fell down around me."

"After seven years," Sam said, "how did he ever recognize you?"

"By this," she said. She raised the hair on the side of her head and revealed a small blue heart tattooed just below her right ear. On either side of the heart were the initials *RG* in fancy Old English–style writing.

"Rowan Garrity . . . ," Sam said, translating the initials for himself.

"It was his way of always being able to find us if we tried to run away," said Shelly. She smoothed her hair back down into place. "Cadden had already said I looked familiar to him, but he couldn't recall from where. Then he managed to see the tattoo while I was passing his tray through the food slot. He said, 'Now I know where I've seen you before.' " She paused for a second, then said with a bitter tone, "He remembered everything about that night as clearly as if it had happened yesterday."

"And he started right away, threatening to tell if you didn't help him and his brother escape," Sam said, filling in the rest of the story for her.

Shelly only nodded her bowed head. "I — I thought about poisoning him," she said. "But I couldn't bring myself to kill anyone, even someone as no-good as Cadden Cullen."

"I understand, Miss Shelly." Sam drew her to him and held her, comforting her.

After a moment, she took a deep breath and straightened. "All right, Ranger. I'm ready to admit what I did and take whatever comes my way."

Sam considered it. He took a step back from her and scratched his head under his hat band. He'd asked for the truth, and now he felt he'd gotten it. The problem with truth, he realized, was knowing what to do with it — how to use it wisely. He'd learned from experience that truth served no good unless wisely used.

"Here's a problem I have, Miss Shelly," he said to her. "This is not my town. Wild Wind has an agreement with Western Railways. With Chief Bell dead, it's up to Detective Longworth to decide what to do about you giving the key to the Cullen brothers. All I can do is report to Longworth what you've told me. Then it's up to him to deal with the matter, best he sees fit."

Shelly looked heartbroken. "Once you tell him, he'll have to arrest me," she said, visualizing the shame she would have to face.

"Under the circumstances, I think it would be best if you told him yourself. I know he cares for you, Miss Shelly. I see it in his eyes."

"And I care for him, Ranger," Shelly replied. "This makes it all the harder for me to do." She winced at the thought of what lay ahead of her.

"Yes, I can see how it does," Sam said. "But you've got to do it. Maybe your telling him will make it go easier for you."

"I'm not asking for mercy, Ranger," she said. "I know I don't deserve it."

"It's not my job to decide who deserves mercy and who doesn't," Sam said, "nor is it yours. But you've got to tell Longworth, mercy or no."

She paused in dread, then said under her breath, "I'll tell him. You have my word." She looked ashamed. "If my word means anything now."

"It does," Sam said without hesitation. "I want your word you'll tell Longworth you gave the Cullens the key, and the reasons why you did it." He stared deep into her eyes. "I also I want your word that you won't tell him I know anything about the matter." He raised a finger for emphasis and added in a firm tone, "Tell him and nobody else. Do you understand me?"

The young woman looked a little confused. "But why, Ranger?"

"Because that's the deal, Miss Shelly," the ranger said. "It's Longworth's town. It's his call. Who he tells is up to him. I'm backing away from it."

"I'll — I'll tell him this evening, as soon as I can get him alone."

"Good," said Sam, "see that you do." He looked off toward the cantina, then back to her. "Now go on to the restaurant. I've got to take care of some business at the Belleza Grande."

"That's it?" Shelly said, looking surprised and relieved that she gotten her ugly secret off of her chest.

"Yep, that's it, unless you want to argue with me," he said.

"No, Ranger," she said in a serious tone, not catching his attempt at lightening the mood. "I don't want to argue with you." She turned and walked away, her arms folded across her chest, her head bowed in contemplation.

The ranger watched her for a moment, knowing how Longworth felt about this woman. He shook his head slightly. Hearing this from her was either going to destroy Detective Clayton Longworth, or make him all the stronger. *Welcome to the law, Detective,* Sam said to himself.

Inside the Belleza Grande Cantina, Chug Doherty was busily railing against the law and the unfairness of what the ranger had done to Fred Elliot. He did not see Sam walk in through the open doors and head straight across the floor toward him. With a shot glass full of whiskey raised in his hand, he gazed upward toward the ceiling, not seeing the worried faces of the men turn away from him and toward the ranger.

Standing a few feet away, Vernon Reese didn't see the ranger either, until it was too late. He did see Mama Jean cross herself with a fearful look on her face and duck down behind the bar. But by the time he realized trouble was coming, it had already arrived. The ranger's rifle butt stabbed him hard in his stomach right where his ribs met. He had started to move for the Colt on his hip, but instead he buckled and fell to the floor with a sickening wheeze.

"And I'll say this too!" Doherty continued, staring up, not hearing Reese fall, nor seeing the crowd of drinkers suddenly pull away in every direction. "Lynching is too good for some sonsabitches — !" His words stopped short. *"Whoa!"* he shouted, flailing his arms and legs wildly, feeling himself suddenly rise into the air.

His whiskey flew from his hand as the ranger hurried across the floor with him, holding him overhead by his neck and the seat of his trousers, and hurling headlong through the large, dusty glass window.

"Madre Santa de Dios!" Mama Jean said to herself, rising in time to see and hear the loud crash of glass and the scream of the airborne outlaw.

Along the bar the townsmen stared, wide-eyed and stunned, seeing Doherty come down onto the dirt street, rolling in a spray of glass and dust.

"My God, he's killed the man!" someone

whispered, seeing Doherty lying limp in the street.

"*Help* me," Reese rasped.

Sam walked back to the bar and picked up his rifle from the bar top where he'd laid it. Reese lay gasping for breath on the floor, clawing at the front of the bar. Sam looked down at the Colt in the outlaw's holster, but made no effort to take the gun from him. Instead he turned with his rifle barrel aimed loosely at the shocked townsmen.

"I see none of you explained my position on *lynching* to these men. Now look what it's got them."

Joe Clancy found the courage to step forward and say angrily, "Ranger, you and Longworth can't ride roughshod over this town! If we have to, we'll tear up the agreement we have with Western Railways and send him packing. *You too.*"

"Make no mistake, any of you," Sam said, looking from one man to the next, "Clayton Longworth and Western Railways have nothing to do with me."

"You belong in Arizona Territory," said Joe Clancy.

"Ordinarily, yes," said the ranger, "but today I belong where I'm standing."

"Now see here, Ranger," said Clancy. He stepped forward, growing bolder as his anger flared. "You can't threaten us and bully your way —"

Clancy stopped in his tracks as the tip of the ranger's rifle barrel jammed into his chest. Sam stared coldly at him and said, "You haven't seen *roughshod* yet, mister. Keep up this lynching talk, somebody's going to get hurt." The hammer of his rifle cocked beneath his gloved thumb.

Going to get hurt? Fred Elliot glanced through the broken window at the outlaw lying moaning in the street. Then he glanced down at Reese, lying at the ranger's feet, gasping for breath. "Easy, Ranger," he offered, sobered enough to see that the ranger was making no idle threat. "There's not going to be a lynching here."

Sam stared at him. "It sounds like you're starting to get my message," he said, his bark still on, his demeanor still cold and unyielding. He gestured his free hand down toward the outlaw gasping at his feet. "Do any of you know this man?"

The townsmen stood silent, afraid to reply.

"Well, I do," Sam said. He reached out a boot toe and nudged Reese over onto his side, just as the man had managed to get a hold on the brass bar rail and start to pull himself up. Reese let out a painful groan and rolled back into a ball.

"His name is Vernon Reese. That one out there in the dirt is Chug Doherty. They are both known to ride with Silva Ceran, the same man the prisoners in your new jail ride for."

"Christ," said Elliot, "then why are they talking up a lynching, if those are their cronies in jail?"

"Just to stir up trouble between you men and the law, so they can keep this town and the law divided against each other," Sam said. He looked down at the groaning outlaw and said, "Isn't that right, Reese?"

Reese could only make a pained face and let out a strained, gurgling sound. A string of saliva bobbed from his lips.

"See? He won't deny it." Sam uncocked his rifle. Reaching down, he pulled the helpless gunman to his feet. He picked up Reese's crumpled hat and stuffed it atop his head. "You and Chug get mounted and get out of here," he said through clenched teeth. "Stop running your mouths."

"You're just letting them go?" Clancy asked.

"Yes, I'm letting them go. I've got nothing to hold them on," Sam said, giving Reese a shove toward the open doorway.

"But what if they bring Ceran and his gang here?" said Elliot.

"Have you thought of that?" Clancy asked.

"Yes, I have," said Sam. "There's a strong possibility they will bring him here, if he wasn't coming here already." He looked from face to face among the townsmen. Then he said to Elliot, "It'll be up to me and Longworth to defend this town, unless you still want to send him packing . . . *and me too.*" He stared Clancy in the eyes, letting his message sink in.

CHAPTER 19

Longworth had walked out front of the sheriff's at the sound of breaking glass coming from the direction of the cantina. He stood looking at the cantina, rifle in hand, and saw the outlaw in the dirt, trying to struggle to his feet. The young detective bit his lip and paced back and forth, fighting the urge to go running to the ranger's side. *But I said I'd wait at the jail, and that's what I'd better do,* he told himself. He stopped and watched, feeling better when he saw the second man stagger, bowed at the waist, out of the cantina and make his way to the hitch rail.

When the two men struggled up into their saddles, they headed down the dirt street. But at the sight of Longworth facing toward them with his rifle at port arms, they turned their horses and crept away onto a back street, out of town.

From the restaurant Shelly Linde stepped

out with a fresh bucket of water in one hand and basket full of cloth in her other. On her way across the street to Longworth, she looked toward the cantina and saw the glass and broken window frame lying in the dirt. She'd heard the noise from inside the restaurant as she'd gathered spare cloth for bandages.

"What was all that?" she asked as she reached Longworth.

"It was the ranger," he replied, as Sam walked out of the cantina and started down the street toward them.

"Did he . . . ?" Shelly's words trailed as she looked at the glass and pieces of wood in the dirt.

"Yes," said Longworth, "he threw one through the window."

"A townsman?" she asked, looking shocked.

"No," said Longworth, "it was one of the strangers Porter was talking about."

"Oh," said Shelly. She stood in silence for a moment as the ranger drew closer. Then she let out a breath. "Detective Longworth, I have something important I need to tell you."

"Call me Clayton, please, Miss Shelly," Longworth said.

"I will, if you still want me to after I tell

you what I've got to say," Shelly said. "Can we go somewhere and talk, please — somewhere private?"

Longworth saw the serious look in her eyes. "Of course," he said. He turned and directed her toward the empty boardwalk out in front of the sheriff's office.

"No, back here," she said, directing him away from the boardwalk and toward a deserted alley running alongside the new buildings.

"Yes, ma'am," Longworth said with a bewildered look on his face.

Sam saw the two of them headed for the alleyway and realized that she must be getting ready to tell the detective what had happened. To give them the privacy they needed, he swung wide around them and walked on. When he was well past them, he cut across the street and entered the sheriff's office quietly, closing and locking the door behind himself.

With the door locked, he leaned his rifle against the battered desk, walked to the Cullen brothers' cell and gestured Cadden over to the bars. When they were only inches apart, the bars between them, Sam said in a quiet but firm tone, "Give me the key."

"The key?" Cadden looked bemused; he grinned. "Ranger, are you kidding? I don't have the —"

Sam's hands streaked between the bars, grabbed Cadden by his ears and jerked him forward. The outlaw's face and forehead banged against the iron bars with a deep twanging sound.

Cadden almost went limp. But Sam shook him by his ears and said, "Want me to ask you again?"

"No, stop!" Cadden managed to say while the bars still rang from the impact of his forehead. "I've got it right here under my shirt!" He hurriedly unbuttoned his shirt and slipped it off of his left arm; the ranger turned loose one ear while he did so.

The ranger looked at the large brass key ring that Cadden had slid up over his elbow. The cell key hung under his arm.

In her cell, Kitty Dellaros stood watching, shaking her head in disgust at Cadden giving up the key, even though the doors were now chained and padlocked. "Damn tinhorn amateur," she said under her breath.

Sam took the key. He let go of Cadden's ear but held him against the bars by the front of his shirt. Between the two of them, he said, "Now, what's this I hear about you threatening to tell lies about my friend Shelly Linde?"

"Hold on, Ranger," Cadden replied in the

same secretive voice. "It's no lie. I was in Abilene. She was there working in a broth—"

His words cut short; his face struck the bars again. This time the ranger jerked him forward by his shirt. "Are you sure you're not mistaken, Cullen?" Sam asked into his bloody face. "We can discuss this for hours on end, if we really need to, to get it straightened out."

"I — I could be mistaken," said Cadden. He felt the ranger grip his shirt tight, ready to jerk him forward again. "I mean, I *was* mistaken. It wasn't her, I'm certain of it."

"I'm glad to hear that, Cadden. If we need to discuss this some more," Sam said close to his ear, "you let me know. I'm going to be right here, ready to help you talk it through."

An hour had passed before the ranger opened the front door and Longworth and Shelly Linde walked inside. From the stunned look on Longworth's face, the ranger could see that Shelly had told him everything and he was struggling with it. Now the ranger would have to wait and see if Longworth would tell him or cut him out. It made no difference to Sam whether or not Longworth told him. But what the detective did about it would reveal the kind of lawman he was going to be.

"We just saw the horse doctor, Horace Stanton riding into town," Longworth said to the ranger, avoiding his eyes.

"Good," said Sam. He pulled the brass key ring from his belt and handed it to Longworth. "Here. You might need this again someday."

Longworth looked surprised, but he took the key ring and inspected it in his hand. "Who had it?" he asked.

"Cadden Cullen," Sam replied. "He had it looped up over his shoulder, beneath his shirt."

"What do you suppose made him decide to give it back to you?" Longworth asked.

"That's anybody's guess," Sam said, staring back toward the cells as he spoke.

Shelly busied herself with stoking a fire in the woodstove and pouring water from the bucket into a small kettle to boil. Longworth glanced at her, then said to Sam in a lowered voice, "Ranger, there's some things we need to talk about."

"All right, go ahead," said the ranger.

"This isn't going to be easy . . . ," Longworth said. He paused in silence for a moment, a troubled look on his face.

Sam finally said, "If this is going to take a

while, maybe we'd best wait." He gestured a nod toward the door where the sound of hoof beats had just stopped at the hitch rail.

Longworth let out a breath. "Yeah, maybe we better. It might take a while to talk about this and get it all off my chest and clear the air."

"Oh . . . I didn't realize the air need clearing," Sam said. "Is everything all right?"

"With you and me? Yeah, everything's all right," said Longworth. They heard boots walk across the boardwalk from the hitch rail.

"Okay, then," said Sam. "Anytime you're ready to talk, just let me know, Detective." He paused, then said, as if in secret, "But remember this: sometimes getting things off your chest *does* clear the air. Other times all it does is leave a mess on the floor."

Longworth gave him a curious, questioning look.

"It's just something to think about," Sam said quietly as the two heard the knock on the door and turned toward it.

Shelly Linde opened the door and stood aside as a black man in a frayed and faded green suit walked in, a shotgun in the crook of his arm.

"I'm Dr. Horace Stanton, DVM," he said, looking all about the new office and back at the cells. "The blacksmith's boy fetched me. Said you are in need of medical services here."

"Yes, we do. Please come in, Doctor," said Longworth. He and the ranger both stepped forward to meet the man. "You already know Miss Shelly Linde," said Longworth. "She's volunteered to assist you."

"Much obliged, Miss Shelly," the doctor said, bowing slightly and sweeping his tall, battered top hat toward her.

Shelly smiled and nodded, but continued preparing the hot water and bandaging.

"I'm Detective Clayton Longworth. This is Arizona Ranger Samuel Burrack." Longworth gestured a hand toward the ranger, then toward the cells. "These are your patients back here."

"Pleased to meet you, gentlemen," said the doctor. He carried a frayed canvas bag hooked over his shoulder by a wide leather carry strap. Nodding toward his shotgun, he said, "The blacksmith's boy also said there is talk of a lynching here. So I *heeled* myself appropriately."

"It's true there's been some lynching talk, Dr. Stanton," said Longworth. "But I don't think you have anything to worry about. The ranger here has quieted it down considerably."

"Indeed . . ." The doctor eyed the ranger up and down appraisingly. "I've heard a lot about you, Ranger Samuel Burrack," he said, "and I hasten to add that it's all been good."

"Obliged, Doctor," Sam said modestly.

"But I like to clearly set forth from the start that in regards to *lynchings,* I will tolerate no man, white or colored, to lay hands upon me, sir," the doctor said in a serious voice.

"Duly noted," said Longworth, reaching out and taking the big double-barreled shotgun from the doctor's hand and leaning it against the desk.

"That being said" — the doctor swung his canvas bag down from his shoulder and held it in hand — "I will proceed with treating your prisoners." He glanced around at Shelly Linde as he turned toward the cells. "Miss Shelly, if you please . . ."

"I'm coming right behind you, Dr. Stanton," Shelly said.

At the door to the Cullen's cell, the doctor and Shelly stood aside and watched as Longworth unlocked the padlock and unwrapped the chain. Cullen eyed the brass key ring stuck down behind Longworth's gun belt and gave the ranger a look. Sam stared back coldly at him. Cullen looked away from Sam and focused a hard stare at the black doctor.

"Say, what the hell is this?" Cadden said, appearing offended.

"It's the doctor," said Longworth. "He's here to treat all of you."

"Like hell," said Cadden. "He's not laying hands on us Cullens."

The doctor had started past Cadden toward Price, who lay sprawled on his cot. But he stopped and looked at Cadden. "What? You have a problem with me attending you, young man?" he asked coolly.

"You're damn right I do," said Cullen. "No horse doctor is treating me and my brother, especially not some Negro horse doctor."

"You knew we had a horse doctor coming, Cadden," said Longworth. "Everybody here knew it."

"No, I didn't," Cadden lied. "An even if I did, I had no idea it would be a *Negro.*"

Dr. Stanton had already stopped at Price's cot and slipped off his faded green suit jacket. "As you wish, sir," he said to Cadden. He rolled down the shirtsleeve he'd just rolled up and turned back toward the iron-barred door. "On to the next cell, Miss Shelly," he said.

"Jesus . . . Wait, Doctor," Price said in

267

weak, pleading voice. "Don't . . . listen to . . . that idiot."

Cadden looked over at him and said, "I'm sorry, brother, but you have to draw a line somewhere."

"I'm dying . . . Cadden, you damned fool," Price Cullen rasped.

"What's it going to be, mister?" the black doctor asked Price. "Is a colored horse doctor going to treat you, or do you prefer to die in your own blood?"

"White doctor . . . black doctor, *horse doctor* . . ." Price gasped and said in a failing voice, "I don't . . . give a damn. . . . Doctor, please . . . help me. . . ."

At the Belleza Grande Cantina, Mama Jean stood a fresh bottle of rye on the bar in front of Fred Elliot, Joe Clancy and the rest of the townsmen. The men strung along the bar had fallen quiet, and drank almost in silence ever since the ranger had rifle-butted Vernon Reese and thrown Chug Doherty through the large front window.

"I have to say, I never in my life seen nothing like that," said a townsman named Robert Samples. He shook his head.

"Nor did I," Clancy said as he refilled Samples' shot glass and his own from the new bottle.

"I did," said Elliot, his hat off and lying

atop the bar, the long welt on his forehead still purple and swollen.

"I'm both stunned and mortified," said Clancy. He raised his shot glass and drank half of it.

"Hear, hear," said Elliot, halfheartedly raising his shot glass. He sipped the glass empty and set it down with a sigh.

Clancy looked, bleary-eyed, around the quiet cantina, and saw the bowed heads and slumped shoulders. Then he sipped down the rest of the glass and let out a long breath.

"Well, that'll do it for me," he said. "I'm headed home for some supper and hot coffee — try my best to forget this day ever happened."

"Whoa, wait a minute!" said Samples. He was younger than both Elliot and Clancy, and he hadn't started drinking as early in the afternoon. "You mean you're just going to pretend none of this ever happened?"

"Yes, something like that," said Clancy.

Another younger townsman named John Rader cut in and said, "We're just going to be shoved around and put in our place by one damned tinhorn territory ranger, because he don't like us talking about taking the law into our own hands?"

"Yes, we are, exactly," Clancy said with a

whiskey slur, picking up his bowler hat and setting it atop his head.

"Hell, I'm not," said Rader.

"Me neither," Samples put in. "You old folks go on home, if that's what suits you. Us younger men will do what's right for Wild Wind."

"Jesus, here we go again," Fred Elliot muttered to himself. He turned and faced Samples and Rader. "That *tinhorn ranger,* as you call him, threw a man twice his size through the front window."

"So?" Samples said defiantly.

"Doesn't that tell you young bucks anything?" said Elliot.

Samples and Rader looked at each other, and both shrugged. "Don't let that ranger sneak up on us the way he did those two?" said Samples.

John Rader turned to some other, younger townsmen who had gathered at the cantina, drawn by the earlier commotion and all the broken glass in the street. "Everybody who ain't heeled, get heeled." He said to Mama Jean, "Keep 'em coming, Mama. We've got some planning to do."

"Hell, I can't go home now," said Clancy, seeing the rest of the crowd starting to come back to life. He took off his hat and laid it

back on the bar beside Fred Elliot's.
"Mama, set me up," he said.

CHAPTER 20

Silva Ceran stood at the spot where Clayton Longworth had crushed his hand trying to change the wheel on the freight wagon. Having followed the tracks of the ranger and the woman to the spot, he looked all around and saw the wagon tracks wind away alongside two riders on horseback. He nudged his boot toe against the discarded wagon wheel lying on the ground. He saw the crudely filed *X* on the busted steel wheel band, but it meant nothing to him.

"How'd she manage to get herself tangled up with this damned ranger? She's not even wanted for anything," he grumbled to himself. He spit in the dirt and stared along the trail toward Wild Wind. *At least she's not wanted for anything I know of,* he reminded himself, realizing that Kitty Dellaros was a woman apt to do most anything that suited her, legal or not.

"Your woman is riding with this one?"

Quintos asked, pointing at the hoofprints on the ground.

"Yeah, this *one* lawman has her riding with him," Ceran said. He turned and looked Trueblood up and down with contempt. "This tells me there was only *one* lawman in Wild Wind, *Delbert*. Do you follow me?"

"Well . . ." Trueblood furrowed his sore and throbbing brow in contemplation. "No, I expect I don't follow you, Silva," he said finally.

"I'm saying, if you and the others had stayed and killed this *one* ranger, we wouldn't have to deal with all this."

"Oh . . ." Trueblood lowered his head. He offered no reply. All he could think about was what would happen when he and Kitty Dellaros were face-to-face. If she told him about her deal with him and Weeks, he was a dead man.

Ceran looked away from Trueblood and back curiously toward the trail into Wild Wind. "Now I'm starting to wonder what's taking Paco and Buckles so damn long. We should have met up with them by now, on their way back from town."

Quintos gave a smug little grin and said, "Maybe this same lawman has killed them too. Maybe he kills all of your men." He turned slowly and looked at his warriors with a slight nod. They stared back at him as if to say they knew he was the one who should be in charge.

Ceran stared coldly at him, but he made no reply. He stepped back up into this saddle and turned toward the trail. "If you're all finished, let's get going and see what's happened to them."

But Quintos wasn't finished. He called out to Ceran, "I bring my warriors to join you, so that together we can rob and make money to arm my people against the white men. I did not bring them to help you find your men or keep watch on your woman."

Ceran turned his horse back at a walk and stopped only a few feet from where Quintos and his men had gathered, facing him. "Listen to me, *Bloody Wolf,*" he said, his rifle across his lap, lying beneath his gloved hand. "We're going to rob lots of places together if everybody plays their cards right."

"I'm not playing cards," said Quintos. "I'm here to make money," he repeated, "in order to wage war." He spat on the ground.

"We're going to make enough money for you and your people to do as you damn well please. But right now, this needs doing first." He gestured his free hand toward

Wild Wind.

Bloody Wolf sat staring for a moment; then he jerked his horse around in a huff and turned his back on Ceran.

Son of a bitch . . .

Ceran grumbled under his breath, turned his horse and rode off along the trail, his men following behind him, keeping eye back on Quintos and his warriors.

Two hours later they rode down onto the flatlands between the hill line and main trail to Wild Wind. Riding ahead of the others, scouting the trail, Little Tongue raised an arm and directed their attention to the two riders coming at them, rising up as if out of the dirt, brush and rocks.

"It's Paco and Buckles," Ceran said with relief in his voice, "and it's about damn time."

"It's — it's not them, Silva," Trueblood said reluctantly, squinting out at the riders, his stitched and swollen face throbbing in pain.

Ceran jumped his horse ahead of the others and stood in his stirrups, staring as Reese and Doherty rode up to Little Tongue on the trail. As they approached the silent Indian, the two circled slowly with their hands on their gun butts.

Reese said to Little Tongue in a strained

and shallow voice, "Who the hell are you?"

Little Tongue made a squawking sound through his thin, parted lips and pointed his rifle back at the trail toward Ceran and the rest of the riders.

Hearing Little Tongue's strange sound, Doherty said to Reese, "Jesus, he must've swallowed a mockingbird."

Seeing Ceran ride forward toward them, followed by the rest of the riders, Reese replied, "This is just what we need — a *squeaking* Indian." He looked Little Tongue up and down with contempt.

Little Tongue stared at them in silence until Silva Ceran rode up at a gallop and reined his horse to a halt. Dust billowed; Vernon Reese fanned it away with his hat. Doherty sat slumped in his saddle with dried blood streaking his battered face. Granules of glass glistened in the afternoon sunlight on the shoulders of his fringed deerskin shirt.

"Evening, Snake," Reese said to Ceran. "I bet you didn't expect to see us again so soon." He sat bowed forward a little in his saddle, his voice still weak and strained from catching the ranger's rifle butt in his stomach.

"No, I didn't," said Ceran. "To tell the truth, I thought you were both dead when you didn't show up right away for your share of the payroll money."

"We got sidetracked for a few days in Cimarron, but we're here now," said Reese. He couldn't wait to tell Ceran about Paco, Buckles and Kitty Dellaros being in Wild Wind's new jail. But he held back, waiting for just the right moment.

"What happened to you, Chug?" Ceran asked Doherty, noting his ragged, bloody condition. He swung his eyes back to Reese, seeing the way Reese sat bowed forward. "Hell, what happened to the *both* of you?"

"I was what you'd call *blindsided* and thrown through the window of the Belleza Grande," Doherty said.

"I took a rifle butt right here," said Reese, touching his upper stomach where his ribs met.

"At the Belleza Grande?" Ceran asked, looking back and forth as the rest of his men rode forward to catch up with him. "So you just come from Wild Wind?"

"Yeah, we just came from there," said Reese. "That *loco* ranger who killed Junior Lake did this to us. The son of a bitch is running roughshod over everybody in town. There's nobody there to stop him."

"I sent Paco and the Comanchero, Huey Buckles, to Wild Wind," said Ceran. "Any idea what might have happened to them?"

"Yep," said Reese, but then he sat in silence staring at Ceran, making him dig for it.

"Listen, you son of a bitch," said Ceran, "you do not want to give me reason to kill you today. If you know something about Paco and Buckles, give it up."

"They're both in jail," said Reese, seeing that this was no time to play games with Silva Ceran. "So is Kitty Dellaros."

"Damn it to hell," said Ceran. "That's what I was afraid of."

"Is that what Paco was doing, snooping around in Wild Wind for you?" Reese asked.

"Yes, he was," said Ceran. "Why? What's going on there?"

Reese and Doherty looked at each other. Then they turned back to Ceran. "From what we heard, the townsmen there are about to stretch their necks for them, vigilante style."

"We both heard them talking about a lynching while we drank at the Belleza Grande," said Doherty. He sat fidgeting in his saddle.

"A lynching, eh?" Ceran gave them both a questioning look. "But I suppose you two had nothing to say about that?"

"No, not a thing," said Reese, with a

278

shrug. "We was drinking, keeping our mouths shut."

"Then why'd the ranger single you two out?" Ceran asked.

"Beats me," said Doherty. He gave Reese a look.

"Wild Wind is in an uproar over somebody killing their doctor and their chief detective," said Reese. "I expect the ranger had to single somebody out. It happened to be us. But what he doesn't know is that I'm going back there, and I'm going to kill him for it."

"You can ride back in there with us," said Ceran. "I'm getting Kitty out of there before somebody makes good on their lynching threat."

"I'm glad to do it," said Reese, touching his battered hat brim in salute.

"Who is this chief detective you're talking about?" Ceran asked.

"He worked for Western Railways," Reese said. "The town signed an agreement for the company to handle the law in Wild Wind until they can manage to have themselves an election."

"You don't say." Ceran gave a slight grin. "Western Railways wouldn't be doing it if they didn't have money there they want protected."

"That's my thoughts on it," Reese agreed.

"Who else is watching about the town besides the ranger?" Ceran asked.

"Some young, snot-nosed railway detective named Clayton Longworth," said Reese. "As far as I know, that's all, just those two."

"One ranger and one Western Railways detective," said Ceran. "It all sounds pretty good to me."

"Here's something you might find of interest. Your gal Kitty and the Cullen brothers, Cadden and Price, made a jailbreak," said Reese. He kept himself from chuckling aloud.

"The Cullen Brothers? Those no-good, pig-mongering sonsabitches," said Ceran. He spat, as if the thought of the Cullens raised a bad taste in his mouth.

"Yeah," said Reese, "seems the Cullens and your gal Kitty set up an ambush on Paco and Buckles, who were leaving town in a hurry." He shook his head, stifling a grin. "It appeared they must've shot the hell out of one another."

Doherty said, "Then they all five ended up in jail together."

Ceran sat staring, hardly believing his ears. Finally he shook his head as if to clear it. "God almighty," he said. "What a foul-up." He turned to the others and said, "All right, we're riding to Wild Wind, getting Kitty and Paco and taking every dollar Western Railways has sitting there."

"What about my Comanchero, Huey Buckles?" said Quintos. He sat staring at Ceran with a determined look on his dark face.

"Yeah, don't worry, Bloody Wolf," said Ceran. "We'll get Huey Buckles out of jail too." He looked around at the other men and raised his voice for all of them to hear. "And we'll kill a ranger and a railway detective while we're at it."

CHAPTER 21

Darkness had fallen by the time Dr. Stanton had finished with the last of the prisoners. He had treated them in the order of the most severely wounded first, and down the line from there. When he entered Kitty's cell and looked down at the bullet graze striping her side just above elbow level, she opened her unbuttoned shirt and spread it outward and off her shoulder.

"Seeing that you're a man of medicine, I suppose a gal can bare all for you." She offered a seductive smile to the gray, aged doctor.

Shelly looked away, embarrassed. The ranger stood at the door to the cell, watching but not allowing himself to be moved by her show of round, ample bosom.

"You need to save your charms and, uh, other assets for the judge when he gets here, ma'am," the doctor said, lowering his head and looking above his spectacles at her. "I'm just a poor, colored horse doctor. I can't help you any way in the world." He smiled tolerantly and stooped down to examine the wound.

"You can't blame a gal for trying, can you?" she asked coyly.

"No, ma'am," said the doctor. "I even appreciate the effort."

As he took a warm, wet cloth from Shelly and wiped the wound carefully, Kitty said to him, "Doctor, I don't suppose you'd give a gal something for all this pain, would you? I'll look you up and repay you *in kind* once the judge turns me loose."

The old doctor continued cleaning the bullet graze and said quietly, "I don't have anything like that, ma'am." He smiled. "My patients never ask for it. When they're in pain, they usually kick their stall."

"That's real funny, Doc," said Kitty. "But come on. I know you've got laudanum, rye whiskey, something."

The doctor busily applied some ointment over the wound with his fingertip. "This will soothe your pain some," he said. "It's the best I can do."

"Please, Doc," she whispered. "I meant what I said. I'll take really good care of you when I'm out of here." As she spoke she ran her free hand along his upper thigh while he took a strip of bandage from Shelly to put over the wound.

The old doctor reached down and removed her hand from his leg before she reached his crotch. "Ma'am," he said flatly, "do I look stupid enough to believe the judge is going to let you go, after you participated in a jailbreak, maybe even murder?"

"What?" Kitty looked stunned by his words. "I didn't kill anybody!" She looked over at the ranger. "Ranger Burrack, I didn't break jail. I hadn't been charged with anything."

"You have now," Longworth said, stepping over to her cell. "I'm charging you with breaking jail, for now. It's up to the judge to decide if you were involved in murdering Dr. Ford. If he says so, you'll be charged with murder, the same as everybody else."

"Hold on, lawmen!" said Cadden Cullen from his cell, gripping the bars. "Brother Price and I had nothing to do with killing the doctor or Bell or any-*damn*-body. Sure, we broke jail" — he shrugged — "but that's more or less a prisoner's duty, ain't it?"

Longworth and the ranger exchanged glances. "In a time of war, maybe," Longworth said. "But this is not a war. You two are criminals."

"See?" said Cadden, pointing his finger through the bars of the cell. "That's the kind of thing the law never makes clear."

Kitty stood up as the doctor finished wrapping the strips of cloth around her ribs. She started to walk toward the ranger. As she did, he reached sidelong and swung the cell door shut. "That's close enough, ma'am," Sam said.

"I just want to talk, Ranger," she said, stopping and spreading her hands. She had a troubled look on her face.

"Talk from there," Sam replied.

Outside the cell, Longworth stood watching, listening, his rifle in the crook of his arm.

"Look, both of you," Kitty said with an expression of shock on her face. "You can't believe I had anything to do with killing the doctor."

Sam caught a quick flash of Weeks lying dead in a pool of blood, his throat sliced deep and wide. "It's got nothing to do with what we think," Sam said. "I keep telling you it's going to be up to the judge when he gets here."

"Yeah," said Cadden, "and if he believes we did kill the doctor, it means we'll be tried and hanged. Tell her the whole truth of it, Ranger."

"You just told her," Sam said. He'd been listening to everybody closely and watching their actions and expressions. Kitty was scared. So was Cadden — scared and angry. But as Sam looked at Paco and Buckles, both sitting on the edge of their cots, he saw no fear, no anger, nothing. Their lack of response told him a lot.

"What about you, Paco Stazo? You, Huey Buckles? Have you two got anything to say on this?"

Paco only shrugged and spoke for them both. "If they are guilty, they will hang." His dark eyes studied the ranger from across his cell. He shrugged again. "What do you want from me?"

Yep, those two are the ones, Sam told himself. Everything he'd heard and seen from Paco and Buckles had made him more convinced. They didn't care who hanged with them; they weren't admitting anything. There was nothing Sam could tell the judge about who had killed the doctor, but he would give the judge his thoughts on the matter, for whatever it was worth.

"Well, that's all I can do," Dr. Stanton said, standing and rolling down his shirtsleeves.

"Step back over to your cot, ma'am," Sam said quietly to Kitty. "Give Miss Shelly and

286

Dr. Stanton room to leave."

"But I'm not through talking," Kitty said.

"Yes, you are," Sam said. "For now anyway." He gestured toward her cot.

"Damn it, Ranger," she said. But still she turned, walked back and slumped down on her cot.

"Jesus! You two sonsabitches!" Cadden shouted, turning in the other direction toward Paco and Buckles. "I know us three didn't kill anybody. You two did! Tell the ranger, damn it, before this thing gets out of hand and her and my brother and I get hung!"

"Shut your stupid mouth, Cullen," Paco said in a menacing tone.

As the two argued back and forth, Longworth chained Kitty's cell door and padlocked it. The doctor and Shelly stood outside the cell, the doctor slipping into his frayed green suit coat.

"But we're innocent. You know we are!" Cadden bellowed, grasping the bars and shaking them violently, as if to rip them down.

"You have never been innocent of anything in your stinking life," said Paco.

"Ranger Burrack, here's the one who killed the doctor," Cadden railed, stabbing his finger toward Paco through the bars.

"This one right here, Paco Stazo. I'll testify that he did."

"I get my hands on you, I'll rip your tongue out," Paco growled.

"All of you, shut up and settle down," said Longworth. Both he and the ranger turned toward the front door, having heard the sound of scuffling boots out front.

"Detective Longworth," a voice called out from the street out in front of the boardwalk.

"Here we go," Longworth said, raising his rifle from the crook of his arm.

"Yep, here we go," said Sam. He looked at Dr. Stanton and Shelly and said, "Both of you can leave through the rear door."

"Begging your pardon, Ranger Burrack," said the horse doctor, "but if it's all the same, I'd just as soon go out the way I came in." He gave a grin and a slight bow of his head. "Call me superstitious . . ." He walked toward the front, where he'd left his long shotgun.

"Whatever suits you, Doctor," Sam said, following him.

"And if you don't mind, Detective," the doctor said to Longworth, his right hand turned palm up. "For my services . . . ?" He picked up his battered top hat and placed it atop his head.

"I'll pay you tomorrow, Doctor, if it's all the same to you," Longworth said.

"Detective Longworth," the same voice out front repeated, "we come for all them murderers. Hand them over to us."

"Tomorrow?" The doctor's smile flattened. "I'd feel better not having to count on tomorrow, Detective, if you don't mind my saying so." He cut his eyes toward the sound of the drunken mob outside the door.

"I see your concern," said Longworth. He looked to Sam. "Ranger, have you any money on you?"

Sam reached into his trouser pocket and pulled on some folded bills. Without counting he said, "Doctor, there's twelve dollars. Is that enough?"

"More than enough, Ranger," the doctor said. "I'll have your change tomorrow, if all goes well here."

"You keep the change, Doctor," Sam said. He picked up a short, double-barrel shotgun he'd loaded earlier and laid atop the oak desk.

Looking at Shelly and the doctor, Longworth stood close to the door and said loudly, "I'm bringing Miss Shelly and Dr. Stanton out. I want to know nothing's going to happen to them."

"Send them out, Detective," said the

voice. "We're not animals. They won't be harmed."

"I'm not going," Shelly said suddenly. She looked at Longworth. "I'm staying here. It's the least I can do after what happened."

Longworth shot the ranger a guarded glance and said to her, "Miss Shelly, you're nervous and you don't know what you're saying. Now, please, you go on out of here with the doctor, and go home." Again he shot Sam a glance. Sam looked down and checked the shotgun in his hands.

The townsmen stood in a half circle surrounding the front door. Some of them held torches and ropes in one hand and rifles or shotguns in their other. In spite of their drunken rage, they allowed Shelly Linde and Dr. Stanton to walk slowly through their midst without incident. The doctor carried his shotgun at port arms, his canvas bag hanging from his shoulder.

At the outer edge of the men, Shelly stopped and looked back at Longworth, who stood on the boardwalk, rifle in hand, a foot in front of the ranger, who stood quietly observing.

"Clayton," Shelly said, "I — I need to say something here."

"Go, Shelly!" Longworth insisted, taking

a step forward. "There is nothing for you to say here. Now leave!"

Sam watched, knowing what was going through both of their minds.

"We wouldn't hurt Miss Shelly for the world," said a red-faced townsman named Dean Shalen, who held at his side a rope with a hangman's knot tied in it. "All we want is a share of justice for these buzzards killing our doctor and Chief Bell." He held up the rope and shook it by its noose.

"Please, Shelly." Longworth jerked his head toward the restaurant.

"Come along, Miss Shelly," the old horse doctor said, coaxing her. "These lawmen need to do their jobs without having to worry about us being in their way." Taking her by her arm, he directed her away from the angry crowd and out of the flickering torchlight.

"What did Miss Shelly have to say?" Elliot asked. He had discarded his hat to keep it from irritating his swollen forehead.

"Nothing," said Longworth, tight-lipped. "She's scared and upset."

"It sounded like she had something that needed saying," Elliot persisted.

"She didn't," Longworth snapped back. He stared hard at the faces around him. "Neither do any of the rest of you. Now break up and go home before we start doing things we'll regret."

The two younger men, Robert Samples and John Rader, now stood at the head of the gathering. Fred Elliot, Joe Clancy and some of the older townsmen had lagged back and given them the lead. Selectman Tyler had managed to disappear as soon as the talk of lynching had begun.

"We're not going anywhere until we've hung those murderers from the boardwalk rafters," said Samples, nodding upward toward the timber framing.

"It's not going to happen," said Longworth. He jacked a round into his rifle chamber just to make his point. "We wait for the judge."

"Like hell we do," said John Rader. "The *judging* has all been done. It's *sentencing* time now." He took a step closer, noose in hand.

Longworth answered his step with one of his own. His rifle butt came up to his shoulder and he took aim at Rader's heart from a distance of less than ten feet. "I will drop you dead where you stand."

Rader stopped; the crowd hushed.

Behind Longworth, Sam stayed calm, motionless. But his gloved thumb reached over both hammers of the short, double-barreled shotgun and pulled them back slowly, quietly.

Breaking the silence, Robert Samples said, "He's bluffing . . . I think."

"You *think?*" said John Rader. His whiskey suddenly left him flat, and his eyes took on a strange look. He wanted to take a step back, but he didn't know how to go about it.

"Don't worry, John. I'm backing you," Samples said, then realized he'd just said the wrong thing to a man looking down the open bore of a Winchester rifle.

Inside the cells, Kitty stood on her cot, listening intently through a barred window. In Paco and Buckles' cell, Paco did the same thing. Even all the way at the rear of the building, the two could hear the angry talk out front as it amplified and rolled down the alleyway to them.

"What're they saying?" Cadden asked, unable to climb onto his cot and up to the window on his wounded leg.

"Shut up so we can hear them," said Paco.

"It sounds like Longworth and the ranger have them cooled down," Kitty said. She went back to listening.

Out front, Samples looked the ranger up and down as he said to Longworth, "We know how you sent this tinhorn ranger to the Belleza Grande to bully everybody out of doing what needs to be done. But that's not going to work this time." He turned his cold, hard stare to the ranger's eyes and said, "I'm in *no way* afraid of this gun-toting *territory* lackey."

"Really?" The ranger took a step forward, and Samples stepped back. But the young townsman kept his right hand poised at his holstered Colt.

"Don't think you'll catch me off guard, Ranger," Samples said. "I'm not some saddle tramp you can throw through a window. I'm fast enough to take you down if I have to."

"Really?" the ranger repeated. "Then what's all this arguing for?" He took another step, making a show of uncocking the shotgun. "Why don't the two of us settle this thing between us like gentlemen?"

"Like gentlemen?" Samples asked, confused.

"He means a duel," said Rader.

"Yeah, I know," said Samples. He turned his stare back to the ranger. "Suits me, Ranger, if you've got that kind of guts."

Good enough . . . Sam sensed a relief come over the crowd. The thought of two men shooting it out seemed to settle them, as long as they weren't one of the two. But he'd take what he could get. He wouldn't kill this man if he could keep from it. But he'd sure put a bullet in him, if that was what it took to resolve this.

"Then let's get to it," Sam said. He stepped down from the boardwalk and leaned the shotgun against a post.

"My God, you're not serious," said Fred Elliot.

"Most serious," said the ranger, stepping sidelong to the middle of the street. Robert Samples did the same only twenty feet away.

"But — but this is *madness!*" Elliot said. "It's not civilized."

"Not *civilized?*" Sam stared at him and the others, ropes and rifles, pistols and shotguns in their grasps.

Elliot got the point and looked embarrassed. "You know what I mean," he said. "You can't fight a duel to see whether or not we hang these murderers. This makes no sense at all."

"Back off, Elliot," said Samples.

"Ranger, you're a lawman," Elliot said. "For God's sake! Don't do this."

"Get out of the street, Elliot," the ranger said grimly. "You've been aching to see somebody die. You're getting your chance."

CHAPTER 22

Cadden limped back and forth in his cell, incapable of sitting still and unable to climb up and listen for himself. "What the hell's going on out there?"

Kitty kept her ear turned to the barred window as she said, "It sounds like the ranger just challenged one of the townsmen to a gunfight?" She sounded as if she didn't believe what she'd heard.

"No," said Cadden. He stopped limping back and forth and stood staring through the bars at her.

"Yes," Paco said from his position at his own barred window. "I did not hear the ranger say it; he talks too low. But I heard the townsman accept his challenge."

"Listen up!" Kitty said suddenly. Her eyes took on a look of deep concentration in the direction of the trail into town.

"What is it?" Cadden whispered.

"Horses' hooves, I think," Kitty said, her

head cocked in the opposite direction of the alleyway and the angry words from the street.

Paco listened intently with a tight grin of satisfaction coming to his dark face. "It's about time," he whispered to himself.

Cadden limped over to Price's cot and shook his shoulder slightly. "Listen, brother. It sounds like riders coming. Maybe Kitty and her boyfriend will get us sprung out of —" Having gotten no response, he stopped and leaned down closer. "Price . . . you okay there, brother?" he said, worried.

"Keep it down," said Kitty, "I'm trying to hear what's coming."

"Oh, man," Cadden said in a saddened voice. "My poor brother, Price, is dead."

"All right, he's dead," said Paco. "Now shut up about it." He turned his attention back to the growing sound of horses' hooves.

Out front, in the middle of the dirt street, the young townsman spread his feet shoulder width apart and shook out his gun hand as if to loosen it up. Longworth stood watching, not sure what to think. Sam's move had taken him by surprise, but he knew he had to back his play. What choice did he have? At least there were fewer guns pointing at him now that the townsmen had all turned to the ranger and Samples.

"Somebody give us a count," Samples said, squared off toward the ranger, eyes locked on him.

"A count?" said Fred Elliot, who had backed away and stood staring, stunned in disbelief. "A count to what?"

"How about to three, Ranger?" Samples asked, sounding calm and ready. "Does *three* sound right to you?"

"Three?" Sam seemed to consider it as he eased his Colt up from his holster, inspected it, cocked it, and raised and leveled it toward the young townsman.

"Yep, it sounds all right to me," he said.

The Colt bucked in his hand; an explosion of orange-blue flame erupted from the barrel. The bullet nailed Samples high in his shoulder, spun him backward and flipped him over. His right boot flew up eight feet in the air and hit the ground a second behind him. His hat sailed away like a freed bird.

"Good God almighty!" said Joe Clancy. "You killed young Samples!"

"No, I didn't," Sam said with quiet confidence. "He's alive." He swung the Colt toward the rest of the townsmen. "If you're his friends, you'll get Dr. Stanton before he leaves town. See to it this man gets proper medical attention."

"Oh, is that it, Ranger?" John Rader asked in an ugly tone. "You shoot a man down like a dog, to get all of us —"

He stopped and backed away as Sam raised, cocked and leveled the big Colt toward him.

"There's nothing fair about this!" Dean Shalen shouted. "You didn't stick to the rules. You cheated the man."

"You thought this was a sporting event, an adventure of some sort?" Sam asked. He swung the Colt from Rader to Shalen.

Fred Elliot tried to be the voice of reason. "Ranger, what they're saying is, you didn't give the man a chance to defend himself." He shrugged. "You just shot him."

"So I did," said Sam. "Sort of the way all of you want to kill those prisoners without giving them a chance to defend themselves in a court of law."

"Come on, Ranger. That's different and you know it," said Elliot.

"It's only *different* if you want to look at it *different*," said Sam. He gritted his teeth and swung the Colt toward Elliot. "Is anybody going after that horse doctor? We're going to be needing him real bad, *real* soon."

"Don't shoot, Ranger," Elliot said, raising his hands chest high. "I'll go get him. The rest of you stand down. Don't give him a reason to kill you."

Longworth stood staring as Elliot loped away down the dirt street to catch up with Dr. Stanton, not realizing the doctor had walked only a short few yards into the darkness and eased down behind a wagon to offer the ranger and the detective cover if they needed it.

Longworth couldn't believe what he'd just seen. But he had to admit, it took everybody's attention away from the lynching — for the moment anyway. He wondered what other tricks the ranger had up his sleeve.

Dean Shalen said to the others, "All right, fellows, he can't kill all of us. When I say the word, everybody rush them both. Don't stop even if I go down. Don't stop until you've got the prisoners ready to swing from a rafter."

All right, he's next . . . , the ranger told himself, leveling the Colt back at Shalen.

Shalen started to make his move, but the feel of pounding hooves on the ground beneath his feet caused him to stop and look off down the trail out of town.

"What the hell is this?" he said. He turned away from the ranger and stared toward four glowing lights swaying overhead above the trail.

"It's those murderers' gang!" a frightened townsman called out in a shaky voice. "They've come to kill us all and set them free!"

"Oh no," said Mama Jean, who'd been standing back from the crowd, watching. "It is not man — it is the devil! He rides on four balls of fire! His horses are half man, half demon!" She crossed herself and kissed the tip of her thumbnail. Tears ran down her plump, trembling cheeks.

Silva Ceran . . .

The ranger shot Longworth a look; the detective reached around, snatched the ranger's shotgun from against the building and tossed it to him. From the darkness, Elliot and Dr. Stanton came running. The doctor had dropped his bag in the middle of the street and carried his shotgun high and ready.

"He who craves battle has found it," the horse doctor called out in biblical tone.

"Hold it," the ranger said in a quiet voice. "It's not outlaws."

"Who is it, then?" Shalen asked. All of the armed townsmen had turned toward the rumble of horses' hooves and the creaking of wood and metal.

Every man ducked slightly at the loud crack of a whip along the dark trail. The four fiery lights rose and fell in a circling glow.

Mama Jean whispered again with her thumb pressed to her lips, "It is *the devil.* . . .

"It's a stagecoach," said the horse doctor with a dark chuckle.

"A stagecoach, at this time of night?" said Longworth, stepping sidelong on the boardwalk, but keeping himself between the door and the crowd on the street.

"It's the judge's coach," Sam said with a sound of relief in his voice that only Longworth noticed.

The torches slumped in the townsmen's hands as the big Studebaker coach began braking to a halt in a roil of dust and flickering firelight. The four horses pulling the coach came to a thundering halt, three of them as black as the night, the fourth a pale white dapple.

"It's the judge's horses, all right," said Joe Clancy, sounding more sober than he had all evening. He jerked his bowler hat from his nearly bald head and swiped a thin wisp of hair sideways.

Longworth stepped back over to the door, shook it to make certain it was locked, then stepped down onto the street beside the ranger. He brushed a hand down the front of his black linen coat and looked himself

302

up and down.

The ranger gave him a nod, letting him know he looked presentable.

As the coach settled in its rise of dust, the shotgun rider scurried down from the passenger's side, yanked a thickly built footstool from its steel hook and hurried around to the door. He set the footstool in the dirt beneath the door and sawed it back and forth into place. Then he reached out and swung the door open. All of this he did with a sawed-off shotgun in his gloved hand.

The townsmen milled and stared. Ropes with nooses tied in them dropped lower and closer to the men's sides, in order to get them out of sight.

The shotgun rider called out as a thick leg reached down toward the footstool, "His Honor, Territory Judge Lawrence Olin."

"They all know who I am, Mr. Burns," said a gruff, husky voice. The judge, a three-hundred-thirty-pound man in a flowing black suit, a twisted black tie and a white shirt open at the collar, stepped out and down onto the ground.

The townsmen stood in rapt silence as the huge man ambled closer to them and stopped and looked at the torches, firearms and ropes in their hands.

Selectman Tyler, who seemed to have

vanished earlier, appeared as if from out of nowhere. He stuck his long hand out to the judge and shook hands vigorously. "Your Honor, what a pleasant surprise this is. We weren't expecting you for another two weeks."

"Yes," the judge said. He rubbed his released hand up and down on his suit coat, his eyes still going warily from man to man. "Apparently I've arrived with not a moment to spare."

Longworth and the ranger watched as the judge's eyes sought them out. As the crowd moved away to make a path for him, the large man strode over to the two lawmen and stopped and looked them up and down appraisingly.

"Young Ranger Samuel Burrack," he said with a stiff, thin smile. "I'm happy to see that no one has . . . *well,* that no one has *killed* you as yet."

"Not as yet, Your Honor . . . not that they haven't tried," Sam said respectfully. His eyes went past the judge to the townsmen. But only for a second. Then he gestured to Longworth and said, "This is Detective Clayton Longworth, Your Honor."

"One of Western Railways' employees, I presume," the judge said, taking over the ranger's introduction. "One of the reasons I have traveled here ahead of schedule. "I've heard so many good things are happening here, I could not wait to see for myself."

"Pleased to meet you, Your Honor," said Longworth, shaking the judge's thick hand.

"We would have been here before dark were it not for a washout along the hill trail," the judge said, rubbing his hand on his coat again as soon as Longworth turned it loose. "Pleased to make your acquaintance, Detective," he added, as if in afterthought. He looked all around the street. "Where is Detective Bell this evening?"

"I'm afraid Chief Detective Bell has been killed, Your Honor," the ranger said quietly. "His killer is inside in a cell."

"Chief Bell killed, you say?" The judge looked around again at the gathered townsmen and put two and two together. But rather than mention what he knew was going on, he said instead, "I see I must have arrived at the ending of a public event — some sort of target shoot, no doubt."

Shalen stepped forward and said, "It is what it looks like, Judge. We were about to lynch a band of murdering dogs."

"I see," the judge said in an understanding tone. "Take it upon yourselves to deliver justice, as it were?" As he spoke he turned and ambled over to Shalen.

"Yes, sir, exactly, Judge Olin," said Shalen, feeling encouraged by the judge's tolerant demeanor. "We pride ourselves in knowing right from wrong, and in being able to take care of —"

Longworth winced at the sound of the judge's big hand slapping a hard, full swing across Shalen's unsuspecting face. The ranger stifled a slight smile, watching the young townsman fly sidelong and turn a flip in much the same way Samples had earlier when Sam's bullet had hit him.

"How dare you intercede in matters of the law!" the judge raged down at the half-conscious Shalen. Olin pounded a thick finger on his chest. "This is *my* world! You do not . . . *do not* presume to compromise it. How dare you, sir!" He turned his glare at two townsmen standing nearby. "Get this man onto his feet so I can smite him down again!"

The townsmen hurriedly drew Shalen to his feet. He stood wobbling in place. The judge drew back his open palm. But before he could administer another slap, Shalen melted back to the ground.

Turning, tugging at the open collar of his white shirt and black tie, the judge said, "If there is any other man who thinks he can usurp the power of my court, let him step forward and look me in the face. I will *consequently* box his jaws forthwith." The townsmen milled and backed away, some dropping coiled ropes to the ground.

"The judge *does* have his ways," Sam said quietly to Longworth, the two of them watching, Longworth in rapt fascination.

Inside the cells, Kitty and Paco had both dropped from their windows at the sound of the talk and scuffling boots moving from the street into the sheriff's office. "We are all screwed," she repeated under her breath, having said the same thing only moments ago when she realized that it was not Ceran and his men riding into town. "Silva isn't coming. . . ."

"Right this way, Your Honor," she heard Longworth say, as the four men stepped inside and Selectman Tyler closed the front door behind them. Longworth picked up a burning lantern from atop the desk and walked a step ahead of the judge, who was followed by the ranger. Selectman Tyler followed the ranger.

"I'm certain these two lawmen would have tidied up some if they'd known you were coming, Your Honor," Tyler said nervously.

"These two young lawmen are doing fine work, Tyler," the judge said gruffly over his thick, broad shoulder. "You are damned lucky to have them here."

"Yes, of course. My feelings exactly," Tyler said meekly.

In preparation for the judge coming to her cell, Kitty fluffed her disheveled hair and tugged her shirt down off one shoulder. She formed a sensual, seductive smile and sat poised on her cot. "My, my, who is this big, handsome man coming to . . ." She looked crestfallen as the judge walked right past her cell as if he hadn't seen her. He stopped out front of Cadden Cullen, who stood clinging to the bars with both hands, sobbing quietly, his head bowed against the bars.

"Why is this man crying?" Judge Olin asked Longworth.

Longworth looked dumbfounded.

"My poor brother is dead," said Cadden, raising his eyes, which the ranger noted right away were dry, in spite of his pitiful weeping.

The four looked over at the still body lying on its cot. "Step to the side, Cadden. We're coming in," said Longworth, already unlocking the padlock in order to loosen the chain on the door.

Eyeing the Colt holstered on Longworth's hip, Cadden did take a short step back. But

Sam could see his intentions were to grab the gun, probably the judge too as a hostage, and make an escape. In foresight, Sam reached through the bars as the door swung open, slapped one handcuff around Cadden's wrist and hooked the other cuff around an iron bar.

Judge Olin saw the ranger's move and the surprised look on the outlaw's face. Shaking his large head, he gave a deep chuckle as he followed Longworth into the cell. "I never feel so safe as when I know this young ranger is around."

CHAPTER 23

Down the hall from his own room, in the judge's room, the ranger and Territory Judge Lawrence Olin spent most of the night seated at a small table, discussing the events that had taken place in Wild Wind. In the soft, round glow of an oil lamp, the judge spoke over a tall glass of Old Bourbon Whiskey, a cup of strong black coffee and, on the side, a three-pound apple pie from the restaurant. In return, the ranger spoke over a cup of coffee, a half-filled shot glass of Old Bourbon sitting close at hand.

With a large serving spoon in his huge fist and a checkered napkin stuffed down into his open shirt collar, the judge looked contemplative as he chewed, then swallowed, then took a gulp of steaming coffee.

"I call where we're sitting tonight as being at the high point of the legal triangle, Ranger Samuel," the judge said in his gruff, guttural voice. "The triangle of truth, if you will."

The ranger only gave him a curious look.

"Down there, in the dirt, is where most *law* is broken." He stabbed the big spoon in the direction of the dark street below. "Who broke it, how and why it was broken, is all weighed and considered over there, in more civilized surroundings — a *court* of law." He swiped the spoon straight across the air toward the new sheriff's office, a temporary place for court to convene until a better location was established.

"But before the matter goes from the dirt to the court, it has to come up here to me, on high." He grinned and drew another line with the spoon, from down toward the sheriff's office upward toward himself, almost touching his head. "You see it, don't you?" he said, stifling a slight belch as he drew a triangle with the spoon, connecting all three points.

"I see it." Sam nodded. He continued to watch attentively as the large man lifted the edge of his napkin from his massive chest and wiped it across his thick lips. Setting the coffee aside, Olin raised the water glass of Old Bourbon to his lips and drank.

"Now then, Ranger Samuel," he said, "while you have the rare, if somewhat *dubi-*

ous, privilege of presiding up here beside me, explain *exactly* what happened down there in the dirt."

Sam said in a measured tone, "Your Honor, I can't tell you exactly what happened. I can only give you my *opinion,* my *hunch,* on the matter."

"Ah, but you see, Ranger," the judge said, "your *opinion,* your *hunch,* might be as close as we'll ever come to knowing the truth about who killed Dr. Ford, or the detective chief." He pointed a thick finger and advised critically, "So be careful with your words. They may carry the weight of life or death for these people."

"You sound like you're making me judge and jury for all four of them," Sam said.

"Yes, that is what I'm doing," said the judge. "There will be no jury, of course." He shrugged. "These outlaws never want to throw their lives at the mercy of a jury. That was their *jury* standing out front with ropes and torches last night. They'll throw themselves at the mercy of the court."

"On you," Sam said.

"On me," Judge Olin said, almost tapping the pie-smeared spoon on his chest. "I sit at the top of the triangle. Here is where the measure of mercy is weighed and portioned — here, in the hour of night."

Sam nodded, deliberately not looking at the glass of Old Bourbon in the judge's hand, or at the brown-tinted bottle sitting nearly empty beside the remnants of un-eaten apple pie.

"I will not go to bed tonight until I know what my verdict is going to be." Judge Olin grinned, then took a deep breath and in-sisted, "So, you must tell me the truth, the whole truth and all the truth that will ever be known on this matter, Ranger Samuel."

Sam started to reach over and pick up the shot glass, but he changed his mind and sipped his coffee instead. Judge Olin took note of his action and smiled faintly to himself.

"The way I see it, Your Honor," he said, setting his glass back down but keeping his hand around it, "the woman and the Cullen brothers had no part in killing the doctor or Chief Bell. They just happened to be break-ing jail at a time when Paco Stazo and the Comanchero were doing the killings."

"That's what she would have had me believe," said the judge, considering the conversation he'd had earlier with Kitty in her cell. He smiled. "I have to admit she was persuasive, especially when she implied what fun she and I might have after the trial." He chuckled in reflection and shook his head.

"She's scared, Your Honor," said Sam, "and she's playing the only card she has."

"She is a striking woman, Ranger, and no doubt a fine *piece of tail,* as they so crudely say," the judge said. "Wouldn't *you* say?" He smiled and took another deep drink of Old Bourbon. "Now, don't tell me she didn't offer it up to you as well."

"She did," said the ranger. He shifted in his chair, never comfortable in such conversations. "I turned her down, Your Honor."

"I know you did," said Judge Olin, "otherwise she wouldn't be in jail in Wild Wind. I didn't mean to imply that she has prejudiced your opinion on the matter with her feminine charm."

"Obliged, Your Honor," said Sam. "All that aside, I believe she's innocent."

"Innocent of killing the doctor and the detective chief, perhaps," the judge shrugged. "But what about the man Weeks, the one you said you found at the water hole where she'd left him?"

"I'd have to call it self-defense," Sam said with a deep sigh. "I know that's giving her an awfully broad benefit of the doubt."

"Indeed it is," said the judge. He grinned again. "But I'll either give *you* that for her sake, or I'll give *her* that for your sake. I believe the woman has gotten to you a bit."

"Maybe she has, some," Sam said. "But it's not like you think." He reconsidered the shot glass of Old Bourbon, picked it up and tossed it back. "When I found her dead horse along the trail, I went through her saddlebags. I found a locket with a picture in it of her as a young girl. She didn't say it's her, but I know it is." He paused, then said, "It keeps coming back to my mind — that young face, the clear, innocent eyes. . . ." His words trailed.

After a silent pause, the judge cleared his throat and said, "All right, now. She didn't kill the doctor or the detective chief *that we can prove.* Although she and her allies, all four of them, were prowling loose at the time of the two murders. This man Weeks was *self-defense,* although we have no way of proving that, except *her word* on what happened." He gazed at the ranger skeptically. "Are there any other murders she's been around that we *cannot* convict her of?"

The ranger slid the empty shot glass aside and sipped his coffee. "You asked me, Your Honor," he said. "I'm telling you what I think."

"Indeed you are, Ranger," said the judge. He reached over with his spoon and swiped up the last thick, moist bite of sugary apple pie and wolfed it down. He chased it with a swig of Old Bourbon, followed by a drink of coffee. Then he wiped his mouth again on the edge of the napkin, which he jerked out from beneath his collar.

"You needn't worry, Ranger Samuel," he said. "I'm not known as a hanging judge, except in cases where the amount of evidence is too high to question." He raised a thick finger for emphasis. "But make no mistake, she's going to jail."

"For how long?" Sam asked.

The judge shrugged. "I've convicted her tonight. I'll sentence her come morning." He winked and shoved back his chair. He started to rise, but he stopped and asked, "What about that jailbreak? How did they get out of the cells?"

"Cadden Cullen had the key, Your Honor," Sam said. "How he got it across the room to open the cells, I don't know."

"You don't know?" The judge studied him closely. "But you have a theory — another *hunch?*"

"It would be best if Longworth talked with you about that jailbreak, Your Honor," said Sam. "I wouldn't want him feeling like we've left him out."

The judge studied his face for a moment. Seeing that the ranger wasn't going to offer any more on the matter, he said, "No, we wouldn't want that."

It was daylight when the ranger awoke, back in his own room. He dressed in the gray hour of dawn and walked to the sheriff's office, rifle in hand. When he knocked quietly on the front door, Longworth unlocked the door and opened it, standing in his sock feet as the ranger walked in and shut the door behind himself.

"How did your talk with the judge go?" Longworth asked, leaning his rifle back against the edge of the desk, where he'd spent the night sleeping.

"He's a talker," Sam said, keeping his voice down in order to prevent the prisoners from hearing him. "He feels like we'll never know exactly who did the killings here. None of the four is going to admit to it or tell on the other." As he spoke he leaned his rifle against the desk alongside the detective's.

"So, they'll all four hang?" Longworth asked.

"In most any other territory, yes," Sam said. "But the judge is not known for hanging."

Longworth considered it. "Then they'll all go to prison for the rest of their lives?"

"Yep," Sam said.

"I don't know if that's better or not," said Longworth. "Hanging might be more humane." He shook his head slightly. "Did you tell him what you thought happened — what *we* thought happened, that is?"

"I told him," Sam said. "I can't tell whether he agreed or not."

The two had discussed the possibility of Kitty and the Cullen brothers managing to escape while Paco Stazo and Buckles were going about the killing of Detective Bell and the doctor.

"If I didn't believe it happened that way, I'd have an awful lot of guilt weighing me down," Longworth said, not realizing that the ranger knew about Shelly Linde and the cell key.

Sam just looked at him, offering no reply.

"What did he think about the cell key?"

"The cell key?" Sam said, appearing to have given little more thought on the matter.

"Yes. I mean about how the prisoners might have gotten it and let themselves out," said Longworth, trying not to sound as concerned and anxious about the matter as the ranger knew him to be.

"It was getting late," said Sam. "We didn't talk much about it."

"Oh . . . ," said the detective.

"I'm going to talk to Kitty," Sam said quietly. "Try to give her an idea that she isn't going to hang. Maybe it'll settle her down some."

"Settle her down?" Longworth said skeptically. "I don't think anything bothers her."

"I think all this bothers her," said Sam. "She just tries hard not to let it show."

Longworth stepped over to the woodstove, picked up the coffeepot and shook it as if to make sure it was empty. The ranger turned away from him and walked back to the cell where Kitty sat on the edge of her cot, smoking a cigarette in the gray morning gloom.

"Morning, Ranger," she said quietly, beneath a low buzz of snoring coming from the other two cells.

"Morning, Kitty," Sam replied in a lowered voice to keep from waking the others. "You're up early."

"Why not?" Kitty shrugged. "Care for a smoke?" She opened her hand and showed him three other cigarettes she had already rolled for later.

"Obliged, but no, thanks," said Sam.

"What can I do for you this morning, Ranger?" she asked. There was the slightest hint of a proposition in her voice, even though the ranger was certain she hadn't intended it to be there. *Maybe she can't help herself,* Sam thought, *or maybe I can't help but interpret her that way.*

"I spent some time talking to Judge Olin about you, Kitty," he said.

"Oh . . . ?" She took a draw; the cigarette's fire rose and fell. "What about me?" She blew out the smoke.

"Do you want to talk from here?" Sam asked.

"No," said Kitty. "Why don't you come inside?"

"I've got a better idea," said Sam. He stopped talking and waited.

Kitty sighed, stood up and walked over to the chained and padlocked cell door. "Why is it I can never get you to go along with me on anything, Ranger?" She reached her hand for his as he held on to a bar.

"Hardheadedness, I suppose," Sam said. He dropped his hand before she could take it. He stood with a few inches and a wall of iron bars between them. "I told the judge I didn't believe you had a hand in the two killings here," he said almost in a whisper.

"Yeah?" she replied in the same tone, eyeing him as if wondering what he might expect in return. "I never tell the law anything," she said guardedly.

"I'm not asking you to," Sam said. "I told him that because I believe it's true — that's all."

"Yeah?" she repeated, still uncertain. "Then I'm obliged, Ranger." She eyed him more and asked, "What about Weeks? Did you tell the judge about him?"

"Yes, I did," said Sam. "And I told him I believed it might be self-defense, just like you said."

"Jesus, Ranger . . . ," she said, as if suddenly understanding that he was not out to harm her if he could keep from it. "I *do* owe you something." She looked around at the other cells and the three sleeping prisoners, as if she was prepared to offer herself to him somehow, right then and there.

"No, you don't," Sam said quickly. "I did it because I believe it. The self-defense I had some trouble seeing, but I managed, knowing the kind of men you ride with."

"What about the jailbreak?" Kitty asked. "Am I going to learn *to sew* because of that?"

Sam knew what she meant. The women's prison she'd go to trained its prisoners to become seamstresses. "I'm afraid so," he said.

"How long?" she asked with a grim expression.

"I don't know," said Sam. "We'll find out today when he holds court here."

"All right," said Kitty. "It looks like this beats what I could have gotten — hoisted up and hung from the boardwalk rafters." She looked at Sam with stripes of black bar shadows falling across her in the grainy light. "Nothing has gone right for me since I met you, Territory Ranger Samuel Burrack."

"I wish it wasn't that way," Sam offered.

Kitty shrugged it off. "Anyway, what about the key? Does the judge know anything?"

"There's nothing to know," Sam said. "Cadden had it. I took it back." He gave her poker-faced stare.

"Don't try bluffing me around, Ranger. I was here. Remember?" she whispered.

He stared at her.

"Don't worry, I'm not saying anything," Kitty said. "I don't want to harm the girl. She got here the same way I did, on an orphan train."

"You came west on the orphan train?" he asked.

"Yep," Kitty said, "around the same time she did. It seems like a hundred years ago." She raised the side of her hair and showed him a scar where once a brothel tattoo had been crudely removed. "I'm glad she made it." She offered a tired smile.

Sam started to say something more, but before he could speak, a bullet sliced through the front window at an angle, ricocheted off the rifle rack and sped all the way back to the cells. It struck an iron bar with a loud ring, then bounced over and thumped into the wall.

"Get down!" Sam shouted as more shots slammed the front of the building, and the thunder of horses' hooves and war cries resounded along the dirt street.

CHAPTER 24

Running in a crouch, the ranger reached the desk, where Longworth had ducked down and taken cover. The detective had one boot on and one boot off, having started to put them on while he waited for the coffee to boil. On the floor lay the coffeepot, a bullet through its center and a pool of hot coffee steaming around it. Sam reached around the desk and grabbed his rifle and Longworth's from where they'd both leaned the firearms when he'd arrived.

Sam handed Longworth his rifle. "Are you hit?" he asked the shaken detective as the sound of hooves rumbled farther along the street, then came to halt and turned at the far end of town.

"I'm good. You?" said Longworth, excited. He reached up and grabbed his gun belt from atop the desk and swung it around his waist. "It sounds like Indians," he said.

"I'm betting it's Silva Ceran and his

bunch," said the ranger, his Colt out, cocked and ready. They heard the gunfire continue as the riders attempted to keep the street cleared of any townsmen who might offer resistance.

"They're coming back," said Longworth.

He and the ranger hurried to the front window and looked out through the shattered glass and up the street toward a billowing cloud of dust from the horses' hooves, as the animals bunched up, making their turn. Seeing the rough-looking band of Indians, outlaws and Comanchero that would be boring down on them any second, Sam ran to the gun rack, jerked up a small wooden box of rifle ammunition and headed for the door.

"Hold this place down. I'll get across the street and draw their fire," he said over his shoulder.

"I've got it," said Longworth.

As the ranger left, the detective hurriedly locked the door, shoved the oak desk over against it and ran back to the window as hooves began to rumble back down the street.

"I'm the one they've come for, Detective," Kitty shouted from her cell. "Turn me loose while there's still time."

"She's right — listen to her," said Paco.

"Silva 'the Snake' wants her free — and me too. The Snake will destroy this town if you do not let us go! Bloody Wolf and his warriors are riding with him!"

"Bloody Wolf!" said Cadden Cullen. "Holy God, Detective! They're telling you the truth! Turn us all loose! Save yourself. They'll tear this town down around you."

Longworth ignored the three. At the front window he rounded his rifle barrel inside the frame, knocking the remaining shards of glass from his line of fire.

Across the street, the ranger had taken cover at the edge of an alley. He looked toward the riders just as they'd made their turn and started back toward the sheriff's office. "Bloody Wolf Quintos . . . ," he said to himself, seeing the Indian at the center of the gathering riders.

He pulled his rifle butt to his shoulder to take aim, but as he did so, Little Tongue let out a terrible screeching sound and jumped his horse over in front of Quintos, blocking the ranger's shot. Blocking, but not stopping; Sam pulled the trigger and cut the screeching short. Little Tongue flew from his horse and landed dead in the dirt.

Seeing his top scout go down, Quintos let out a war cry and charged forward, leading the riders along the dirt street. Sam levered a fresh round into his Winchester as Silva Ceran came into sight out of the swirling dust. *The Snake,* Sam said to himself. *I knew you'd be here.*

As Sam fired, a bullet grazed his shoulder. But his shot still found its target. Ceran flew from his saddle and rolled away on the ground. Sam saw him rise to his feet and hurry out of sight into an alley. "Trueblood! You son of a bitch!" Ceran bellowed, seeing Delbert Trueblood make a break for it, now that he knew Ceran was down and couldn't stop him.

Firing erupted from doorways and second-floor windows, from townsmen who had spent the night in town. They were still armed from the night before and ready for a fight, especially with members of the gang associated with the prisoners who'd killed their beloved Dr. Ford and their detective chief.

The ranger took quick aim and fired; one of Quintos' warriors flew from his saddle. Two more bullets from two other directions twisted the outlaw back and forth before he hit the ground. Sam saw the black horse doctor step out of a doorway in his faded green suit and his battered top hat. He raised his long shotgun and emptied both barrels into the former Reverend Alvin Prew as Prew tried to take aim at him with a big Remington revolver. The ex-minister's head exploded in every direction in a spray of blood, brain and bone matter. The doctor dropped back out of sight to reload.

Seeing Prew's frightened horse run in an aimless circle, Silva Ceran leaped forward from his cover, grabbed it, swung atop and rode off the street as the others charged forward in a thick cloud of dust. *Uh-uh, Ceran. You're not getting behind the cells,* the ranger told himself, running back across the street, firing into the riders as he went.

From the broken window, Longworth shouted at Sam as he continued firing into the charging riders. "Where are you going?"

"I'm going after the Snake. He's trying to circle back behind you. Keep watch on the back door."

"Will do. Go get him," Longworth shouted loudly, excited both by the gun battle and the fact that the town appeared to be winning.

As the ranger headed into the alleyway alongside the new buildings, he heard a loud war cry from the balcony out in front of the judge's room overlooking the street. In a quick glance, he saw Judge Olin standing in his long, striped nightshirt, firing wildly with a long Colt Horse Pistol. Then he saw the judge hurry back inside just in time as the balcony boards began to pop, buckle and fall beneath his weight.

At the corner of the wide alley running behind the new sheriff's office, Sam stopped and raised his Colt from his holster. He took a quick peep around the edge of the clapboard building and checked the Colt while he waited, knowing this was where Ceran would be headed. From the cell window he heard Kitty calling out in a guarded tone of voice, "Silva, in here. I'm in here."

"So am I, Snake. Come and get us," Paco called out, not as quietly.

Sam waited, hearing the melee in the street continue to rage. But he noted that the war cries from the Indians, the outlaws and the Comancheros had diminished, replaced by the whooping and cursing of the townsmen taking control of the battle.

When Trueblood had ridden off of the street, he had no idea that Ceran would be riding right behind him. At the corner of the alley four blocks from the jail, he dropped from his saddle and looked at the bloody wound in his upper arm.

"I've had it," Trueblood gasped, out of breath. He leaned back and bowed his head for a moment, the pain in his arm throbbing, his tightly stitched face showing no signs of improvement, no letup in pain. Hearing the fight in the street not going well for his side, he said, "I'm out of here," and started to swing back up into his saddle.

"Not so fast, you coward son of a bitch!" Ceran said, sliding his horse to a halt at the edge of the building, seeing that Trueblood was about to run out on him. He held a Colt pointed at Trueblood from less then twelve feet away. "You've still got to settle up with me."

Trueblood was tired and aching and right then couldn't care less if he caught a bullet in the head. "What do you want from me, Silva?" he asked, no longer afraid of dying.

"What do I want? I want to see your face when I have Kitty out of jail and standing face-to-face with you. I want to hear what happened out there, with you and her and Weeks, after this ranger chased all of yas out of here."

"You want to know, I'll tell you," said Trueblood, as the firing on the street still roared. "Kitty's horse went down. She bargained with me and Weeks for a ride."

"Bargained what?" Ceran asked, an even darker look coming over his face.

"What do you think?" Trueblood said boldly. "We bargained for some of that fine

330

tail we've been watching you sniff along behind all these months."

"Why you —" Ceran gripped the Colt tighter, taking aim.

"Go on, get it done," said Trueblood, liking the feeling of no longer being afraid of what Ceran would do to him. It would be over fast, not like all the pain he had coursing through him. *To hell with it,* he thought. He gave a tight grin. "There's not enough bullets made to kill every range bummer who screwed Kitty behind your back. She rolled over quicker than a trained circus dog." He shook his head. "She's the one offered it up for a horse ride."

Ceran listened and gritted his teeth. On the street the battle raged. Quintos had led the men to the other end of town and turned them for another sweep. But the few still in their saddles had lost heart, seeing most of the numbers lying dead or dying on the dirt street.

"Funny thing is, I never even got any," Trueblood said with a pitiful laugh. "My whole damn life, I hardly ever got any — not enough anyway — and *never* from a woman that looks as good as Kitty Dellaros."

"That's too damned bad, Delbert," Ceran said, blood running from a bullet hole in his shoulder. He squeezed the trigger. The bullet nailed Trueblood in the forehead and sent his head slamming back against the clapboard building with a solid thud and a wide splatter of blood and brain matter. The outlaw fell straight forward and landed facedown in the dirt. Smoke curled from the gaping exit hole in the back of his head.

Four blocks away, Sam singled out the gunshot from the rest of the fighting on the street. Standing ready, he eased forward for another peep, but stacks of crates and piles of debris behind the long row of buildings blocked his view. "Come on, Snake. Don't start getting bashful on me now," Sam said to himself under his breath.

From their cells, Kitty and Paco had also singled out the gunshot. "Silva!" Kitty cried out loudly, no longer caring who heard her, as long as she caught Ceran's attention.

But Ceran did not hear her, nor did he care anymore about breaking her out of jail. *To hell with her,* he thought, examining the blood on his shirt, feeling the burn and the ache of the fresh gunshot in his upper shoulder. He stared down at the body of Delbert Trueblood lying facedown on the ground.

"This big tub of shit . . ." He let out a breath, then said, "You're right, Delbert.

She's been screwing anything that can screw back." He turned his horse away and rode off across the alley and onto a thin back trail leading out of town.

Sam saw Silva Ceran for only a second as Ceran rode across the alley and out of sight. But it was long enough for Sam to realize that the outlaw leader was getting out of Wild Wind while the getting was good. Sam was surprised to see that he wasn't coming to break Kitty out of jail. But he didn't have time to wonder why. He hurried to the rear door of the sheriff's office, stood to the side and knocked hard.

"Longworth, it's me, Sam. Open up," he called out above the waning but still present gunfire.

"Ranger? I'm coming," Longworth called out. Turning from the front window and running back to the rear door, he lifted the latch and swung the door open, rifle in hand, in case it was a trick.

"Easy," Sam said, seeing Longworth's rifle pointed at him. "Ceran is getting away. I'm going after him. Are you going to be all right here?"

"This bunch didn't know what they were riding into, Ranger," Longworth said. "The whole town is still stoked from last night. They've just about wiped these outlaws out.

Yeah, I'm good here. Why'd Ceran leave without his woman?"

"I don't know," Sam said. "But he's getting away." He shot a glance toward the cells, where the prisoners stood staring, their hands wrapped around the bars. Kitty wore a bitter, hurt look on her face, but she tried to hide her feelings.

"He'll be back for me, Ranger. You can count on it," she said.

"He has forgotten about you, *you pig*," Paco called out angrily. "He has forgotten about me too."

Kitty turned and looked away, her arms folded across her chest.

Sam said under his breath to Longworth, "Watch yourself, in case this is a trick and he does come back for them."

"Do you think he might?" Longworth asked.

"No," said Sam. "He's wounded. He's running to save his skin. That's why I'm getting after him right now." He gave Longworth a questioning look.

"It's my town, Ranger," Longworth said. "These townsmen and I will take care of things here. Go get Silva Ceran."

"I'm gone," said Sam.

He ran from the sheriff's office to the livery, where he had left Black Pot in a stall.

The gunfire from the street had fallen off considerably, he decided as he bridled the stallion, threw a blanket and saddle up over the big animal's back.

As he straightened up, looping and fastening the cinch, a noise from the direction of the side shed caught his attention. His Colt came up cocked and ready from its holster. He eased over to the door that opened from inside the barn into the side shed. As he reached for the door handle he heard another rustling noise from inside the shed.

With no warning, he threw open the door and aimed his Colt inside. But instead of seeing the face of one of the outlaws hiding there, he saw the wide-eyed face of Tommy Tinkens, the son of the restaurant owners.

"Don't shoot me, Mr. Ranger!" the frightened boy managed to say, sticking his thin arms straight up in the air.

The ranger stopped and let out a breath. "Don't worry, young man. I'm not going to shoot you. What are you doing here anyway?"

"I was in here when the shooting started," said the excited child. "I come in here sometimes and play like I'm driving one of these. I was afraid to go to the restaurant, so I hid in here underneath." He pointed to the wagon Longworth had parked inside the side shed. "Was that the right thing to do?"

Sam holstered his big Colt. "Yes, that was the right thing to do." He listened to the fighting on the street, which was settling down but still going on. "Maybe you should stay there awhile longer, until the gunfire is over."

"All right, Mr. Ranger," the boy said. "I like it down here anyway." He backed away and ducked down under the freight wagon.

The ranger went back to Black Pot, led the stallion out the rear of the barn, stepped up into his saddle and rode away. Behind him he still heard gunfire, but the battle had lost its intensity.

On the street, Robert Samples, John Rader and Dean Shalen ventured out onto the street from the open door of the Belleza Grande and walked warily along the street, spreading out as they went. With his shirt bearing bloodstains and a bullet hole, Samples carried one arm in a sling that the black horse doctor had made for him.

"I've got this one," he said, stepping over to where one of the renegades tried pushing himself up from the ground with both hands, a wide puddle of blood spreading beneath him.

With his free hand Samples reached down with his Colt toward the struggling ren-

336

egade. The Colt bucked in his hand as the shot exploded and the renegade melted back to the bloody earth.

"Jesus, Bob," said Dean Shalen with a sly grin, "the judge said take them prisoner if they're still alive." He bore a purple handprint on his jaw where Judge Olin had slapped him the night before.

"He was making a run for it," Samples said, walking on as if nothing had happened.

"Can't fault you for that," said Rader with feigned sincerity.

"Hell, there's two more making a run for it right now," said Shalen, gesturing his Colt along the street at two more wounded men, one of them a renegade, the other Chug Doherty. The two were done for. Chug Doherty had managed to sit up, gripping his bloody chest with both hands. The renegade lay flat on his back and slashed aimlessly at the air above him with a knife.

"You take one; I'll take the other," said Shalen with a grin. "Don't let them get away."

"What are you men doing?" Judge Olin asked, stepping barefoot out of the hotel door, wearing his trousers, his nightshirt half-stuffed down into the waist of his pants, one suspender hooked over his thick shoulder. He carried the big horse pistol swinging in one hand.

"Cleaning up," said Shalen, "just like you told us to."

Rader pulled the trigger and sent Chug Doherty flopping back dead on the ground before he saw the judge walk out onto the street. Judge Olin quickly looked away as if he hadn't seen what Rader did.

"All right," said the judge, looking all around. "But I'll have no shenanigans, be forewarned —" He stopped as he saw a two-horse buggy racing into town from the direction opposite that of the attack. "Whoa. What have we here?"

He stood at the head of the armed townsmen until the buggy slid sidelong to a halt a few feet away. The buggy driver sat quietly. Beside him a man in a black suit stood up with a hand planted atop his derby hat and said, "By God, sir! Good show." He looked all around at the dead renegades and outlaws, then said, "I came as soon as I heard the shots."

"Well, that's good of you," Judge Olin said, his horse pistol at ready. "Now, who the blazes are you?"

"Who am I?" the man took a stiff attitude. "I'm Devon Hollister, sir. I'm the chairman of Western Railways, Frontier Division — the man with the balls and the bank book."

He stepped down from the buggy and stood only inches from the judge's face. "Would you like to see either of them, sir? If so, which do you prefer?"

The judge gave a belly laugh. "Begging your pardon, Mr. Hollister. I should have recognized you from the periodical covers. Welcome to Wild Wind. I'm Territory Judge Lawrence Olin. I've heard wonderful things about you."

"Yes, I'm certain you have," said Hollister, looking past the judge and off along the street. "Where is Hansen Bell? I'm here to *observe* progress and *give* direction."

"Bell is dead," said the judge, "murdered by outlaws. But there's a young detective, Clayton Longworth, at the sheriff's office who has proven himself quite well."

"Bell, dead, you say?" Hollister stopped and looked all around. "In that case I'll decide whether or not we'll want to pursue an investment in this godforsaken hole." He looked the big judge up and down. "I'll also decide how well this Longworth person has proven himself," he added gruffly.

"Of course you will," said the judge, gesturing a thick hand toward the sheriff's office. "Just let me know how my office can assist you."

CHAPTER 25

Before Ceran had ridden a mile out of Wild Wind, he saw Charlie Jenkins cutting across the flatlands two hundred yards to his right, riding in the same direction. The two looked at each other and continued spurring the horses on until their trails intersected a half mile ahead. They loped the last few yards and brought the horses to a halt at the crest of a sandy, low rise.

"I don't want you thinking I ran out on you, Silva," Jenkins said as soon as they'd stopped their horses. "That was a flat-out trap waiting to be sprung on us." He handed Ceran his bandana from around his neck and watched him fold it and stuff it inside his shirt against his bloody shoulder wound.

"I know," said Ceran. "They had us set up like tin ducks. You did the smart thing getting out of there." He looked back toward Wild Wind, unable to say much, since he himself had fled and left all his men to fend for themselves. "Did you see Quintos or any of his men get out alive?"

"Yeah, I saw him and Two Horses and somebody else cutting out over in that direction, heading for the hills," said Jenkins. "I didn't try to catch up to them."

"It's just as well," said Ceran. "After this, I never want to see his cowardly face again." He offered no explanation as to why Quintos had suddenly become a coward. But it didn't matter to Jenkins; he'd just as soon never again talk about what had happened. "We're only riding with our own kind from now on," Ceran said.

"Did any more of our men make it out alive?" Jenkins asked.

"I don't know," said Ceran, the two turning their horses toward the hill line in the distance. "If they did, they'll show up. Don't forget, I still owe some of them money."

"I haven't forgot," said Jenkins. "I'm one of the ones."

"Right," said Ceran. He paused, then said, "Your money's safe. Don't worry about it."

"I'm not worried," said Jenkins.

"What's that mean?" Ceran asked. He stopped his horse and looked at Jenkins.

"Nothing," Jenkins said. He shrugged. "I just mean I'm not worried about getting my money, is all. With so many dead, there's plenty more of it now."

"You think I planned this?" said Ceran, getting more agitated, more angry and paranoid. "You think I wanted to get my men killed just so there'd be more money for me?"

"Hell no, Silva!" said Jenkins, seeing that the outlaw leader was starting to rage out of control. "All I'm saying is that we —"

"I know what you're saying, you son of a bitch," said Ceran, his Colt streaking up from its holster.

"No, Silva, no!" Jenkins shouted.

Two miles back on the stretch of flats, the ranger watched through his battered telescope. He saw Jenkins fly from his saddle and hit the ground; he saw Ceran grab the reins of Jenkins' horse to keep it from racing away. Then he lowered the field telescope from his eye and shook his head. *Another one down,* he told himself, collapsing the telescope between his gloved hands.

Now that he saw Ceran had two horses, he knew this could turn into a longer chase than he might have first anticipated. *But that's all right,* he told himself. He wasn't going to push the stallion in order to catch up to the outlaw. He nudged Black Pot forward and kept the big animal at a steady pace.

It was afternoon when Ceran rode up off the flatlands onto the hill trail, leading the spare horse behind him. He traveled along the rocky trail until afternoon shadows stretched long across the hill peaks and the valleys and canyons below. At dark he moved back deep beneath a cliff overhang and built a small fire that went unseen from the trail or from the flatlands below.

But having followed the outlaw for most of the day, the ranger moved up closer as night set in and led Black Pot along a path that lay above the overhang. From there he watched the flames for a few minutes, then stood and dusted his trouser seat and said quietly, "Come on, Black Pot. It's time we go calling."

Moments later, huddled at the campfire beneath the overhang, Ceran had dozed off for a moment, his head lowered onto his forearm, his other hand pressing the bandana against his shoulder wound. But he awakened instantly and sprang to his feet, Colt in hand, when a sound from the trail pierced his veil of sleep. He listened intently as he slipped away from the glow of the fire into the surrounding darkness and behind a rock at the edge of the overhang. Once behind cover, he slipped the Colt back into its holster, eased his big bowie knife from his boot well and waited.

A full five minutes passed before he heard another sound in the night. This time he made out the faint sound of a hoof clicking against stone on the rocky trail. He stood poised, tense and ready, knife in hand as he heard the quiet sound of footsteps walking up the last few feet toward his camp. *Whoever it is deliberately left his horse behind in order to slip in on me,* he reasoned.

All right, let's see what good it did you. . . .

As the silhouette came into view in the grainy moonlight, Ceran leaped forward. In spite of his shoulder wound, he grabbed the man by the hair below his hat brim and jerked his head back, exposing his throat. He swung the knife in a vicious, sidelong stab. But the dark figure ducked even with Ceran holding him.

Instead of the big blade slicing through the soft tissue of the throat, it sank four inches deep into the man's ear and stuck there. The sudden impact of the blow caused Ceran to turn loose the handle as the man staggered aimlessly, screaming at the top of his lungs.

Damn it! So much for quiet. Ceran leaped forward, caught the screaming man by his shoulders and hurled him across the ground into the firelight. The screaming man landed

344

facedown, the knife sticking from his ear, blood squirting with each rapid beat of his heart.

Ceran ran over, leaped atop the man's back and began bashing his face and forehead on the rock shelf beneath the overhang. "Shut up . . . you son . . . of a bitch!" he bellowed, until the man's voice fell silent and his body fell limp beneath the outlaw leader.

"Jesus!" Ceran said, knowing the screams had been heard out across the flatlands below. He had used a knife in order to keep from being heard and having to break camp and travel on. *Now, that's exactly what I must do,* he told himself. He wiped a hand across his blood-smeared face and breathed deep, trying to catch his breath.

"That is Dad Lafrey," said a deep voice from the edge of the darkness.

Ceran jerked around toward the voice, his fingers already grasping for his holstered Colt, but it slipped off because of the thick blood covering his hand. "Damn it, Bloody Wolf!" he said, recognizing Quintos and Two Horses, the two of them staring at him as they stepped forward from the edge of the grainy light. "Don't ever sneak up on a man that way." As he spoke he wiped his hand on his trouser leg.

"We didn't," said Quintos, "he did." He nodded toward Dad Lafrey lying dead, his face flattened against the bloody rock shelf, the big knife sticking from his ear.

Ceran stood and shook his head. "I liked Dad. He should have known better than to do that."

"He does now," said Quintos. He dismissed the matter and walked over to the fire. Two Horses remained standing, rifle in hand, as if keeping watch on Silva Ceran.

"You know, first thing in the morning I was going to come looking for you, see if you or any of your warriors made it out of Wild Wind," Ceran said, wiping his gun hand some more, this time on his shirt.

"The town was armed and waiting for us," said Quintos. "I want to cut off my ear for ever riding there with you."

"I was as surprised as you were, Bloody," said Ceran, stepping sidelong around the fire to get closer to him. Two Horses' eyes moved right along with him. "I never seen a town so stoked up, or well prepared for a fight."

Quintos stared into the low flames and said, "I asked myself, did Silva 'the Snake' Ceran take me and my men there knowing we would be killed?"

"No. Hell no, Bloody," said Ceran. "I went

there for my woman and for the money."

"But we got neither," said Quintos, still not raising his eyes from the flames.

"That's the breaks of this game," said Ceran. "But there's money there. I know there is. We just didn't get it."

"You made money," Quintos said flatly.

"Oh?" said Ceran. "How do you figure I made any money in Wild Wind?"

"It came to me on the trail that all the money you would have to share with your men, you would not have to share if they were all dead," Quintos said in the same flat tone.

"Well, that's one way of looking at it, I suppose," said Ceran. "But here's another way: you and Two Horses and I can ride to where I stashed that money. We split it up and go our own ways." He offered a slight wry grin. "You can buy arms to kill the *white man.* I can go to Mexico and get so high on *mescal* and *mescaline* that I can't even count my toes."

Quintos nodded slowly. "You think quick. That is good. That is why I came to ride with you. I also heard that you are a man to be feared and held in honor. I said to myself, Here is a man who will show us how to make the money we need."

"Well, Bloody," Ceran said with a thin

smile, "riding with me *is* what you're doing. We *are* going go get some money."

"I know," said Quintos, standing slowly. "But now that I have witnessed how you are, I want to kill you so bad that it makes my head hurt."

Ceran watched Quintos' hand ease toward the Colt sticking out of his waist sash. "Hey, you stupid Injun," he said in harsh tone. He saw Two Horses' thumb go over his rifle hammer and cock it. "You and this idiot kill me, you'll never see that money."

"I know," said Quintos. "But there are things more important than money." He started to grab the Colt; Two Horses started to swing his rifle up. Ceran's hand stood poised, ready to go for his own Colt, noise be damned. But they all stopped at the sound of a rifle lever jacking back and forth from the edge of the firelight.

"Everybody freeze up," said the ranger. But he knew it was a waste of time telling them.

"Freeze up?" Ceran turned toward him with a sneer, his hand going for his gun butt. But Ceran's wound slowed him down. Sam saw that his first shot wasn't meant for Silva Ceran. Quintos had also turned toward him, his Colt already coming up out of his sash.

Sam's rifle shot hit Quintos dead center, sending him flying backward, his heart's blood spraying on the jagged wall of the overhang. The ranger levered his rifle as he swung it toward Ceran, seeing the outlaw's drawn Colt explode toward him in a blue-orange streak of fire. But Ceran's shot went wild. The ranger's aim was deadly.

Silva Ceran fell backward onto the rock shelf less than two feet from Dad Lafrey's bloody corpse.

Quickly levering another round into his rifle chamber, Sam swung toward Two Horses, who had only managed to get his cocked rifle half raised as the ranger's Winchester seemed to stare at him with ill intent. "Drop it," Sam said, seeing there was time to hold his shot and keep from killing him.

Two Horses let the rifle fall from his hands. But instead of standing still, he began chanting and dancing slowly in place. "I do the *death dance,* to honor you as a great warrior," he said, gesturing his hand toward the bodies on the rock shelf.

"No dancing. Stop it," said the ranger.

But Two Horses didn't stop. He bowed slowly, letting his hands sweep low, close to the edge of his high-topped moccasins. "This is what my people do when we know we are in the presence —"

"I've already seen it," the ranger said, cutting him off. The rifle bucked again in his hands. Two Horses flew backward and hit the ground, his hand managing to pull the knife from his boot well even as the Winchester's bullet struck him dead.

Sam lowered the rifle, walked over to the fire and stooped down beside a boiling pot of coffee. He picked up a clean cup sitting nearby and rounded his gloved thumb inside it, inspected it. Then he picked up the coffeepot and poured a cupful, and sat slumped beside the fire. "Don't mind if I do . . . ," he said under his breath.

CHAPTER 26

It was late evening the following day when Tommy Tinkens ran into the sheriff's office, out of breath, and said to Longworth and Shelly Linde, "He's back! He's back! You said to tell you when he's back!"

"Tommy, take it easy," said Shelly, catching the boy before he fell forward into the desk.

Longworth gave Shelly a look of dread as he stood and walked toward the front door. "Maybe I ought to meet him alone," he said, taking his hat from a peg on the wall and putting it on his head.

"I'll — I'll wait here while you tell him everything," Shelly said in a worried voice, her arms looped around the small boy's shoulders.

Longworth just looked at her.

"You are going to tell him about me?" she asked, not wanting to say too much in front of the boy.

"I'll tell him what I need to tell him," Longworth said. As far as he was concerned, he wouldn't tell the ranger or anybody else about what Shelly had done. *It's nobody's business,* he convinced himself. Besides, the ranger had almost certainly figured it out for himself. He didn't need to be told. *Some things go without saying between lawmen,* he told himself.

Out front, a few townsmen started to walk up to the ranger as he slowed on the dirt street, leading the bodies of Silva Ceran and Quintos tied across their horses behind him. But as Sam slowed and veered toward the hitch rail out front of the sheriff's office, the men lingered back, looking hesitant to get too close to him.

As Longworth walked over, looked up and took the reins to the two dead outlaws' horses from him, he said, "We wondered if you'd run into much trouble out there. Some of the men wanted to ride out and see. I told them to give you another day first."

"Obliged," Sam said, still looking all around at the men standing back, some of them drifting away. "It was better I went alone." He gestured toward Ceran and Quintos' bodies. "There's the main two. There's three more strung out between here and the high trails."

"I can send somebody out," said Longworth.

The ranger nodded. He looked around at the front of the hotel, where workmen were already repairing the fallen balcony.

"Where's Judge Olin?" he asked.

"He's gone," said Longworth.

"He's gone? What about the court — the trials?" he asked.

"He held court this morning," said Longworth. "Now he's gone. He left right afterward."

Sam looked surprised. "He didn't want me to testify?"

"He said he knew everything you had to say," said Longworth. "There was no jury. Everybody threw themselves at the mercy of the court."

"We figured they would," Sam said. "But still . . ." He looked all around the street again. "What's going on here?"

"We need to talk, Ranger," said Longworth. "Why don't you step down? We'll go inside."

"Talk about what?" Sam said, feeling suspicious but not knowing why. He made no effort toward stepping down from his saddle.

"It's been a fast day," said Longworth.

"Mr. Hollister, from Western Railways, came to town after you left yesterday. He heard about everything that went wrong and started to fire me on the spot. But the judge came to my defense and saved my job." He paused, then said, "He not only saved my job; I managed to get a promotion out of the deal."

"Congratulations, Detective," Sam said, but he noted that Longworth wasn't smiling about his good fortune.

"It helped that Tommy Tinkens had just come to Shelly and me and told us about a strongbox full of Western Railways' money lying hidden under the ore samples in the freight wagon."

Sam just stared at him for a second, then said, "That was a piece of luck."

"I'll say," Longworth said, lowering his voice a little. "I acted as if I knew it was there all along. Hollister couldn't praise me enough. That's when he put me in charge here."

"Good for you," said Sam. He stared at Longworth for a moment, then said, "But this is not what you want to talk to me about, is it?"

"No, it's not," said Longworth. He let out a breath and said in a shaky voice, "It's about the prisoners, Ranger. The judge hanged them, every one. He said they were all involved . . . they were all guilty."

The ranger sat staring, stunned, unable to speak for a second. Then he swallowed a dry knot in his throat and said, "Every one of them? Even Kitty Dellaros?"

"Yes, Ranger, even Miss Dellaros," Longworth said. "I hope I never have to see anything like that ever again." He looked away. Then he looked up at the expression on the ranger's face. "Are you all right?" he asked.

Sam didn't reply. He sat staring at the rope marks on the timber along the front of the boardwalk. "He hanged them right there? No different than the lynch mob was going to do?"

"Yes," said Longworth. "He said this was *different*. Said it was *official,* so that made it more civilized." He paused, then added, "He also had some chairs set up, and had them shoved off the chair instead of drawing them up by hand and strangling them, the way the lynch mob was going to do."

Sam still didn't answer. He looked back and forth along the dirt street and said, "I told Kitty that she had nothing to worry about — that Lawrence Olin wasn't a hanging judge."

"She said you told her that," Longworth

said quietly. "Shelly talked to her some. . . . You know, to help settle her down at the end."

Sam just stared at him.

"She asked Shelly to tell you that it was okay; she never would have been a good seamstress anyway." He reached into his vest pocket and pulled out the tin locket and handed it up to the ranger. "She said she wanted you to have this. It's what Shelly calls an orphan locket. She was given one just like it when the orphan train brought her out here. She said they put a child's own picture in it and would say, 'This is so you never forget who you are.' "

Sam took the locket, gripped in tight in his gloved hand and gave a sigh, his eyes closed for a moment. "Why did the judge do this?" he asked no one in particular, shaking his bowed head.

"Hollister pressed him into doing it, Ranger," Longworth said. "I work for Western Railways, but I'm not a fool. I see how they are. They are powerful and they are mean-spirited. They get what they want, and they trample who they want, in the name of progress."

Sam looked off toward the hotel, where the fancy two-horse buggy sat at the iron hitch rail. "Is that Hollister's rig?"

"Yes," said Longworth. "He said Western Railways is the law here now, and that I'm the man wearing the badge for them. You can go talk with him, if you think you should. But I think it's best if I'm there with you."

"No, I don't want to talk to him," Sam said. He pictured the triangle of law Judge Olin had talked about and drawn in the air with a spoon. "That's a level of law I expect I don't yet understand."

"Me neither," said Longworth. He paused, then said, "But we're both young. We're still learning."

"Yeah," the ranger said, "learning something new every day. . . ." He touched his hat brim and started to turn the big stallion.

"Wait, Ranger," said Longworth, standing in the dirt street, still holding the reins of the two horses. "Spend the night at the hotel — get some rest. You can leave early in the morning."

"Tonight's a good night for me to be out under the stars," Sam said. He gave the stallion a touch of his boot heels. "Take us on, Black Pot," he said, and he rode away toward the darkening badlands.

ABOUT THE AUTHOR

Ralph Cotton is a former ironworker, second mate on a commercial barge, teamster, horse trainer, and lay minister with the Lutheran church. Visit his Web site at www.RalphCotton.com.

The employees of Thorndike Press hope you have enjoyed this Large Print book. All our Thorndike, Wheeler, and Kennebec Large Print titles are designed for easy reading, and all our books are made to last. Other Thorndike Press Large Print books are available at your library, through selected bookstores, or directly from us.

For information about titles, please call:
  (800) 223-1244

or visit our Web site at:
  http://gale.cengage.com/thorndike

To share your comments, please write:
  Publisher
  Thorndike Press
  295 Kennedy Memorial Drive
  Waterville, ME 04901